HARDLINE

Meredith Wild

CORGI BOOKS

TRANSWORLD PUBLISHERS
61–63 Uxbridge Road, London W5 5SA
www.transworldbooks.co.uk

Transworld is part of the Penguin Random House group of companies whose
addresses can be found at global.penguinrandomhouse.com

Penguin
Random House
UK

Originally published in the United States by Forever, an imprint of
Grand Central Publishing, part of the Hachette Book Group, Inc.

First published in Great Britain in 2015 by Corgi Books

A CIP catalogue record for this book
is available from the British Library.

ISBN
9780552172516

Typeset in Bembo
Printed and bound by CPI Group (UK) Ltd, Croydon, CR0 4YY

Penguin Random House is committed to a sustainable future for
our business, our readers and our planet. This book is made
from Forest Stewardship Council® certified paper.

1 3 5 7 9 10 8 6 4 2

For the family who opened their hearts to me,
and the two people whose love made that possible.

CHAPTER ONE

My phone dinged.

B: *I'm leaving work in twenty minutes.*

I silenced my phone, ignored Blake's message, and turned my focus back to Alli. She tucked a lock of long brown hair behind her ear and continued to update the team on the weekly stats for our Internet startup, Clozpin. I listened attentively, grateful to have her back on the team.

Alli had been back in Boston only a few weeks, but she was finally sharing a city and an apartment with Heath again. Heath was happy, she was happy, and I was thrilled to have her reclaim her position as the marketing director after the debacle with Risa. I'd invited Alli back even before letting Risa go for sharing confidential information about the company.

I winced at the thought. Alli was a fountain of optimism, but Risa's betrayal still stung me. I hadn't heard from her since our last meeting, and somehow the silence between us filled me more with dread than anything else. I wanted to doubt her ability to start a competing site with Max, our almost-investor and Blake's sworn enemy, but the unknown worried me. What if they successfully lured our advertisers away? What if they were able to build something that was legitimately better and filled a need that Clozpin didn't?

With the kind of money Max was bringing to the table plus Risa's inside information gleaned directly from everything I'd learned in my short tenure as CEO of the company, anything was possible. And something about the way she left, filled with so much venom and resentment, spoke to every insecurity I had about running a business. I was still fledgling, without a doubt. I wanted to believe I could hold my own, and in many ways I had, but I had a lot to learn.

Another text message arrived on my phone, no less distracting as it vibrated against the glass top of the conference table.

B: *Erica?*

I rolled my eyes and quickly tapped out a reply. I knew he'd pester me until I acknowledged him.

E: *I'm in a meeting. I'll call you after.*

B: *I want you naked in my bed by the time I get home. You should leave soon.*

E: *I need more time.*

B: *I'll be inside you within the hour. Your office, our bed, your choice. Wrap it up.*

The air in the room was suddenly too cool against my hot skin. I shivered and my nipples beaded, grazing uncom-

HARDLINE

fortably against my shirt. How did he do that? A few well-placed words, delivered via text no less, had me checking my watch.

"Erica, do you have anything else you want to cover?"

My eyes locked with Alli's. She cocked an eyebrow like maybe she knew I wasn't paying attention. All I could think about were the consequences of keeping Blake waiting, and the physical response to that anticipation was already becoming difficult to ignore. I corralled my thoughts away from Blake's promises and back to the present.

"No, I think we're good. Thanks, everyone." I collected my things quickly, eager to get moving. I waved off the rest of the group, and they dispersed to their workstations. Alli followed me into my partitioned office.

"What's up with Perry? I didn't want to bring it up at the meeting since it's kind of an odd situation."

"Not much. He emailed me again, but I haven't replied yet." I didn't have time to get into the complexities of that situation right now If I wanted to meet Blake's deadline.

"Are you thinking about taking him on as an advertiser?"

"I'm not sure." I was still conflicted on the matter.

Her big brown eyes were wide. "Does Blake know he reached out to you?"

"No." I gave her a pointed stare, making it clear without words that I didn't want him to either. The last time I'd seen Isaac Perry, Blake had him pinned to the wall by his throat threatening to de-limb him if he dared touch me ever again. I didn't want to make excuses for Isaac's bad behavior that night, and I didn't want to forgive him any more than Blake did. But this was business.

3

"He's not going to be happy if you end up working with him."

I stuffed my laptop into my bag. "You think I don't know that?"

Blake's associations colored more strategic business decisions than I cared to admit.

Alli leaned against my desk. "So what are you going to do? Perry must be offering something impressive if you haven't completely shot him down yet."

"Perry Media Group represents a dozen multimedia publications that span the globe. I'm not saying I trust him, but I can at least hear him out."

She shrugged. "Whatever you think is best for the company I'll support. I don't mind dealing with him directly either, if you're more comfortable with that."

"Thanks, Alli. I'd rather get to the bottom of this myself though. We can talk about it more later. I need to head out. Blake is waiting for me."

"Oh, are you going out?" She brightened immediately, her business persona vanishing, replaced by the energetic best friend who made every day a little brighter.

"Um, we have plans. I'll see you later," I said, trying not to sound cryptic before slipping out of the office and waving my goodbyes.

A minute later I stepped outside into the early August heat. Rush hour traffic pushed by, and my phone rang before I could take my first steps toward home. I groaned and fished it out of my purse. Blake could be maddeningly persistent. When I retrieved it, a Chicago phone number appeared instead.

"Hello?" I answered tentatively.

"Erica?"

"Yes, who is this?"

"It's me, Elliot."

I brought my hand to my mouth, muffling the sound of my shock at hearing my stepfather's voice. "Elliot?"

"Do you have a minute? Is this a bad time?"

"No, this is fine." I pushed through the doors of Mocha, the café downstairs, for a reprieve from the heat. "How are you? I haven't talked to you in forever."

He laughed. "I've been busy."

I smiled to myself. I hadn't heard that sound in so long. "Of course. How are the kids?"

"They're doing really well. Growing up too fast."

"I bet. How's Beth?"

"She's fine. She's back to work now that the kids are in school, so that keeps her busy. We've both got our hands full." He cleared his throat and took an audible breath. "Listen, Erica, I know I haven't been very good about keeping in touch. Honestly, I feel terrible about it. I really wanted to come to the graduation. Things were just really hectic here—"

"It's fine, Elliot. I understand. You have a lot going on."

"Thanks." He sighed quietly. "You've always been so level-headed. Even when you were younger. Sometimes I think you had it together more than I did. I know your mother would be proud of the woman you've become."

"Thanks. I hope so." I closed my eyes, letting a remembered vision of my mother take over my mind. Despite the strong facade I kept up, my heart hurt at the memory—times when the three of us were happy. That time had been cut short abruptly when my mother was diagnosed with cancer, a disease that ripped through her at an alarming speed and took her from us too soon.

While our lives had gone in different directions after her death, I hoped Elliot had found happiness with his new wife and their children. Even if it had come at the expense of any normal childhood for me. Boarding school and then college had raised me, yet I couldn't imagine it any other way. This was my life, and the journey had brought me to Blake, to a life that was finally beginning to take shape now that school was behind me.

"I have been thinking about Patricia a lot lately. I can't believe it's been almost ten years. Life runs away from you sometimes. Made me realize how long it's been since we talked."

"It's true. The past few years have really been a blur. Especially lately. I was crazy to think I was busy before." Between the business and my relationship with Blake, my life had been turned upside down a few times over. Just when things started to calm down, life seemed to throw us something new.

"Well, I'm going to see if we can make it out to Boston soon. I can't stomach the thought of letting ten years go by without...you know, some kind of acknowledgment. We owe her that much."

My mouth curved into a sad smile. "That would be nice. I would like that."

"Great. I'll see what I can do."

"Let me know if you pick dates, and I'll coordinate things on my end too."

"Perfect. I'll talk to Beth about it soon and let you know what we decide."

"I'll look forward to it. I'd love to see you again, and of course meet your family." *Your family.* The words sounded strange as they left me.

"Take care, Erica. I'll be in touch."

I said goodbye, but the second I hung up another call came in. My heart sped up when I saw Blake's number.

Shit.

★ ★ ★

I stepped into the apartment and dropped my bags onto the counter in the kitchen. The lights were off, but the afternoon sun peeked in through the shaded windows. As I moved into the living room, I heard Blake's voice.

"You're late."

I spun to find him at the bar on the other side of the room. He was shirtless, barefoot, and held a half empty tumbler in his hand. His face was void of emotion yet somehow filled with an intensity that had me immediately on edge. His green eyes seemed to glow in the dim light of the room. His jaw was tight, loosening only briefly to take a drink.

"I'm sorry. I got a call—"

"Come here."

I let my next words fizzle out unspoken. We weren't going to be discussing Elliot's unexpected call, at least not right now. Something was off about the way he looked at me, the unforgiving edge in his voice as he uttered those two little words.

I walked slowly toward him until we were inches apart and the heat radiated between us. Blake was undeniably gorgeous, male beauty perfected. Tall and lean, his body had my brain regularly short-circuiting. This was no exception. I touched his chest, unable to resist in our proximity. The muscles flinched in response.

"Take your shirt off," he said.

I searched his eyes a moment but found no humor there. He stood before me like a statue, a beautifully carved work of art, cold and unmoving. I feathered my fingers over his abs, trailing them to the band of his jeans slung low on his hips.

"You okay?" I murmured. I'd seen him like this before. He didn't need to tell me, because I already knew something or someone had gotten under his skin today.

He winced, a nearly imperceptible response. "I'll be better in a minute."

Knowing what could get him there, I pulled off my blouse and let it drop to the floor.

"Better?" I cocked my head, hoping to draw out the playful lover in him.

His eyes were unchanged, steely as ever. "Don't make me wait again, Erica."

His voice was dangerously low. I held my breath, trying in vain to harness control over my own body's reactions to him. That potent mix of desire and anticipation welled up inside of me. The details of the day blurred into the background, secondary to the here and now and the domineering man who was moments from fucking away his release and using my body so very well to do it.

I lowered my hand to the hard outline of his erection and stroked him through the soft worn fabric of his jeans. "I'm here now. Let me make it up to you." He caught my wrist. "You will, trust me."

I looked up through my eyelashes. He released me and brought his hand to my chest. He traced the lace hem of my bra and the skin beneath. The simple contact warmed me. He pushed the cup of the bra down roughly, palmed my freed breast, and thumbed my nipple. I leaned into the slow circular motions as a flicker of desire took root in my belly.

I moaned, and he pinched tightly. I sucked in a breath through my teeth but didn't push him away. His lip turned up at the corner and a flash of terrible mischief passed over his eyes.

"Undress and bend over the table."

Playful had arrived, but so had someone else.

I frowned in the direction of the dining area and the large wooden farmhouse table at the center of it. Before I could argue, he swatted my ass and gave me a gentle shove in that direction. I moved quickly and removed my skirt, bra, and panties. I faced the table, resting my hands on the warm textured wood. On the center of the table, lengths of rope were curled into a pile.

"Down," he said in a clipped tone.

He placed his hand between my shoulder blades and pressured me lower. I slid my hands out in front of me, exhaling sharply as the front of my body touched the cool table, the tops of my thighs pressed firmly against the edge. The anticipation held me hostage, robbed me of the ability to make sense of anything but the surety that Blake was taking control now.

And I'd given him that.

As soon as I'd walked out of my normal working life and into the apartment we now shared, I went to war with damn near every instinct I had. I handed over all control to the man I loved, trusting that he'd take care of us both. He always did, but sometimes I couldn't resist the urge to push back just a bit, so he knew I was still there, fighting.

He ran a cool hand over my ass. I tensed in response to the simple touch. I bit my lip, steadying myself for what always came next.

"You were twenty minutes late. Do you know what that means?"

Before I could speak, his hand made sharp contact with my ass. I whimpered at the sharp pain. Then the sting melted, setting off a fiery heat through my body. I arched, pushing back against him.

"Are you going to punish me?" I asked quietly.

"Is that what you want?"

"Yes." The meekness of my responses still surprised me, considering how far we'd gone and how much I loved those dark places we found in each other. Admitting how much I loved it still took a certain amount of courage.

"Lucky for you. You're going to get twenty lashes. I want you to count. Don't forget, or I'll get the belt."

Without delay he slapped my ass again, hard enough to echo through the room. The second I caught my breath, I rushed to speak.

"One."

"That's it." He delivered another.

"Two."

With every punishing swat, I tightened and grew wetter, a circumstance I still couldn't quite grasp. But getting spanked drove me fucking crazy. By the time we were in double digits I was clawing at the table, more than ready for the pleasure that came after the delicious pain.

Twenty.

I sighed and rested against the table. The relief was short-lived as Blake caught my ponytail and coaxed me up to stand.

"Up."

I straightened, and he spun me. He dropped his jaw, as if to speak, but instead he pulled our bodies together. His skin scorched under mine, and suddenly I wanted him even more. He sealed his lips over mine with a hard kiss. The aroma of scotch mingled with the musk of him. I opened my lips to him, inviting him, wanting his taste on my tongue. He yanked my ponytail gently, breaking the contact.

"You're too greedy."

I pouted.

"You're spoiled, and you don't listen."

"I listen," I insisted.

"You may listen, but you don't obey worth a damn. Playtime is over. You need to learn, and tonight I'm going to teach you."

I fought the fear that coiled in my gut. Fear of the unknown. "I'm sorry."

"That's a good start. Get on the table."

I hesitated a second and then quickly lifted myself onto the edge. He shook his head and scooted me back.

"In the middle. Hurry up."

I lifted my eyebrows, but rather than question him, I shimmied to the middle. As I did, he circled the table and retrieved the rope from my path.

"Lie down."

I obeyed, and he caught my wrist, extending my arm to reach the corner of the table. With shocking speed and dexterity, he bound my arms to the legs of the table. As he moved to my ankles, I pulled against the rope, testing its security. No give.

He bound one leg, and then the other, until I was spread eagle on the table.

"That's better." He gave my calf a small squeeze.

My skin heated all the way to my cheeks as the extent of my vulnerability sank in. I wanted to tell him this was too much. The words were on the edge of my lips, but I was already wet and needy for him, for whatever he was cooking up in that devious mind of his. Adding to my growing unease, Blake moved away until he was out of my range of vision.

"Where are you going?" I tried to hide the anxiety in my voice.

"Don't worry. I'm not leaving. Not when you're spread out for me like a fucking banquet."

I heard ice hitting the inside of a glass and then the quiet guzzle of it being filled. He returned and stood before me, bringing the glass to his lips, obscuring the ghost of a grin on his beautiful face. Something in his expression promised I was in for a slow torture. The need that pulsed through me doubled. I was entirely at his mercy now.

Seconds that felt like minutes passed. My breasts heaved in time to my breathing, which ticked up as I waited. For what? I had no idea, but the possibilities thrilled me.

He lifted the glass once more, drained its contents, and dropped the tumbler loudly onto the table between my legs. He dipped his hand into the glass, and the clink of the ice was followed by the silent shock of the cold on my skin. He traced a slow wet path down the inside of my leg, along the sensitive skin of my inner thigh. I shivered, tensing, as he traveled over my hips to my belly. The cube melted slowly at my navel while he reached for another.

He rounded the table, coming to my side. With the next cube, he circled my nipples, lingering on each. On the brink of pain, I suppressed my protest. I couldn't risk more punishment if it delayed him being inside me. He lowered his lips, replacing the numbing cool of the ice with the wet heat of his mouth. His teeth clipped the hardened points while a cool hand found its mark between my thighs.

He hummed, sliding easily through my folds, teasing my clit. "You like when I tie you up, baby?"

I licked my dry lips, nodding quickly. Did I? I wasn't sure. All I really knew was that I didn't want him to stop. I didn't want to say anything to keep him from giving me the pleasure that only he could. He kept me right on the edge, a state so heightened and helpless that it bordered on unbearable. I tugged against the restraints, the rope biting into my skin.

"Stop fighting, Erica."

He straightened, depriving me of his touch and his closeness.

"I thought you were in a hurry," I complained, trying to get a grip on the desire that burned through me a little more fiercely with each passing minute. Goddamn him and this rope.

He grinned. "I was, but the thought of punishing you tempered that sense of urgency. Now I'm just enjoying myself."

I closed my eyes. My chest expanded with a deep breath, and I willed myself to relax. As I did, I felt a shock of cold between my legs.

I cried out, from surprise and the sensation that I wasn't convinced yet was discomfort. My clit was throbbing against the ice as he maneuvered over the nub, between my folds. I released a breath as he lowered it away from my most sensitive parts and dipped the tip gently into my pussy. When I thought he might relieve me, the hint of a touch gave way to the ice. How long could he do this to me and keep his own desires in check? How long could *I* do this? I was ready to burst and scream.

"Blake, I can't…I can't do this anymore. You're killing me."

"How does it feel to wait…to want?"

I clamped my jaw tight, trying to distract myself from the terrible ache between my thighs. I squirmed despite myself, knowing it wouldn't bring him any closer to fucking me.

"I hate it."

"Should we end it?"

"Yes," I said, the desperation plain in my voice.

He leaned closer, his lips grazing the sensitive skin of my neck. He traced the curve of my ear with his tongue, a slow torture all its own.

"Beg."

Chills broke out over my skin. I arched my chest into the air, into nothing because he was barely touching me now.

"Tell me how much you want it. I need the words."

"Blake…please, just fuck me."

"That sounds like an order. I want begging."

I groaned and he pulled away, no longer touching me anywhere in any way.

"Blake!" I was furious and desperate.

"*Submit.*"

I jolted at the sharp edge of his voice.

"You need to submit to me, Erica, if you want to come. No more playing games. No more testing me."

I swallowed hard, fighting the instinct to rile at his order. *Submit.* My throat tightened, as if the word had lodged itself there and wouldn't pass until I accepted it. That word meant so much. Submitting was easier when I was coaxing him into taking what he needed from me. Now he was taking what he wanted. He wasn't asking and we weren't negotiating.

I closed my eyes, straining to hear the voice in my head telling me to relax, to let go. "You're not making it easy." I wanted him to understand my resistance, maybe even let it slide. Even when he went all Dom on me, sometimes he'd give me room to push back.

"I've been putting out fires all day. I want to come home to you, and I don't want to have to break you every time. If I have to, I will, but I won't always be asking nicely and making it easy for you. So you should get used to submitting. You're naked, tied to the table, and one stroke away from coming. Do you want to come?"

"Yes, badly."

"Then *beg.*"

"Please..." The plea was weak as it left my lips.

"I'm listening, Erica. Please what?"

"Please, make me come. I want your hands on me. I'll do anything...I swear."

"Will you be home, naked, when I ask you next time?"

"Yes."

His fingertips grazed my throbbing clit. I sucked in a sharp breath and lifted my hips to meet his touch, but he evaded me as quickly as he'd arrived.

"Promise?"

"I promise. Jesus, I'll do anything."

"And I won't have to give you directions about how to submit again, will I?"

"No," I promised, shaking my head emphatically.

The heat of his hand radiated where I badly needed him. I resisted the urge to coax my body centimeters closer. *Fucking hell, this is torture.*

Every cell in my body strained toward his touch, and yet I had no control.

This was the reality I fought to accept. Somehow I had to trust that he'd get us there. With that realization, something inside me released. I weakened against the table, no longer fighting the restraints. My muscles let go but my mind spun, no more in control than my body was over how badly I wanted him.

Then he touched me. Covering my pussy with the palm of his hand, he gripped me firmly.

"This is mine. You don't come unless I want you to. Do you understand?"

I gazed at him, bleary eyed with my own need. I was seconds from crying for how on edge I was, as if somehow his own frustrations from the day had passed right through me.

"I'll be whatever you need, Blake."

His eyes softened a fraction at my concession. Then he entered me with two fingers. My jaw fell, releasing a gasp of relief. He twisted inside me, exploring my wet depths.

Trembling, I tightened around him, wishing I had more of him there but grateful I had anything at all. He pumped gently and thumbed my clit with quick circles.

I released a small cry at the potency of that one motion, relieved and coiled up again all at once. My nerves came back to life, my flesh hot and ready for him all over again. God, the man had a gift for making me painfully aware of how much my body thrived with his touch. I caught myself when my hips lifted a fraction on their own accord.

Beg. His demand echoed in my head, both sultry and unforgiving. My core pulsed. Blood thrummed through my veins, humming in my ears. The beginnings of an unstoppable orgasm crept up on me, and I wasn't about to let it go. Not for pride, not for anything.

"Don't stop. I'm begging you, please don't stop."

"That's what I want to hear, baby. You want all of me in there?"

"God, yes."

"Want me to let you come first?"

Colors swirled behind my eyes and every muscle tensed now with anticipation. My eyes flashed open when I realized he hadn't yet given me explicit permission to come. I met his dark gaze, his eyelids hooded with the same brand of desire that was rushing through me at this very moment.

"Please let me. Blake, please …"

He lowered and caught my mouth in a rough kiss. Our lips rushed over each other, our tongues clashed and sucked. All the while his fingers continued their ministrations, gently fucking me, coaxing me to the edge. The searing pleasure of it overtook me, as if the only sense in the world came from the places where our bodies met, the pleasure he was gifting to me. And I was as grateful as I was desperate to have it. An all-consuming heat swept over me. I began to shake with the effort not to orgasm.

"Oh God," I whimpered, losing my hold on reality, on anything. "Please, please, please."

"Come, Erica. Right now," he rasped into my mouth, his intimate touch deepening.

I gasped for air, arching off the table. Bound by the rope, I could hasten nothing, control nothing. The words, the order, had stripped me down. I was owned. *His.* At his mercy and command, I crashed over the edge with a wail. I clenched my fists, tight and tautly held as the climax ripped through me.

The world went silent in that perfect moment. I was still trembling when he left me. His fingers went to work loosening the rope around my ankles. Somewhere in the delirious aftermath of the orgasm, I registered relief at this new freedom. Seconds later he was fully naked, covering my body with his. He hooked my legs around his waist and with the thick head of cock against my entrance, he pressed into me a bare inch.

"I'm so fucking hard it hurts. I'm going to fuck you deep, so deep that next time you won't forget who owns you, baby. I'll have you coming again and again, until you trust me to give us what we both want."

My voice was lost in my delirium. I was reeling, barely prepared for what he'd give me next. The muscles of his torso were hard and taut as he wrapped an arm around my waist. His green eyes were dark and dilated, and they locked with mine. I saw him then—the man, but also the animal that lived below the surface.

He needed this. He needed me this way.

"Blake." I licked my lips, now dry from my ragged breathing. "Kiss me...please."

The tension in his gaze, the dominant determination, gave way to something else.

And I felt it when our lips met, with more care now than before, but no less passionate. Love. I recognized it. With all his kinks and maddening control issues, I loved this man. As much as he needed this, I needed to be this for him.

"I love you." The words rushed out when I broke our kiss.

Those intense eyes burned into me once more. The need that vibrated through his body seemed to still for a moment. Then he lowered again. His lips brushed over mine gently.

"I can't breathe without you, baby. You undo me and then put me back together whole again. You take it all, and you still love me for it."

The questioning in his eyes and the doubt in those last few words broke my heart a little.

"Blake...I'm yours. I want this. I want every part of you." My throat tightened, for reasons altogether different now. Desire and a soul-wrenching love worked its way through me, radiating between us.

Our lips met again and he pushed into me, dipping his tongue into my mouth as he did. My sex gripped around him, stretching around his thick cock. Then he was deep inside me. We were so close, our souls joining as our bodies did. He withdrew and thrust again, hitting me deeper. I gasped. His body was hard above me, rippling with strain as he held back. I felt it too, that need to burst, to be engulfed in this wild desire.

Heat blazed in his eyes as he cupped a hand at my nape, leveraging his weight on his elbow. I locked my ankles around his waist as his bicep flexed into the flesh of my waist. Then he drove hard, just the way I wanted him to. The friction of his entry hurled me to the sharp edge of an orgasm. My jaw dropped with a soundless cry that found its voice as he pounded into me.

Hard. Fast. Merciless and rough. One of the many ways I loved having him.

The relentless pace had me coming again quickly. My pussy tightened around him, as I clung to his hips with my thighs. One climax crashed right into the next until he began to come with me. He ground his hips into me, pinning us to the table in a rabid race for relief, for release...my name on his lips.

CHAPTER TWO

I straddled Blake's hips, massaging my thumbs over the pro-
truding muscles of his shoulders. His muscles barely gave,
and I wondered if I was having any effect on him at all.
Then he breathed out a soft moan. I smiled and lowered
so my front covered his back. I kissed his skin, breathing in
the fragrance of the lotion mingled with his scent. By some
magic of nature, my own muscles let go. His musk, the sweat
from our lovemaking, nearly overwhelmed me. I could lie
like this and smell the man all damn day.

"You smell amazing." I pressed my lips against him,
kissing him, inhaling him.

He released a soft chuckle.

I darted my tongue out to taste him, like the smell of
him wasn't enough. As if getting screwed to oblivion on a
dining room table, bound like the bad little submissive I was,
wasn't enough. Blake Landon was my drug, my obsession—
a habit I had no intentions of ever quitting.

I worshipped him with my lips and my teeth. I massaged him, my fingers trailing over him with the same kind
of obsession.

In a flash, he bucked me off and I was on my back, his
gorgeous naked body between my legs.

"Are you trying to get fucked again? Because if you are,
you're doing a damn good job of it."

I giggled. He smiled broadly, capturing my wrists on

either side of my head. He rubbed the tender spots where the rope had bitten into me.

Recognizing a whisper of familiar worry in his features, I slipped out of his grasp. I cupped his cheeks, holding his focus on me. "I'm fine. Don't start with the guilt, okay?"

"I didn't mean to hurt you."

"Trust me, I didn't feel a thing. In the heat of the moment, all I can feel are your hands on me, you inside me. It's all consuming. Something that might hurt normally just adds an edge to whatever pleasure you're giving me. And you know damn well I like it, so don't start acting like I'm some wounded kitten."

"But it hurts you now. What if you bruise?"

"Who cares? I won't fight so hard next time. You wanted to teach me a lesson, didn't you?" I shifted my hips beneath him, teasing him as his erection throbbed hot against my belly. I twisted my lips into a crooked grin. I wanted playful Blake, and I wasn't about to let him fall back into shaming his needs—needs that were quickly becoming mine too.

After what I'd been through with the man who'd raped me four years ago, I never thought I'd be able to give someone the kind of control I'd given Blake. But he'd shown me how to enjoy letting go. He'd opened my eyes to the craving, to something deeper and infinitely more intense than anything I'd ever experienced.

I fought for control only to have him strip me of it in that masterful way that he always did. He broke me down until I was mindless with desire, and I didn't want it any other way now. I couldn't imagine it.

I ran two fingers over the frown that curved his brow. "What's eating you, anyway? You seemed upset earlier."

He rolled off of me and onto his back, his gaze fixed on the ceiling. Before I could press him, a door slammed and I heard muffled voices. I hopped up quickly, shut the bedroom door, and locked it. I joined Blake back on the bed, snuggling into the nook of his arm. I tossed my leg lazily over his strong thigh.

A loud thud from the hallway in the apartment echoed through the room. The sound was followed by a woman's giggle and then a moan. I smirked. Alli and Heath were at it again, but who was I to talk?

Thank God they hadn't walked in on Blake's little stunt in the dining room. I couldn't imagine explaining any of that to Alli. She was still mercifully in the dark about all of Blake's kinks and quirks in the bedroom, and at least for now, I'd rather it stay that way.

"We should take a trip," Blake said suddenly.

I sighed. "I'm sure they'll get a place soon."

"Not soon enough. Plus, we haven't been away together since…well, since Vegas. We could use a long weekend. I want to spend some time with you. Just us. No distractions."

An unexpected series of events, many of them orchestrated by Blake, had brought us here. Vegas had been a turning point among them, and the memory of our first time together still warmed me from head to toe. There had been only lust between us then, but lust had turned to obsession and somewhere in that wild blur, I had fallen in love with him.

"I'm not sure I should take time away from work right now." The past few hours had pushed Risa and Max and their whole scheming madness out of my mind, but slowly reality crept back in.

"I think you've earned it. Let me take you away for a few days. There will always be something we need to do and someone who needs us. But there's nothing that can't wait an extra day or two."

I raised my eyebrows, the compulsive worker in me not entirely believing him. "You sure?"

"Positive. In fact, I've just decided I'm not giving you a choice. We'll leave after work tomorrow." I grinned, a little thrill working its way through me. "What should I pack?"

"I'll put a bag together for you."

"You don't have to do that."

"I'm not sure you'll be wearing clothes much anyway, so it doesn't really matter, does it? Bikini, some thongs. That should do fine."

I laughed and playfully swatted his face. He caught my hand and growled, hauling me on top of him.

"Until then, I think we need to make a little noise of our own."

I laughed again and shook my head. "Not to be out-done, Blake. You are incorrigible."

"Trust me, I have no interest in hearing my little brother getting laid. The only way I can send a message is to return the favor. All I need to do is figure out a way to make you scream for me."

My smile slipped a little. He wrapped his arms around me, holding me tight and stoking the fire with every soft graze of his fingertips over my skin.

"I have a feeling you already know how to do that very well."

★ ★ ★

A loud knock woke me. Blake stirred behind me but didn't wake.

"Erica, are you up?" The muffled voice came from behind the door.

I slipped on Blake's T-shirt and glanced back to make sure Blake was decently covered. I opened the door a bit. Alli was wide-eyed and already dressed for work.

"What?" I frowned. "What time is it anyway?"

"It's eight o'clock. Get dressed. I need to show you something."

I studied her with tired eyes, not awake enough to comprehend anything beyond wanting to curl up in bed with Blake again. "What is it?"

"Just get moving and meet me at the office."

"Why—"

Before I could finish she'd disappeared down the hallway and the door clicked shut a few seconds later. I turned back into the bedroom and headed to the bathroom. Blake was still sleeping when I finished my shower. I dressed quickly and hovered over him a moment, enjoying the rare peace on his countenance as he slept. Of the two of us, he was typically the early riser, but it had been a long night. Some nights we couldn't get enough of each other, and last night had turned into the morning before sleep finally found us. I pressed a soft kiss to his cheek and left for work.

When I walked into the office, the entire team was huddled around James, their eyes glued to something on his display monitor. I joined them, unsure at first of what I was looking at.

"What's going on?"

"This site, PinDeelz launched last night," Alli explained.

"All our Clozpin users were messaged about the launch, including us. Very discreet."

I leaned over James's shoulder as he navigated through pages of a site that, though different in its branding, displayed very similarly to ours. My stomach fell when each page displayed ads from Bryant's, one of our major advertisers who had yet to renew their contract with us for the following month.

Motherfucker.

I straightened and disappeared to my office. I whipped open my laptop and investigated the site further. The about page listed Max as its founder and Risa as its chief operating officer. Not surprisingly, Trevor's role wasn't mentioned, but I knew damn well that the hacker who'd spent months, maybe years, trying to ruin Blake's ventures had been pivotal in getting this competing site off the ground. Even if that meant taking a break from relentlessly attacking my and Blake's businesses.

Anger surged through me. I could barely process that this was happening. Sid and I had spent months fine-tuning Clozpin, making it what it was today. All our success, all the mistakes and the lessons, had been swiftly copied and enhanced.

Alli joined me and sat in the chair across from my desk, my concern reflecting in her features. She worried her lip but said nothing. Inside I was flying into a psychotic rage. I wanted to throw the biggest temper tantrum anyone had ever seen. I wanted to curse, and God help me if I could get Max and Risa…and Trevor…in front me, there would be blood.

"I can't believe they really did it."

"I know," she said quietly.

"I'm in disbelief that someone would harbor so much hatred for me and for Blake that they would do something like this. Total sabotage."

"They won't last, Erica."

I let out a short laugh. "Why not? What's keeping them from it? You met Risa. You know how determined she is, and with Max's money, I see no reason why they can't completely wipe us out now. This market isn't big enough to support two sites with such similar offerings."

"Don't think like that. We're far from doomed. I have been talking to a lot of new prospects since I've been back. It's a process, but we're close to closing more. We're established, and we have the track record. I'm shocked they could get Bryant's to take a risk with them being so new."

I was pissed all over again imagining what Risa must have said to lure one of our biggest advertisers away. "What am I supposed to do now?"

"We keep going. They want to distract us and scare us. Don't let them do that."

I shook my head. Nothing she said would improve my present mood. Deep down, I didn't believe her either. The sky was falling, and I couldn't sit back and watch them tear down everything I'd worked for.

The morning passed, and I didn't feel any less exasperated by the situation. I'd wasted hours obsessing over every detail of their new site, comparing every bell and whistle to ours. My insecurities were at the wheel, and they were steadily driving me right off the tracks. By lunch, most of my adrenaline rush had worn off and my body reminded me that I'd been up half the night with Blake. I needed coffee.

I walked down to Mocha and took a small table in the corner. I fidgeted with the paper menu even though I always got the same thing. Simone sauntered up, carrying more than a few stares with her as she moved across the cafe. Her red hair, enviable curves, and saucy smile greeted me a moment later.

"How's my favorite techie?"

"I've had better days," I said. "Anyway, I thought James was your favorite techie."

She smirked and leaned against the table. "Yeah, well, he's getting there. I'm not completely convinced he's not still pining over you."

I resisted the urge to roll my eyes. I really hoped James had moved on, and Simone absolutely had my blessing. From his mop of inky black hair to his muscled sleeve of ink, James was her dream man. The only problem was he'd read all the signs wrong when Blake and I had been apart. Or maybe he'd read them right, knowing I was in desperate need of a friend, of anything or anyone to fill the void that being away from Blake had created. I hadn't known until too late that nothing would ever fill that void except for the man who shared my bed now.

"I don't think you have to worry about that, Simone."

She frowned slightly. "You guys never hooked up did you?"

"No." My eyes went wide at the suggestion. "God, no."

She laughed. "Relax. It was just a question."

Except it wasn't. It was an unwelcome reminder of the indiscretion that James and I had shared. Regret washed over me every time I thought of that weak moment outside the office. At the time, I had been convinced Blake was up to no good with Risa, not to mention his ex-girlfriend Sophia who had been ruthless in her pursuit of him. Everything was mixed up and confused. I didn't know what the future held until I found myself in James's arms, swept up in a kiss that quickly faded into the cold reality that if there would be any man in my future, Blake would be that man.

"What's wrong, hon? You look wiped out."

I looked up. "I am. Just work stuff. Long story."

"Want to give me the cliff notes tonight? You can break it down into layman's terms for me over a cocktail. You know I only understand half the shit you guys say anyway."

I gave a weak laugh. "I'm going out of town with Blake tonight, but maybe we could grab a quick drink before we leave. Do you care if he comes?"

"'Course not. Now, what can I get you?"

I ordered and took my time with my food. Most days I'd rush through lunch to get back to work, but today I watched unhurried as people passed by the windows of the cafe, carrying on with their lives. A story hid behind every face, and I couldn't help but wonder if I could ever trust someone outside of our team again. Naively and against Blake's warnings, I'd trusted Max—enough to consider giving him ownership in my company before Blake funded the business instead. And Risa...she'd been hungry, eager to learn and take on all the responsibility that I desperately needed to delegate, only to use all of it against me today.

I fought the tears that threatened. If I'd let them free, they'd be full of anger at having let myself learn this lesson the hard way.

CHAPTER THREE

I scanned the bar for Simone. Not finding her, I chose a seat beside an empty stool. I flagged down the bartender, a little too eager for a cool drink to wash away the bullshit of my day.

As I waited for my drink, the five o'clock news played out in silence on the screens above the bar. My heart thumped as Mark's face appeared, followed by footage of Daniel, presumably on the campaign trail. Along the bottom of the screen, the segment was captioned "MacLeod death still under investigation." A sick feeling writhed in my gut. I wanted that chapter closed maybe as much as Daniel did now. I couldn't imagine what was still in question after Mark's apparent suicide. I wasn't sure I wanted to know either. I was about to ask the bartender to turn up the sound when someone came up beside me.

"Hey."

I jumped slightly only to find James there offering me a tentative smile. He was wearing one of his graphic T-shirts that seemed to perfectly fit the tattooed man beneath.

"Oh," I said. "Hi."

He raised his eyebrows. We hadn't really been alone, or remotely one-on-one for a long time. Work had carried on as usual, but we hadn't talked things through the way we should have. Everything that had been left unsaid weighed on me sometimes. I'd been too wiped out from the drama of reuniting with Blake to really make time to sort it all out with James. Instead it lingered awkwardly between us, in the past but also never far from my thoughts when he was around.

"I wasn't expecting to see you here, sorry," I said, trying to excuse my awkwardness.

"Simone didn't tell you I was coming?"

I shook my head, hiding my surprised expression with a slow sip of my drink. I wondered where this was all going with Simone.

I shifted uncomfortably, as if I could feel his gaze on me, studying my reaction. Did he want me to be jealous? To show me that he'd moved on? If so, all I wanted to convey was how happy I was that someone amazing like Simone held his interest. I hated to believe I'd led him on in any way, encouraged feelings I had no right to encourage in my completely fucked up state of mind weeks ago.

"How are things with you two? Getting serious?" I avoided his eyes, as if that could hide the fact that I was clearly fishing for confirmation.

He laughed quietly and shoved a hand through his wavy black hair, pushing it back away from his face as he stared down at the beer the bartender had just delivered.

"Sorry if I'm not really up for talking girls with you, Erica. It just seems a little strange, I guess, in light of everything."

"You're right, I'm sorry." God, could this get any worse?

He smiled, disarming the moment a little. "It's fine. Anyway, Simone's your friend, right? I'm sure she'll give you the dirt."

I returned his smile, a little relieved. "No, I don't really ask her about it. It's not my business."

"Does she know about…us?" He motioned between us, that small gesture signifying weeks of tension and dancing around an unexpected attraction that had cropped up.

I shook my head. "I mean, kind of, but she knows I'm with Blake."

"Right." He exhaled.

His relief gave me a little hope that he was more than a little interested in Simone. Maybe he didn't want her knowing about our little moment any more than I wanted Blake to. The prospect of Blake knowing roiled my stomach. He was jealous enough of James.

"How are you doing lately? You seemed pretty upset today."

James had a way of picking up on my moods, no matter how carefully I tried to hide them behind my flimsy partition. It would do no good to hide how I really felt or to pretend all was well.

"I'm upset, I won't lie," I said. "To be honest, I wouldn't mind beating someone to a pulp right now. I'm not sure if I'm more upset by Risa stabbing me in the back, or the effects all of this will have on the business."

"I can imagine. You trusted her. Hell, we all did."

I stared at my drink. "I feel so stupid. Like I should have seen this coming."

"There's no way you could have known."

I shrugged. "Maybe. Maybe if I hadn't been so lost in my own head the past few weeks."

"All you did was work. I don't know how you could have been more present with the business. Seriously, you were sleeping at the office most nights."

I shook my head, my thoughts drifting to that time. A

wave of fatigue hit me at the memory. I couldn't remember being more worn down, more determined to wear myself down than I had been. And somehow Risa had been conspiring with Max the whole time, even as I worked tirelessly to move us forward. The whole sequence of events spun in my head, over and over. Every rotation made less sense, gave me that much less faith that I could stop their attempts. What could I really do?

I systematically pushed the sweat of my drink down the glass, saturating the small napkin underneath. James rubbed my shoulder gently.

"Erica," he murmured.

I looked up, my focus returning to the present as I transfixed on James's deep blue eyes.

"You have the rest of us, and you have me. You know we're solid, and we will get through this. Don't give her the satisfaction of knowing she's upset you. Give yourself a break this weekend, and we'll figure all this out next week. I know how you get and worrying yourself into a nervous breakdown isn't going to help anyone. We need you, remember?"

I lifted my lips in a small smile. "Thanks, James."

"Erica."

A man's voice rang out behind me. A possessive hand curved around my upper arm. Blake stood close behind me, his gaze trained on James. The bitterness in his eyes seemed to radiate and reflect back onto him as James barely suppressed a sneer in his direction. I wanted to rise and stand between the two men, to shut down any potential standoff before it could escalate.

"Blake."

I doubted whether I'd said the word out loud until Blake answered, his eyes never losing their focus on James.

"We should go. We're going to be late."

James's gaze went to Blake's hand circled possessively around my upper arm. James's jaw tightened and the muscles in his neck strained. That sick feeling washed over me again. He still believed Blake had hit me. I wanted to put that suspicion to rest, but I couldn't without revealing more information than he needed to know.

"I thought we had time for a drink."

I put a hand over Blake's. His eyes flashed to mine, as if the small touch had broken a trance.

"Change of plans," he said quickly.

I nodded and grabbed my purse, eager to diffuse this tension. I turned back to James and out of Blake's hold. "I'll see you next week."

James nodded and turned away from me. I tensed, wishing I could say something to make all this go away. But Blake's jealousy and James's need to protect me against some imagined threat ran deep. Blake reached into his pocket and tossed a twenty-dollar bill on the bar, threaded his fingers through mine, and led me toward the entrance.

"What was the change of plans?"

We stepped out and into the fading late afternoon sun. Before he could answer, Simone bounded up to us.

"Hey, where are you going?"

"Sorry, Simone. We have to head out earlier than expected," Blake said.

"James is waiting for you though," I added cheerfully, gesturing toward the inside.

Her gaze flashed between us. "Okay. Well, you two love birds have fun, okay?"

I smiled shyly and let Blake guide me toward the idling Escalade at the curb. A second later, I stepped up into the vehicle captained by Clay, the bodyguard who Blake insisted on keeping more available lately.

I slid onto the cool leather seat next to Blake. Before I could say anything, he scooped me onto his lap and pressed his lips to mine. The kiss was urgent, intense as it had been the night before. He swept his tongue over my lips, urging me to part for him. I opened to him and reveled in the velvet push of his tongue over mine. With soft licks, he explored my mouth. Harnessing every wayward thought I'd had, I turned my attention to the passion in his touch, the need I could nearly taste between us.

His scent filled my lungs as we shared breath. I sifted my fingers into his hair, angling him deeper, pulling him closer. The sweetness of his tongue lingered as we teased and nipped at each other's flesh. I stifled a moan, vaguely aware that we weren't entirely alone.

We separated enough to catch our breath. If we went much further, we'd be devouring each other in no time.

"Hey," I said, realizing we hadn't yet said a single word since we'd been in the car, which had been several minutes now.

"Hey yourself," he murmured.

His eyes were dark and determined. He slid his hand up my thigh up to my ass and grabbed me under my dress. I bit my lip, acutely aware of the ache between my legs and the wild desire he could inspire in me in a matter of minutes. I could think of nothing else but the fastest way to have him.

"I have no idea where we're going, but it'll be a long drive at this rate."

He looked toward the front of the car. "We're not driving. Clay's taking us to the airport. I have a plane waiting for us there."

"Where are we going?"

"I figured we'd stay close, but I didn't want to spend half the night in traffic. We'll catch a flight to the Vineyard and be at the house within the hour. I didn't want to waste a minute more than we had to this weekend."

I grinned and met his lips for a sweet kiss. "I can't wait."

★ ★ ★

A predictably small and sporty car was waiting for us when we disembarked and got us to our final destination as quickly as Blake's fancy Tesla would. We pulled up to the sprawling house at the far tip of the island. The small span of time and the miles of separation from day-to-day life sank in as we ascended the steps to the house. The warm ocean air was a welcome change from the muggy city heat. The relief was another reminder of how much I really needed a break.

Blake dropped our bags inside the door and turned to me. He pressed against me as I wove my arms around his neck. He slid his hands down the fabric of my dress until he reached the hem and pushed it up.

"I missed the hell out of you today," he said, his grip tightening on my hip.

"I missed you too. I always do."

"I'll warn you, though, I'm not feeling very patient. Want you fast and hard. Can you take that, baby?"

I gasped, fire rushing over my skin with the promise. Flexing and releasing, he pushed me back against the door. Without waiting for an answer, he hooked his thumbs over my panties and slid them down.

"I want in you now."

My breath rushed out, heat flushing my skin all the way to my cheeks. My heart fluttered with anticipation. I shrugged out of my dress and he separated long enough to let it fall. Then he was back, his mouth at my breast, sucking hard. One, and then the next. I whimpered when his teeth came down around the sensitive tip. There wasn't a cell in my body that didn't want him to deliver on his promises now.

"Okay."

I fumbled with his shirt, tugging it over his head. He unzipped his pants, freeing his full erection before it fell heavily in his hands. I bit my lip hard. He wouldn't wait a moment longer to claim me.

He hooked my leg over his hip and positioned himself at my entrance. He pushed in slow, letting me accommodate him gradually, retreating again only to push deeper. By the time he filled me completely, I'd grown slick around him.

My head fell back against the door with a small cry.

"Blake."

My core pulsed around his thick penetration. We stayed that way, breathless, connected, desire shooting through my veins. I dug my fingernails into his side, pulling him closer, deeper.

"Fuck, you feel amazing. I thought about this all day,

being buried deep inside you. Your body tight around me, coming hard all over my cock. All fucking day, I haven't been able to think about anything else." He pinned me harder, pushing in deeper as he did.

I gasped. "More."

With the small plea, he cupped his hands under my ass, lifting me so my legs wrapped around him. He leveraged me against the wall. The weight of my body combined with the strength of his had us joined tightly. I was tense with anticipation and just as relieved by the welcome sensation of having him there, our bodies united again. It had only been hours, and the tender flesh between my thighs did nothing to lessen my craving for him.

I held his face in my hands, the stubble from the day rough on my palms. He looked deep into my eyes. Lust, love, and that intense possessiveness swam in those green depths, taking my breath away all over again.

"You're mine, Erica."

As the words hit my ears, he pushed upward. I clenched around him instantly, gasping at the bite of discomfort. He was deep, impossibly deep.

"I'm yours," I breathed.

"If I have to remind every man who stares too long, who thinks for a second he could have you, I'll do it."

He surged up again. The friction of our bodies and his tension took over my senses. As urgently as he wanted to claim me, I wanted to be claimed. I closed my eyes, the promise of orgasm suddenly close. Muscles tense, I tightened around him helplessly.

My voice wavered, strangled by the rush of his powerful thrusts, one following the next in rapid succession now. His name filled the air between us, again and again as I begged for more. I clenched down around him, reveling in the friction as it unraveled me, stroke by stroke.

"He'll know it. Goddamnit. He'll know you belong to me."

"He knows, Blake. I'm yours…I've always been yours." I opened my eyes, desire blurring my vision. "Make me yours, Blake."

I ran a hand through his hair and gripped at the roots. Silenced with our kiss, he groaned. He shoved my hips against the hard wood of the door as he drove into me. In seconds I was drunk on his taste, lost. Lost in him, flying high on this feeling, surrendering to it completely. He took me fiercely, love and desperation passing through every touch. We climbed together, in a rush for the release that would bring us together in the only way that mattered right now.

"Blake…oh, God. Oh, fuck."

The grip of my thighs around him weakened as the climax crept up, taking hold of my mind. I couldn't think of anything but Blake, this love. He was the answer when nothing else in my life seemed right. This made sense. I needed this, him, in a way that made no sense and perfect sense.

"Now," he gritted out.

The simple word pushed me over. My mouth opened with a soundless cry as the orgasm took its hold. I clung to him, my focus pinpointed on the throb of his cock plunging into me, guiding me over the edge to that perfect place. A few more powerful thrusts and I came with a scream. He dug into me, his grip rough, until every muscle went taut, his body buried deeply within me.

"Erica!"

His voice was hoarse, sounding as stripped down as I felt. Arms holding me closer, as if I'd disappear if he didn't, he caught his breath, brushing his lips along my neck.

All my strength left with the orgasm, a fact that became evident when he finally loosened his embrace. When my feet found the floor, my legs wobbled. He held me steady, hands at my hips, as he slipped out of me. Warm release dripped down my thigh with his retreat. I went to move, but he stilled me so I was held firmly in place. His gaze riveted on the translucent line it trailed down my skin.

"Fuck, baby. Seeing that just makes me want to fill you up again."

"I'm going to make a mess on your floor."

He laughed. "We might have to make a mess all over the house then, because I'm still hard. I'm wrecked, but all I can think about right now is coming in you again. All fucking night."

A delirious smile spread across my face. "You going to keep me up two nights in a row? You'll wear us both out at this rate."

He smiled and hauled me back into his arms, brushing a soft kiss over my lips.

"We're on vacation, remember? I can make love to you all night and we can sleep all day. Not a damn thing anyone's going to say about it either."

"No house guests," I whispered.

"Thank God. I'm not sharing you with anyone until Tuesday morning."

He moved away, zipping his pants up. Then he lifted me into his arms, taking us to the bedroom and into its adjoining bathroom.

We showered, lathering each other. We stepped out and Blake wrapped me in a fluffy white towel and dried my hair with another. The heat of the shower might have wiped the last of our energy. We collapsed into the bed, weakened by the day, by our lovemaking.

I cuddled up to him, enjoying the closeness, our skin clean and smooth against each other.

"I love you, Blake."

He tipped my chin up so I met his gaze.

"I love you too."

CHAPTER FOUR

I opened my eyes, and the world came into focus. Propped up on his elbow, Blake raked me in with a lazy smile across his lips.

I stretched, curious how long we'd slept. A glide of his hand down the side of my torso sent a tingle of awareness through me. I hummed, leaning against him, all too aware of my nakedness and the mere sheet covering his. His eyes gleamed with pure appreciation and the love that hummed between us. Love. It bloomed in small moments like this, making all the good times that much better, all the tough times worth working through. What I felt for this man took my breath away.

"You're so beautiful in the morning," he murmured.

I tried to hide my smile, turning to the pillow. "Stop."

He brushed the hair off my cheek and kissed me there, lingering by my ear. "I'll never stop. As long as I live, I'll never stop."

I arched to kiss him, melting so easily for him. I took it all in, let it soak into my skin down to my bones. This new freedom, being away with the man I loved so desperately.

I settled back down, nuzzled against his arm. A part of me was still groggy, like I could sleep for days. I'd recognized that in his tired eyes last night too. I sensed he had been struggling lately, but I still had no idea why. As close as we could be, physically, I hated that distance that crept between us at times. That wall that he kept up, usually to keep me safe.

I traced the ridge of his lower lip with my finger. "I want you to be able to tell me anything. Do you feel like you can?"

He raised an eyebrow. "Yes, why?"

"I feel like you've been…I don't know, tense, lately. I wish you would tell me why."

He released a breath, caught my hands, and pressed a kiss to my fingertips. "It's not a matter of being comfortable sharing anything with you. I know that I can. It's more whether or not I decide to burden you with whatever I'm dealing with."

I waited until his eyes locked with mine, wanting to show him I meant what I said. "You're not burdening me. Not knowing what's bothering you is more of a burden. I never know if it's me, or if there's something I could be doing to help."

His expression changed, masking whatever emotions brewed below the surface. "You can't help with this."

"With what? Just tell me."

He sighed and leaned back into the pillow. "You really want to talk about Max? Not exactly a pleasant topic of conversation."

I frowned. Curiosity over what Max was up to now burned through me. "What is he doing?"

"He's not really doing anything, but that doesn't keep him from being an impressive pain in my ass. I've been trying to get him off the Angelcom board since I found out he was funding Trevor to attack my—*our*—sites."

"Shouldn't that be easy? You're the executive director."

"I am, but this is more like a democracy versus a

dictatorship, which I'm somewhat regretting now. I can't just kick him out. I have to run these decisions by a board. The majority won't agree to vote him out."

"Why? Isn't that a no-brainer?"

"They don't want to piss off Michael, Max's father. He's got more money than God, and risking any potential connection with him isn't worth penalizing Max's complete and utter lack of ethics."

I stared at him, contemplating this frustrating circumstance. No wonder Blake was ready to burst every night lately. To have to tolerate the man who had spent years trying to undermine him, with no support from his colleagues, was hard to imagine. At least the people on my team were on *my team*, and there was never any question who the enemy was. Well, at least now that Risa was gone. I was still struggling to quell my lingering paranoia that I couldn't trust anyone after I'd trusted her with everything, confidential information that she was now using against me. Still, Clozpin was a far cry from white-collar investors and the corporate circles many of them ran in.

"Are you so surprised?"

"What do you mean?"

"I mean, the premise of Angelcom is to make more money for people who already have mountains of it. Seems like those kinds of people have it because they're in the habit of amassing and protecting it. Would you expect them to act any differently than they have?"

He shook his head. "I suppose not. It's pretty ironic though."

"How's that?"

"The company is infested with the greedy fucks I'd wanted to take down in the first place."

"What are you going to do now? If they won't vote him out, what other recourse do you have?"

"I haven't decided my next move yet. I'm not sure how Michael would react if I approached him with what's going on. If I could get him to understand, I could get the support of the board and make sure Max didn't get near another boardroom of mine ever again."

"I thought you and Michael were close."

"We are. At least we were at one point. I haven't seen him in a while, and understandably, I don't want our next meeting to be me telling him that his son is a fraud and a cheat."

I traced a path over his chest as it moved with each breath. My beautiful man. I hated that we had to deal with people like Max, like Trevor. Jesus, the list went on.

"I'm really sorry, Blake. It's a shitty situation. But you'll find a way through it. You always do. And someone like Max can't keep going around stomping on people's dreams and get away with it forever. At least I hope not."

As angry as Blake was with Max, I wasn't sure this was the best time to tell him about his and Risa's new site and how it threatened me now.

He tipped my chin up. Our eyes met. "What's going on?"

I hesitated before I began. "Max and Risa launched their little venture. A competing site. Total rip off of Clozpin, and it looks like they took at least one of our major advertisers with them. Who knows how many users."

His eyebrows shot up. "When were you going to tell me this?"

"Alli told me about it yesterday. She wanted me to be the one to tell you. And frankly I needed some time to make sense of it. I don't know if I have though. I'm mostly feeling like they're going to systematically destroy my business with the same determination that they went after you. Except I'm not you. I don't have your resources or your experience. I'm still trying to figure out how to run a company. I wasn't expecting to go on the defensive like this in the midst of our growth. First Trevor, and now this. I'm trying not to feel hopeless about all of it, but it's kind of hard not to."

"Trust me, he's not going to destroy your business. I won't let him. And as hate-filled as they are, the two of them are no match for the two of us." He brushed my cheek with his knuckles. "It hurts, but it's business. You can't lose faith. That's what they want. If I gave up every time someone took a sucker punch at me professionally, I'd have been done long ago. You're too strong for that."

"I just can't believe someone could be so devious, so hateful. I couldn't imagine ever wanting to do this to someone, anyone, no matter how much I despised him."

"I hate to say this, but get used to it. As soon as you start to do well, someone will want to take that shine away from the things you do, lessen it or make it their own."

My eyes went wide. "You're not making me feel so hopeful about a future in entrepreneurship."

"You'll toughen up. And you have me."

"But what can we do? We have no control over what they're doing. This feels like sabotage, but I'm totally powerless over it."

He was silent a moment, as if he were strategically thinking his way through this one. "Well, I could always hack their site." The corner of his mouth lifted.

I rolled my eyes. "Great. Dueling hackers. I think we can both agree that solves nothing. Beyond that, it's beneath you."

He laughed. "Is it?"

"You said you only use your powers for good, remember? Even if they are terrible, I can't see you destroying their site."

He pursed his lips. "Maybe you're right." He wrapped an arm around me and brought me down to him, kissing me gently. "No more talk of Max. This weekend is for us. What do you want to do?"

I glanced at the clock; it was nearly lunchtime. Our schedule was all kinds of mixed up. Time didn't really matter when it was just Blake and me.

"What do you want to do?"

His eyes darkened with a knowing smile. "If it were up to me, we'd never leave the bed."

I pushed myself up and straddled him. "We didn't come all this way to stay in bed all day."

He groaned, raking over my nakedness. "You're not making a very good argument for leaving."

He followed the path with his hands, palming my breasts and teasing my nipples into hardened points. The carnal appreciation in his stare warmed me instantly. I ached for his mouth, squirming despite myself.

As if he could see my resolve melting away, he cupped my ass and ground me down against the hard erection that strained through the sheets between us. I bit my lip and rolled into the motion, seduced by the unavoidable truth that I wanted what he wanted, and just as badly. My head fell back as the contact rubbed over my clit in just the right way. Fire licked over my skin, heating me through to my core.

He lifted me with his hips, ripping away the sheet the separated us. His cock was as hard as I'd imagined, thick and ready for me. More than ready. His narrowed gaze told me refusal was a lost cause. Finding the slick heat between my legs, he fingered me gently.

"Always ready for me," he murmured.

Answering the silent pleas my body gave, he lowered me down onto the rigid length of his cock. I gasped at the depth, the sharp edge that we always seemed to walk with each other.

"That's it, baby. Take all of me."

My eyes fell shut as I gave myself over to it. All my senses tuned in to the way our bodies fit, all the ways this man owned my pleasure.

★ ★ ★

We left the privacy of the house and wandered into town. The island buzzed with activity. We wasted the rest of the afternoon perusing shops, trying to avoid the now unavoidable throngs of summer tourists. We talked, but never about work. We laughed, always touching in some way. I needed it, and maybe he did too, because I couldn't remember a moment when we weren't connected. Most of the time we were simply together, without words, but in the comfort of being with each other.

We'd been ravenous for each other lately, some all-consuming hunger that only grew stronger once sated. I needed him. And that need pulsed through me every waking hour. In the background of my days, in the demands of our nights, and in the quiet wordless moments that we shared in between. I'd lost all control over it, and I'd given up trying to harness it. We'd spent too much time apart. I couldn't deny any fleeting chances to be together.

From the day Blake derailed my presentation months ago, he'd captivated something in me. What had grown between us since I could no longer be without. Maybe he felt the same way, and that ever present need—to touch, to hold, to be lost in each other through the long nights—was a manifestation of that nameless emotion between us.

Between our afternoon romp, the activities in town, and the fresh air on the island, I was exhausted by the time we pulled up to the house. I shivered when we stepped into the cool air. I much preferred the breezy summer air over the climate control of the indoors. I'd spent too many months cold, yearning for summer. The warm sun was not something to waste.

Always so in tune, Blake rubbed my arms, coaxing some warmth into the chill that had worked its way over me.

"Are you hungry?"

"A little, yeah."

"Go relax on the deck. I'll grab something for us to eat."

I agreed and stepped out onto the deck that gave an unobstructed view of the ocean beyond. I sank into one of the Adirondacks and propped my feet on a stool. I closed my eyes and let the warm breeze dance over my skin as the sun set. The sounds of ocean waves lapping against the sandy shore might have lulled me to sleep if I'd been alone a few minutes longer.

Blake joined me then, setting a plate with cheeses, crackers, and meats on a table. He poured white wine into two glasses and handed me one.

"Thank you," I said.

His eyes glittering warmly. I met his smile, wondering what had inspired that look since I saw him moments ago. "You're happy."

He sat back, smirking before taking a drink. "I am very happy. You have that effect on me, you know."

My heart sang. I tipped the glass, and as the fruity liquid hit my tongue, I knew this had been a great idea. Three days of peace and quiet with Blake was already pure heaven. I relaxed into the chair.

"This is amazing, Blake. I could stay out here forever. It's so peaceful."

"Careful what you wish for. I'll have us moved out here by the week's end."

I laughed. "No kidding. I can't make a wish without you rushing in to make it come true."

His eyes held me steady, serious in their depth. The humor in my words faded away when I thought about what a gift he was to me. I took a breath, suddenly overwhelmed by that truth. What had I done to deserve such an amazing man to call my own?

"You know there's no way I can thank you for everything you do for me. I kid, but seriously, how can I ever repay you for all the wonderful things you've done?"

"I'm sure I'll think of something." He nodded to my glass. "Drink up."

I sighed and took a long sip. I nearly spit the liquid out when something hard fell against my lips. I swallowed quickly and looked inside the glass.

Oh my God.

I straightened, planting my feet on the ground, though nothing could ground me for what I was seeing. I stared stupidly into the glass, frozen and vaguely aware that Blake had moved to kneel at my feet. His palms brushed along the sides of my bare thighs up to my shorts.

"Breathe, baby."

I inhaled on command, my eyes unable to shift from the shiny diamond-studded ring that rested in the empty well of my glass. I couldn't think. I could barely breathe.

"This hasn't been a one-way street. You've given me just as much as I've given you. You've loved me at times when I haven't made it so easy for you to...Erica, honey, look at me."

I swallowed over the tight prickle in my throat. Tears burned my eyes as I met his warm gaze. "This is crazy," I whispered.

"This might be crazy, but this is our life, and I want to spend it with you, as your husband. I want to come home to you and know you'll always be there. I want to make love to you every night and wake up with you every morning for the rest of my life."

I shook my head in disbelief, tears falling. I searched for words, but none came.

He brushed away the wetness on my cheeks and

reached for my glass. Tipping it, he retrieved the ring and set the glass away. He grasped my hand gently and looked up at me.

"Erica, will you marry me?"

I stared into his eyes, now green and bright in the fading daylight. Time stood still as the question echoed in my mind, as the enormity of what he was asking me sank in. Could this be real? Could he really mean it?

"Are you sure?"

He smiled. Somehow he'd never looked so gorgeous. "Yes, I'm sure."

"Are we rushing into this? That's what everyone's going to say."

His eyes widened a fraction. "We've been through enough to fill a lifetime. I don't need any more time to know you're the one I want to be with. And I seriously don't give a damn what anyone else has to say about it. Neither should you."

I looked past him to the steady ebb and flow of the ocean. Our little paradise had become that much more surreal. To be Blake's wife, to tie our lives together, irrevocably. I'd thought of it, of course. I'd tried not to read into his insinuations about a future of forever. Deep down that was what I wanted too, though. As much as the prospect terrified me when I thought about what it really meant, I did want forever with Blake. He brushed his thumb over the skin above my knuckle, sending a rush to my heart. I loved this man, and I couldn't believe anything would ever change that.

"Okay," I said quietly.

He cocked an eyebrow. "Okay?"

I smiled. "Yes."

"Are you sure?"

I laughed softly. "Yes, I'm sure. I—I want to marry you. I love you, Blake. How could I say anything but yes?"

His face split with a smile. He slipped the sparkling band over my knuckle and into place, pressing a kiss where it sat. He stood, bringing me with him and into his arms. We were wrapped together so tightly, I could scarcely take a breath.

"I love you, Erica. You'll never understand how much, but I'm going to try like hell to show you."

I held him back and the reality of our promise settled over me, warming me from limb to limb. Our love filled me, until I thought my heart might explode with it.

In that moment, I knew I could never love anyone the way I loved Blake.

CHAPTER FIVE

The rest of the weekend flew by. Blake took us out on the water, jetting us to outlying islands where we basked in the sun and listened to the steady rush of the ocean water until we were too tired or hungry to stay longer. We explored every quiet corner of the island. We ate and drank and made love. We talked and made promises. Every minute was like its own little paradise.

This commitment between us still felt new, like a dream. But so was being on the island, isolated from our real world. Every time my eyes lit on the sparkle of the band on my finger, my heart leapt. It was a brilliant and overwhelming reminder of Blake's love. Both thrilled and apprehensive of what it meant for our future, I couldn't help but fantasize about our happily ever after.

"Do you like the ring?"

I looked up at Blake, who'd caught me admiring it as our plane approached Boston's dusky skyline. "I love it. It's simple."

"We can pick out something bigger if you want. I took a risk with it. I wasn't sure what you'd want."

"No, I want this. It's perfect."

"Good." He grinned and squeezed my hand gently. "We'll put another one next to it, and then I'll know I have you for good."

I envisioned its companion, and the meaning struck me.

"Like the bracelets."

He nodded.

"You'll have me cuffed and bound to you forever, Blake. You sure you want that?"

He leaned in, taking my lips in a gentle kiss. "That's the idea."

My heart twisted. A tiny flutter of nerves hit my belly at the thought of being Blake's forever. His *wife*.

As our plane floated toward Logan Airport, I regretted that we were returning so soon. The break had been amazing but short-lived. I was still high on it, but less pleasant realities waited for both of us. Whatever trouble came our way, we'd face it together. I'd made Blake a promise that we always would. No more running and no more trying to be strong on my own. Fighting my own independent nature wasn't easy, but sharing my life, the good and the bad, was more important now than ever.

When we stepped into the apartment, Alli met me with a squeal and tight hug. I laughed and hugged her back. The happiness of having my best friend so close compounded with this news, warming me.

Heath's hand slapped Blake's in a shake. "Congrats, man."

A small smile spread across Blake's face. "Thanks."

Heath's focus shifted to me and he pulled me into a tight hug. "Erica, future sister-in-law. You have no idea what you're getting into with this one, but more power to you."

I laughed and pushed him back playfully. The two men wandered into the living room and talked while Alli all but dragged me toward the kitchen so she could inspect the ring. She studied it for several seconds as the light danced off the diamonds. I smiled, thrilled all over again that he'd asked, that I'd agreed. Without even having had the chance to fantasize about what that moment between us might be like, I'd known immediately it was what I wanted.

Alli ran a thumb over the band, one eyebrow raised. "This is different."

I shrugged, not quite sure what to say. I wasn't about to tell her that the bracelets he'd given me months ago doubled as handcuffs, and this ring held a similar symbolism. "Different, but it's us. I love it. Plus, how am I supposed to work on a computer all day with some huge rock on my finger?"

She leaned back against the counter, her gaze lifting from the ring to my eyes for the first time in several minutes. She studied me then, with almost as much intrigue as she'd studied my diamonds.

"So if I know you, your mind must be going a million miles an hour with all this."

I laughed. "A little. I'm just …"

"What?"

I sighed. "I don't know. I think I'm still in shock that he wants this, you know, to make things permanent."

"Blake is crazy about you. You know that."

"It was an easy decision to make. Obviously I'm head over heels for him too. Not like he would have taken no for an answer anyway." I laughed to myself, trying to imagine what lengths he would have gone to get the answer he wanted.

While my thoughts ran away from me, Alli smiled broadly and bounced a little. "I'm so happy for you, Erica! I've been freaking out all weekend. Heath told me after you left, and I've been dying to see you again."

"I had no idea," I said, admiring Blake's gift, his promise.

"This can't have been the first time you've talked about marriage."

My eyebrows shot up. "Why, have you?"

A flush reddened her cheeks. "I'm not talking about me. I'm talking about you. Usually people talk about marriage before proposing. Test the waters and what not."

"He mentioned it once, kind of in jest I think, but I told him he was crazy. And I meant it. I still think this is all kind of crazy. I'm scared to death, but I want to be with him. If this is what he wants and it needs to be now, so be it."

The whole prospect was overwhelming and unexpected. I loved Blake without condition, but solidifying our relationship with marriage was something I wasn't considering as a possibility for years more.

Marriage, to me, implied stability, something sure and reliable. Happily ever after and all good things. Conversely, very little in my life felt stable right now except my love for Blake. Despite his reassurances, the future of the business would worry me deeply until I knew it was safe along with everyone's jobs.

Clozpin was so much more than a job, and seeing it successful was more than a short-term goal. I needed it to work, for so many reasons. If it didn't, I'd be even more dependent on Blake's wealth and security. While I appreciated that he would be that for me and never make me feel less for it, the idea of being completely dependent on someone else was unsettling.

"So have you thought of a date? A venue?"

I laughed at Alli's enthusiasm but also fought a wave of anxiety at sorting out all those details. When on earth would

I have time for that? Did his family expect something big? I'd been so overwhelmed with the proposal, I hadn't even thought to ask Blake what his thoughts were on the matter. I was still trying to wrap my head around the basic concept of marriage.

"I seriously have no idea what we're going to do or when."

Alli's big brown eyes were wide and expectant.

"But of course I could use your help," I added quickly.

She smiled and bounced again. I laughed at her boundless enthusiasm. She was going to be an invaluable resource on all things wedding. If anyone could pull it off, Alli could.

"You're the one who should be getting married. You probably have the whole thing planned out already." My voice was hushed, and I looked behind my shoulder quickly to make sure Heath hadn't heard me.

"I might, but I'll settle for planning yours for now. Who knows when or if we'll ever get around to it."

"Sounds like you two have actually talked about it though?" She shrugged and leaned her hip against the counter. "A little, but that's a huge step. We know we're not quite ready for that. I do have some more good news for you though."

"Oh?" My eyebrows lifted with curiosity.

"Heath and I found a new place. It's pretty close, but I'm sure Blake will be psyched to have his apartment back. We're going to start moving things over this week, so Mr. Broody won't need to share you with me anymore." She smiled and poked my shoulder.

I smiled, happy for her and for us. "You must be excited."

"I am. It's the first time we'll be getting a place together, that's ours. It's already vacant, so we should be moved over completely in a few days."

"That's awesome. Let me know if I can help."

"Don't worry about it. You focus on work. I know you have plenty to catch up on at the office, but pencil me in for dinner next week. Heath wants to invite the family over to see the new place. Plus I'm sure everyone will want to talk wedding details, so that will be fun."

"Okay," I agreed weakly.

The knot in my stomach grew at the mention of Blake's family. I loved them, but they were a little overwhelming sometimes. Was there such a thing as being too nice, caring too much? Maybe by comparison to my family. The thought of inviting the Hathaways into my life to celebrate this occasion was unsettling at best. They'd done little more than shun my mother since the day she told them she was pregnant with me. Would they shun me now too, or feign interest and attend as if they'd cared at all my whole life? Either scenario seemed stressful, but I didn't want to deprive Blake's family of an occasion that might mean the world to them. Heaven help me, our two families could not be more different.

To avoid further inquisition, I pulled Alli back into the living room and we chatted away the rest of the evening with the guys. I relaxed into Blake's side, grateful, in love, and determined to make the most of the last few hours of our break away from the world.

★ ★ ★

The office had been quiet this week, save the quiet hum of machines and tapping of keyboards as people worked. I was doing some quick math when my phone rang. Daniel's number lit up the screen. For the first time in weeks I considered answering. As soon as I reestablished contact with him, the battle to maintain a healthy separation between our lives and business affairs would begin. I hadn't felt up to it, and after learning that two more advertisers would be closing their accounts with us since PinDeelz launched, I wasn't sure why I would be now. Perhaps out of sheer desperation to occupy my mind with something other than the downward spiral of my business, I answered.

"Daniel, hi."

"Hi. I wasn't sure you'd answer."

I wanted to be honest in my response, but I also didn't want to piss him off. I'd really hoped this next chapter of our relationship wouldn't be so contentious. I wasn't sure if I could survive it if it was. Daniel Fitzgerald had proven himself to be both violent and dangerous, but I forced myself to believe I could harness the man behind the political machine, behind the layers of societal pressure to be all that he'd become. Despite all my misgivings, something inside me was committed to salvage what I could from our warped father-daughter relationship.

"I've been out of town," I said, offering a half-truth. "How are you?"

"The campaign has been doing well, so I can't complain. How about you?"

"Um, good."

His silence extended over the next few seconds, and I felt an odd pressure to fill it.

"Blake and I are engaged."

He paused. "I suppose congratulations are in order."

"Thanks." My voice was small. I had a hard time believing he was genuinely happy for me, when he was the reason why Blake and I had spent the most agonizing weeks of my life apart. The separation had almost ruined us.

"Assuming you haven't forgotten about the campaign work we discussed," he said.

I inhaled, steeling myself to hold my ground.

"I needed some time, Daniel, after everything. But no, I haven't forgotten."

"Have you had enough time then? Can we meet to discuss? Time is running down on the clock, and your contribution is still important. I'm not taking anything for granted with this race."

I tapped my pen, my thoughts swirling around my own business problems. "Maybe. When did you want to meet?" The last thing I wanted to admit was the state of the business. That could open a door to him pushing me to work for him permanently. I couldn't imagine any worse punishment for failing at entrepreneurship than being forced into that arrangement. "Maybe next week we can get lunch and meet at the headquarters after. Will has some things to update you on."

"That's fine."

"See you then. And congratulations again, Erica. I'm happy for you."

I frowned, words catching in my throat. "Thank you," I finally managed.

I hung up and stared at my phone. Perhaps I'd never be able to figure Daniel out. Or perhaps this was the beginning of having his trust, and maybe of him earning mine.

The rest of the day whittled away in a flurry of tasks,

large and small, until my energy was thoroughly battered. I glanced at the clock and considered packing up so I could have a few extra minutes to get ready for dinner with Marie, my mother's best friend, and her boyfriend Richard later. Sid stepped into my office and interrupted the thought.

"What's up?" I craned my neck to look up at him.

He folded his thin frame into a seat across from my desk. "I was wondering if you had a few minutes to talk."

I tensed, imagining the worst. The site was wrecked, or he'd found another job and given up on Clozpin. "Is everything okay?"

He shrugged. "Other than the fact that we're losing advertisers and user engagement is slowing. Are we going to sit by and watch this happen?"

I relaxed slightly, but the tone of his question put me on the defensive. "What do you want me to do, Sid? I have no control over Risa's site or the lengths they go to undermine us."

"Exactly." He regarded me quietly with his big brown eyes.

"And?"

"Well, why don't you focus on things that you can control instead of obsessing over what they're doing? They aren't going away any time soon, and if your strategy is to sit idly by hoping they do, we're not going to last long. Sites like ours come and go every day."

"We're maintaining, Sid. All hope is not lost." I worked to believe the words.

"I didn't sign on to maintain. There's no reason why we can't grow. Diversify."

I frowned. "What do you mean?"

"I mean we should up the ante. They've duplicated our concept, and if that's all they know how to do, they'll be the ones who falter. I think we need to start thinking outside the box. What can we do to make the site better?"

I threw my hands up. "I've thought of little else for days, believe me. I mean, I have some ideas but nothing revolutionary."

"Maybe you're thinking too small. You have all these connections now, right? What about a partnership? Maybe we need to take another look at those kinds of opportunities."

"We don't need money. Blake invested."

"That's not what I'm talking about. I'm talking about broadening our target market. Take your brain out of the small service that we're providing and consider what we could do on a larger scale."

I nodded, humbled by the suggestion. "You could be onto something. Do you have any ideas?" He shrugged.

"I'm not really a twenty something female. I just feel like we're looking at the problem from the wrong angle. You're the one who came up with this concept, and I think if you can get past the panic and forget about what Pin-Deelz is doing, you can take us to the next level. Put them in the rearview."

"Thanks, Sid. I'll think about it, okay?"

"Sure. Let me know if I can help."

"Of course." I leaned back into my chair. "How is Cady?"

"Good. We're good." His cheeks reddened.

I fought a smile. "I'm glad to hear it."

He unfolded himself from the chair quickly. "I'm taking off. I'll see you tomorrow."

I waved him off and got lost in thought. I doodled on my notepad until the loss of revenue I'd tallied a few minutes earlier was surrounded with an ornate design. Maybe Sid was right. Why couldn't the answers be easier to find? Every major decision I'd made lately seemed to be reactionary. What happened to the time when we were driven by ideas, not survival? We'd secured the finances from Blake to grow and carry on, but if I didn't figure my way through this, his investment would dwindle quickly. I cringed at the thought of failing him. He'd opened so many doors for me, and all for what?

I was about to give up when a thought occurred to me. I shuffled through my desk drawer until I found a card. I took a deep breath to calm my nerves and dialed the number on it.

★ ★ ★

We stepped into the cool air of Abe and Louie's, the heavy door closing out the light that flowed in with our entrance. My arm hooked around Blake's. The steak house's maître d' disappeared to prepare our table, and Blake turned me, pinning me to his chest. My breath hitched at the sudden contact, our closeness in plain view of anyone nearby.

"Bring back anything?"

I smiled as the memory of our first chance meeting came back to me. Even then, he'd taken my breath away.

"A few. I was ready to haul you into a coat closet and kiss that smirk off your face."

He hummed, tracing my lower lip. The hunger in his

eyes had my heart beating against my chest. "Not too late for that."

"True. But I don't want to get kicked out before Marie gets here."

"You think they'll kick us out for this?"

I sucked in a sharp breath. He cupped a hand at my nape and planted a chaste kiss on my lips. The other slid around my waist to hold me as he dipped me back. I smiled under the soft press of his kiss, wrapping my arms around his neck.

"You're quite the romantic these days, aren't you?"

He grinned and pulled me up, not loosening his hold around me.

"Still celebrating, I take it?"

My loving gaze shifted toward the door, the voice there reminding me that we were far from alone. Marie walked closer, a dark-haired man behind her. Curiosity, pride, and love shone from her eyes, and the look hit my heart. Blake loosened his hold so I could go to her. She pulled me into a warm hug.

She whispered in my ear. "Congrats, baby girl."

"Thank you."

She stepped back and looked up to the man who was at her side now. He was tall, nearly six feet, with short black hair and olive skin. His dark eyes captivated me for a moment.

"Erica, I'm Richard Craven. It's a pleasure to finally meet you."

He captured his hand in mine as I reached out.

"Likewise. I've heard so much about you."

Tall, dark, and unwilling to commit. I looked between him and Marie. Marie, the woman who could be my mother but always seemed to strike me as too youthful and vibrant for her age, somehow looked even younger beside him, her expression soft and almost girlish in his presence.

Blake came up beside us. "Richard, I'm Blake Landon."

Richard grinned and shook his hand. "We meet at last."

Blake's eyes narrowed.

"We've attended a few of the same events around town. I'm a journalist, so I've been there to cover local stories and what not."

"I see. Well, it's a pleasure to meet you formally, Richard. Should we eat?"

Marie clapped and smiled. "Let's."

Blake caught my hand and nodded toward the approaching maître d'.

We settled at our table, and Marie peppered me with questions while we waited for our meal. Where and when would we have the wedding? Who were we inviting? When I was going dress shopping? I answered as many as I could. Blake and I would need to figure out some basic wedding plans before anyone else had the chance to pump me for details. Not having answers was driving me crazy and adding to the mountain of anxiety I was already dealing with.

I turned my attention to Blake's conversation with Richard, desperate for an escape.

"Do you write for a specific publication?" Blake asked.

"I have a staff position at the *Globe*, but occasionally I write for others."

"Richard is asked to travel quite a bit," Marie chimed in.

"What kind of stories do you report on?" I asked.

His gaze shifted to me. Something passed behind his eyes. Curiosity, vague interest maybe, but I couldn't put my finger on it. "The type of reporting I do really runs the gamut, but I take a special interest in political coverage."

"Do you enjoy it?" I hoped the disinterest wasn't evident in my voice when I asked.

A charming grin lifted his lips. "What isn't entertaining about politics?"

I could think of a thing or two. I laughed lightly, unwilling or maybe unable to give him an honest answer that wouldn't open a can of worms not conducive to polite dinner conversation.

"What about you, Erica? Do you have any interest in politics?"

"Not especially, no." I put my napkin on the table. "If you'll excuse me a moment. I have to use the ladies room."

"I'll join you, dear," Marie said.

She freshened her makeup in the mirror, brushing gloss over her bottom lip.

"So what do you think?"

"About Richard? He seems great. Definitely very charming."

She shot me a sassy grin. "He charms the hell out of me."

I rolled my eyes and laughed. "TMI, Marie. Anyway, I thought things were kind of rocky with you two? What changed?"

"He was traveling for a while, and we didn't see much of each other. Honestly, I really thought things had fizzled between us. The past couple weeks have been different though. I don't know. It's hard to explain, but maybe we've just passed a certain point with each other."

"I guess that's good, right?"

"It's good enough for now. I'm having too much fun to push the issue. What about Blake? You must be on cloud nine."

I smiled, warming at the mere thought of him. We'd been apart for all of four minutes and I missed him. Was I ever hopeless.

"I am, yeah. He caught me completely off guard, so I think I'm still getting used to the idea of all this marriage stuff."

She shook her head and patted my cheek. "My little girl. I can't believe it. You're going to beat me to the altar. If I didn't love you so damn much, I might hate you a little."

I laughed. "Blake's the one who seems to be in a rush, otherwise I'd be happy to give you a head start."

She cocked her head slightly. "You sure about this? Blake seems wonderful, but you know you don't have to do this if you're not ready. I don't want you to be an old maid like me, but you have plenty of time."

I looked down, my fingers twisting around the beautiful ring. I couldn't imagine anything, any doubt or reservation, threatening to come between me and keeping this ring on my finger.

"I'm not sure if marriage is something anyone is ever ready for, right? Plus I already said yes, so I'm a little committed already." I laughed nervously.

She brought her hand up, brushing my cheek softly. "Listen to your heart, Erica. There's nothing but noise in this world, and that's got to be the one steady voice in our lives. If your heart says yes, nothing else matters."

I reached for her, holding her in a hug for a long time.

I thought about all the times she'd comforted me, given me advice and solace.

"Thank you, Marie, for everything. Also, you're not an old maid."

She laughed softly and released me, blinking away the wetness in her eyes.

"All right, enough of that. I'm going to wreck my makeup. Let's get back to our men."

The rest of the evening went well. We chatted, and Marie shared stories of our summers together when I was back in school. Any embarrassment that came with her honesty was quickly replaced with gratitude that she was the one person who could represent my otherwise absent family. Blake squeezed my hand under the table, occasionally shooting me a knowing look, as if he too appreciated her little insights into my past. It was the closest to embarrassing baby pictures he was likely to experience in my world.

We finished a decadent dessert, and Richard picked up the check just as my phone rang. I fished it out of my purse and recognized the number.

"Excuse me, I have to take this."

Blake's brow wrinkled, but I slipped away from the table before he could question me.

"Hello?"

"Erica, it's Alex Hutchinson."

"Alex, hi. Thanks for getting back to me. Um, I'm not sure if you remember me."

"Of course. Landon introduced us at the Vegas event. Took a minute to jog my memory, but you've got the fashion site, right?"

"Right. Clozpin."

"So how's it been going?"

"Overall really well. I'm actually brainstorming options for expanding the site, possibly incorporating some e-commerce. You came to mind, of course, which is why I'm calling. I'm not sure if there are any partnership opportunities, but if nothing else, I'd love to just get your advice. I know you must be busy."

"No worries. It'd be easier to talk in person though, I think. Any chance you're coming out for the Tech Awards this weekend?"

"Uh, no," I said, not wanting to admit that the event wasn't on my radar at all.

"I could scrounge up a couple tickets if you can make the trip. We could discuss any opportunities for working together while you're out. And you could write it off as a business expense, of course."

I laughed. "I think I could probably work something out. Let me check my schedule and shoot you an email to confirm, but I'd love to come."

"Great, let me know. If you can't make it for some reason, I'm planning to be out your way in a couple weeks to see some family, so we could always meet up then."

"Sounds good. Thanks again, Alex."

We hung up, and I couldn't hide the smile on my face when Blake approached me in the entryway.

"Who's got you smiling like that?"

"That was Alex Hutchinson."

"Why are you talking to him?"

The furrow in his brow deepened and quickly released when Marie and Richard joined us. We hugged our goodbyes, and Marie made me promise to call her for dress shopping.

My mind spun as Blake led me outside. The valet drove the Tesla up to the curb and Blake opened the door for me to get in. Settled behind the wheel, Blake pulled into the steady flow of evening traffic. After a few minutes of silence he finally spoke.

"So what's going on with Alex?"

"I was talking to Sid about maybe taking Clozpin in a different direction, trying to think outside the box a little, and it occurred to me that Alex had offered to be a resource when we met. I'm not sure if he'd be interested in any partnership—"

"What kind of partnership?"

My excitement over the call waned quickly at the skepticism in his voice. "I don't know if that's something he would consider. His site is huge, and he's obviously doing really well on his own. But Max and Risa are in business competing with us now. I've lost a handful more advertisers, and my revenue is going to take a hit. I just thought—"

"I get it, but you're considering a partnership with Alex Hutchinson and you didn't run this by me?"

I shifted in my seat. "I didn't realize I had to. Is there something with Alex that I need to know about? If it's anything like what you kept from me about Max, I'd like to know before I fly out to San Francisco to see him."

He exhaled audibly, betraying his growing frustration. He parked abruptly down the street from the apartment and stared off a moment. "He's nothing like Max. I'm a little shocked you didn't talk to me about any of this though. I'm the investor in your company."

"I'm grateful for what you've done, Blake. I have every intention of paying you back, but if I have any chance of doing that, I need to get us back on track. Otherwise this is going to be an epic failure and your investment will be lost."

"I don't give a shit about the money, Erica. Four million dollars would be worth losing if it brought you into my life. Every penny I have would be."

My heart twisted at the proclamation. "Thank you, Blake. But this is about me making this business work. I reached out to Alex on a whim, and I honestly didn't think he'd get back to me so quickly. I definitely wasn't expecting him to be receptive to discussing this further, but it seems like an opportunity I should pursue. I'm telling you about it now, literally minutes after it's happened. I'm sorry if you felt I was keeping anything from you, because that wasn't my intention."

He caught my hand and rubbed the back of it gently.

"Are things going okay at work?" I didn't want to argue, but I could tell something was bothering him, hoping it wasn't all me. "Have you been able to talk to Michael yet?"

"I put a call in to him, but I haven't heard back yet. I might make a trip to Dallas. Some things are better discussed face to face."

"Maybe you could go while I'm in California."

He shook his head, his lips pulled into a tight line. "No, I'll go with you. Alex is a friend. We've worked together before, and obviously I don't want you traveling alone."

"I'd like that. There's some technology awards event this weekend, and he said that he could get tickets if I could make it."

His hold on my hand tightened slightly. "Sure. I'll have Cady make arrangements. We can get a flight Friday night."

I leaned over and slid my free hand across his button down. His eyes darkened. We stayed that way, still in the darkness, eyes glittering in lamplight. I sensed he had more to say, but I didn't want to push him tonight. I reached up, closing the small distance between us.

Sealing our mouths together, I sought the sweet depth of his. The kiss deepened. Our tongues tangled. He freed my hand to cup my cheek, angling me to his liking. I reared up, wanting our bodies closer in this small moment, as impractical as it might have been.

"I love you," I whispered, panting for air when we separated.

I lowered my hand, gratified as always to find him hard, his erection straining. I kissed him deeper, teasing him with strokes of my tongue that I imagined lavishing elsewhere.

He pulled back, catching his breath. "Let's go in."

Before he could move I had his fly unzipped, my fingers circled around his length. I kissed his neck, nipping at his skin while I stroked him from root to tip.

"Fuck, Erica, let's go in. Someone's going to walk by."

I smiled against him. "And do what? Tell on us? Maybe they'll want to watch me suck you off." I took his earlobe in my mouth. "My lover's had a bad day. Let me make it better."

He exhaled sharply, his cock twitching in my palm. "I'm going to punish you for this later."

I laughed quietly. "You're going to punish me for wanting your cock in my mouth? I think I can handle that."

"If a cop pulls up before I come, we're going to redefine punishment. You might not like it. Make it fast."

He lifted a fraction, his erection shifting in my grasp.

My mouth watered at the promise of tasting him. I took the hint, lowered, and wrapped my lips around his hot flesh. I swiped my tongue over the head and down his shaft, lubricating my path until my mouth was filled with the throb of his erection.

"Fucking hell. I love your mouth."

I moaned. The taste and his musk overwhelmed my senses. I eased him in and out with a rhythmic pulse. With his hand fisted in my hair, I slowed, letting him take control of my movements. He tightened his hold, guiding me over his cock, forcing himself deeper, faster. I heard his hand hit the steering wheel. His hips arched, holding himself to the back of my throat and then releasing me. I drew in a sharp breath through my nose a second before he repeated the motion, challenging what I could take.

Once more, and with a strangled cry, his muscles jumped. Curses filled the air around us. A warm gush flooded my mouth. I finished him, swallowing the evidence of his release until he was clean. He pulled me off abruptly, his head thrown back on the seat rest.

"You're killing me."

"I know the feeling," I breathed, writhing with need now.

He turned his head, gazing down at me. "You're all wet, aren't you?"

I shifted slightly, the rub of my thighs together doing little to ease the ache there. "Yes, and I'm willing to beg you to do something about it."

He trailed a finger along the low neck of my blouse, grazing the top of my breast. I bit my lip hard, the tension inside me mounting. He lifted his hand to release it with his thumb and pressed our lips together. A deep, possessive kiss, his taste lingered on my swollen lips.

"Touch me," I whimpered.

"I want to, believe me. But as soon as I sink my fingers into your pussy, I'm never going to be able to get out of this car without fucking you. You might want the world to know I'm fucking you straight out of your mind, but if I'm going to jail, I'd like it to be a little more notable."

"Where's your sense of adventure," I teased. I kissed him hard, too wound up for my own good. "I can't wait."

"Trust me, you can wait, and you will wait. You'll wait even longer if you don't get your ass inside now," he growled. "This car's not big enough for all the things I'm going to do to you."

CHAPTER SIX

The sun set over the curve of the horizon as the plane made its way east. I leaned against Blake, tired from my day. I was grateful for the weekend, even if it meant travel and more work. I would have rather enjoyed another break on the Vineyard, but I'd take what I could get.

"We should talk about all this wedding stuff. If I have to sit through another inquisition with Alli I'm going to lose my mind."

He smiled. "She's probably giving Heath a heart attack."

I stayed quiet, not wanting to hint that maybe marriage plans weren't so terribly far away for the couple. Heath still had a long way to go pulling his life together after his stint in rehab. Being back in Boston with his family and now Alli seemed like the right move, but we all cared too much about Heath to take this good stretch for granted. That may have been why Blake hadn't pushed him to move out, even if it had encroached on our privacy now that we were living together.

"Have you thought about what you want to do?"

I sighed. "Not really. I think I'm too overwhelmed to even consider the details. When, where, and who…I can't imagine how I'm going to pull this together."

He slid his hand into mine and squeezed gently. "We can do whatever you want. At the end of the day, all I care about is being married to you. If that's at some lavish affair that will go down in Landon family history, or if we take a weekend in Vegas and tie the knot on our own, I don't really care as long as you're Mrs. Erica Landon at the end of it. Just don't make me wait too long, okay?"

I relaxed a little at the sweet look in his eyes when he said my name, the name that would be mine. "I feel the same way, but I don't want to disappoint your family. If we eloped, they'd probably hate me for stealing their moment."

He laughed softly. "Their moment? Baby, this is our moment. We can do whatever we want. Heath will get around to it eventually, and Alli can go nuts with her planning then. Say the word, and I'll book the Elvis chapel."

I rested my head against his shoulder, closing my eyes. "I don't know. I guess I need to think about it."

"Are you worried about your family?"

The dread in my stomach answered his question before I could respond. "Maybe a little. Too bad my family can't be more like yours. I'm not sure I'd even want to invite them to a ceremony."

"Have you told Elliot?"

I shook my head.

"Daniel?"

"Yeah, I told him. He actually said he was happy for us. Totally threw me off."

"Well he sure as hell won't be walking you down the aisle."

"I don't think we have to worry about that. If anyone would, it'd probably be Elliot. He actually called me out of the blue the other day. We haven't talked in months."

"You never mentioned it."

"I would have, but you had a pressing need to tie me to the dining room table. He's what made me late, by the way."

He squeezed my hand, maybe in a silent apology. I was too comfortable to move and catch his reaction.

"So what did he say?"

I shrugged my shoulders, suddenly wishing I hadn't brought it up at all. I understood Elliot's reasons for wanting to reach out to me, but I hated feeling like he was doing it out of obligation or guilt.

Blake caught my chin, tipping it toward him. "Did he say something to upset you?"

I met his gaze and straightened in my seat. "No. It's just that talking to him again brought back a lot of memories. A lot of those are sad, I suppose. He wants to come visit and commemorate Mom's passing. It's been ten years."

I stared into the darkening night sky through the small window at my side. A vision of my mother as I remembered her passed through my mind, the same way it did every day and at times like these. She was always with me, somehow.

"Funny how years can go by and one conversation can bring me back there so quickly. All of a sudden I was twelve again. I mean, I'm an adult now. I can rationalize and cope when difficult things happen, but I'm not sure I'll ever be able to think about her life or her death without the kind of devastating feelings I had as a child."

"That makes sense."

"Does it? I mean, I should be able to move on by now, but that conversation made me realize how much is still there, unresolved, for me."

"What do you feel is unresolved about it? I mean, it doesn't sound like she had options."

"It's not that. I understand there was nothing that could

have been done to save her. It's more how everything fell apart after she died."

"With Elliot?"

I nodded. "I don't feel like I can be angry with him. When everything boils down, he's not really my father. His commitment was to my mother, and he could have never known she would get sick."

"His commitment was to you too, though."

I lingered on that idea longer than I really wanted to. "It doesn't matter now. I don't even know why I'm talking about it."

"Because it still hurts you."

"I'm a big girl. I can deal with it."

"I know." He brought my hand up and kissed it softly. "You don't always have to be so damn strong, you know."

I laughed quietly. "I don't know how else to be."

"I suppose that makes two of us. Except I'd be a lot happier if you let me shoulder more of the burden for you."

I shot a questioning look his way.

"This meeting with Alex, for example. I could have easily set that up for you, felt him out for possibilities, and negotiated something that would work out favorably for you. But you're so damn headstrong you insist on doing it all yourself."

"Why wouldn't I?"

He laughed softly. "Why would you want to, when I can do it and you can focus on other things?"

I pulled out of his grasp. "Like what? Wedding planning?"

"No, like running other aspects of the business. Isn't that what you enjoy?"

"Building these relationships is part of my job. If anyone should be doing it, I should."

"Suit yourself, Erica. You want to do things the hard way, I'll let you, but I'm not going anywhere so it might be worth a second thought. We're on the same team, remember?"

He took my hand from my lap, laced his fingers through mine, and trailed his lips down my arm. I shivered at the whisper of his breath on my skin. My nipples beaded instantly. I looked out the window, trying hard to be mad, but the innocent touch was a dangerous promise of how easily he could take control whenever he wanted. Blake had enough persistence to break down anyone's defenses.

I could fight, but he'd always win.

★ ★ ★

The expansive function room was teaming with people. All walks of life. From suits to techies to everyone in between. From what Blake had told me, this was the "who's who" event in the tech world, and I could expect to meet an impressive cross-section of people in the industry. Blake wore a dark gray suit, and I'd dressed simply in a deep red wrap dress and black heels.

Blake kept an arm around my waist as we wove through the crowd. The gesture warmed me in more ways than one. I was always nervous at events like this, and as much as I wanted to hold my own, having him there with me was a comfort.

"Landon."

Months had passed since we'd met, but after a second,

I recognized Alex as he walked toward us. His gaze drifted from Blake to me, and then to Blake's hold on me. I considered stepping away, but doing so would only be awkward. If Alex didn't already know about our relationship, he would now. And if he thought my recent success came from Blake's wealth…well, he might be right. I only hoped he wouldn't discredit the pitch I'd planned for partnership opportunities because of it.

I scolded myself silently for reading so much into it. After all, Blake and I were engaged now. *Engaged.* The thought blew me away every time I said it to myself.

"Alex, it's great to see you. Thanks so much for inviting us out." I reached to shake his hand, giving him my best professional grip.

He met me with a broad smile. "Absolutely. I'm glad you two could make it. This is always a fun event. All the hot shots are here, so you'll fit right in."

"Oh, thanks," I said shyly.

"So tell me about Clozpin. What have you been up to?"

I cleared my throat, hoping I didn't look as awkward as I felt. I looked up at Blake. "Um, I'd love a drink."

A crooked grin curved his lips. "Sure thing. Alex?"

Alex raised his glass. "I'm good."

Blake maneuvered with grace toward the bar. My body cooled where he'd held me by his side. I took a quick breath. I needed some space to say what I'd come to say to Alex. I met his eyes with a small smile.

"I'll be honest, Alex. The business has been going great. We've picked up some big name advertisers, and there has been an impressive growth spurt in the very short time we've been funded. The trajectory is strong. However, a competitor site recently popped up. They've essentially cloned us and are now trying to poach our advertisers."

He frowned. "That must be frustrating."

"Very, but it's been an eye-opener too. Our team is stronger than we've ever been, our foundation is very solid, and I think we could transition to the next level pretty easily and leave this copycat in the dust."

He took a sip off his drink.

"How do you plan to do that?"

"That's where you come in. I'm open to suggestions, but this seems like a perfect time to partner with someone who could use our traffic to build sales of their own and help us grow in return. I checked out your site after the conference, and while ecommerce has always been in the back of my mind, I've admittedly had my hands full growing our current business model. I wasn't ready for a major shift until recently."

He nodded slowly. A ghost of a smile curved his lips. "I can see why Landon invested with you."

I laughed nervously, not quite knowing how to respond. My thoughts went to Blake as Alex's words echoed in my mind. I cocked my head and studied him a moment.

"I don't remember mentioning that Blake was an investor, but perhaps that was obvious."

"I might have assumed, but no, we spoke a bit today over the phone. He just wanted to touch base and it came up. Don't worry, he was determined to let you pitch me. He failed to mention the copycat though, which makes me all the more impressed that you were honest with me about it."

My jaw set. I didn't know whether to be annoyed with Blake or proud that I'd impressed Alex. But why was he always meddling? When would he realize I could hold my own? My brain reminded me that he wanted to help, compulsively so, but another part of me wondered if he truly believed I could handle it.

Alex's voice broke me from my thoughts. "Sounds like a promising start though. Let's meet up tomorrow to talk details. I don't want to pull you away from the party. I'm sure Blake's eager to show you around. Plenty of people to meet here."

He nodded beyond me. I followed his gaze, suddenly more determined to find Blake's face in the crowd than I was to butter up my prospective business partner. When I found him, my heart fell into my stomach. The chiseled outline of his profile faced Risa. She twisted a lose strand of her jet-black hair around her finger as she spoke, mouthing words I couldn't read. She looked as put together as ever in an all black designer suit. But her expression was tentative, her eyes wide and her body leaning back slightly from the unmoving column of Blake's body.

"Erica?"

I turned my attention back to Alex.

"Are you fine meeting for lunch tomorrow?"

My thoughts suddenly scattered. "Yes, that's fine."

"Great. Let's meet at the hotel restaurant around noon."

"Sounds good. I'll look forward to it."

Then Blake was beside me, circling a hand around my upper arm. His grip was firm enough to send warning signals to my brain. When had I become so in tune to his moods? And when did my body start reacting so acutely to them?

"Alex, will you excuse us?" Blake's voice was no longer

relaxed and casual. Instead the words came across curt, as if Alex were no longer an old friend, but just another business acquaintance.

"Of course. Have a great night, you two."

Alex waved us off without another word. Blake led me toward the exit we'd just arrived through, his hold on me tightening a fraction. I resisted the urge to yank out of his grasp and call him out on getting to Alex with my pitch before I had a chance to. I wanted to be angry with him for unnecessarily butting into my professional life yet again, but something was definitely wrong beyond all that.

"What is Risa doing here?"

"She's here for the same reason everyone else is here. To see and be seen." The words came through gritted teeth.

My stomach knotted with worry. We slowed in front of the bank of elevators, and he hit the button hard.

"What did she say?"

The bell rang, and we entered the mercifully empty car. The doors closed slowly and he backed me toward the mirrored wall of the elevator, pinning me there with the closeness of his body. He grasped my jaw, forcing us eye-to-eye. I couldn't evade the intense eyes that burned into me.

"I'm going to ask you one last time. And you'll tell me the goddamn truth. If you don't, we're finished. Done."

The knot in my stomach doubled at hearing his threat.

"You lied to me once, because you thought you were protecting me, but if you lie to me right now, it'll be the last chance you'll ever have." He took a short breath. "Tell me the truth, and we'll figure it out."

I thought my heart might pound right out of my chest

at its current pace. I was too stunned to respond for a few seconds.

"Blake...you're scaring me."

His jaw worked, as if wrestling with the words he held behind the firm line of his beautiful lips. "Did. You. Fuck. James?"

My heart stopped. I looked into his eyes, desperately searching for a reason for his unexpected question.

"No," I whispered.

The car came to a stop, and he left me, moving swiftly down the hallway. I hurried out, following him into our room. I lingered by the door, my mind still racing. What had Risa said? What had spurred this intensity from him, seemingly out of nowhere?

Blake tossed his jacket off. It landed on a chair and he moved to the window. Shoving his hands through his hair, he faced the sprawling city view.

I simply stared. In awe, in fear, in love. I didn't know what was happening between us tonight, but I hated how far away he already felt. I took a step toward him and stopped short when he turned to face me. My breath left me when our eyes met again. Stone cold. As dark and unfeeling as I'd ever seen them. No longer my sweet and romantic lover, the man in front of me was the ruthless billionaire who wouldn't be crossed.

"Strip."

The order settled into the silence between us. The word physically chilled me, a shiver working its way up my spine.

"Blake, I don't understand..."

He unbuttoned his shirt, unhurriedly pulling it loose

from his pants. "I want you to strip down. Naked, here in the middle of the room."

"Why...why are you so upset with me?"

The smooth veneer of his controlled expression broke. A frustrating grimace revealed his teeth. "Goddamnit, Erica. I'll get another room, and I'll be on the first plane out of here in the morning. You can sleep alone and go home alone. If that's what you want, you should test me now. See how much room I'll give you."

His skin reddened. Had he ever been this angry with me? But why? His jaw ticked, the muscle bulging as he waited for me to react. I opened my mouth to speak, but I couldn't. I had no idea what I was defending myself against. What had taken us from an enjoyable evening to being swept up in the tornado of this unexpected rage?

As if in answer to my unspoken question, he spoke in low and measured tones. "Risa let me know about James. Remember, your little rendezvous outside the office after I dropped her off? Sounds like things got pretty heated between the two of you." He cocked his head a fraction. "Assuming there's some weight to that story."

No. No, this wasn't happening.

My eyes blurred with the sting of the tears I held back. I was paralyzed. Without consideration, I would have done anything to stop where this was going.

He tossed his shirt aside and came toward me.

"Was it as steamy as the beach? I seem to recall you being pretty worked up after that."

"Blake," I pleaded. He was twisting everything. God-damn her for doing this to me, to us.

He stood in front of me, staring down into my eyes. He

seemed taller, more intimidating than I'd ever remembered. I lowered my shoulders, his posture seeming to demand that I do.

"Is it not true? Tell me it's not true."

I snapped my jaw shut. Anything I said now would be futile. He wasn't interested in my excuses.

He threaded his fingers into my hair, gripping it by the roots to pull me an inch closer. I whimpered at the small pain. My hands found his chest, the leverage holding me up as my knees weakened slightly. The heat of his skin nearly burned mine. He leaned in so I could feel his breath in my hair, against my neck. I could smell him—the man I loved who maybe hated me now.

"Strip." The venom in his voice was now replaced with a dangerous determination that prickled under my skin. "And kneel."

My eyes fell shut. I exhaled sharply, already feeling stripped by his words. I wanted to cry, but I remembered his threat. That he'd leave me. Maybe only for a night, but the thought of him leaving in the midst of all this terrified me. I couldn't believe that he wasn't already considering leaving me completely.

He released his grip. I nearly stumbled as he moved away. I looked down at my feet, my hands sliding restlessly against my dress. Without thinking, because I couldn't make sense of anything right now, I kicked off my heels, one after the other. My fingers went to the knot holding my dress across my body. I fumbled with it, my hands trembling badly now. I loosened it and let the dress fall to the floor around me. Sensing the seconds ticking by and knowing he was counting them, waiting, I quickly released my bra and slid my panties down.

I stood there, starkly naked. The silence stretched between us. I lifted my head to find him. Eyes that stormed with emotion seemed to bark the order in the silence of the room.

With the unspoken command, I lowered, resting shaky hands on my knees. A voice in my head screamed that I shouldn't have to, not this way, answered by another that told me I deserved every minute of it. Either way, I couldn't let him leave me, and if I had to kneel to make him stay, I would.

CHAPTER SEVEN

I stared at the carpeted floor in front of me. This was what he wanted from me. When I wanted to ask why, when I wanted to fight it, Blake's words echoed in my mind.

Total submission. Total control over your pleasure and pain.

He wanted this...my submission. He didn't want to explain himself. I could say sorry. We could talk it out, fight it out, but this is what he wanted now. Maybe it's what I needed too. That tornado of our bodies crashing together, silencing the rest of the world. Except he was furious, and I hated to see that look in his eyes knowing I'd put it there.

He crouched down in front of me, but I kept my eyes down, focusing on his shoes, the way his slacks strained against his muscled thighs. God, but the man was gorgeous. Even when he was angry as hell.

His hand graced my cheek, eliciting a shiver that traveled up my spine.

"If I wasn't so pissed off right now, I might be impressed with you, Erica. My little submissive is finally learning. We'll see how long you can keep it up, because you're going to get the punishment of a lifetime tonight. Do you think you can take it?"

I lifted my head, my eyes narrowing. The fighter in me threatened to spout off to him. I inhaled a slow, steadying breath through my nose. *Ride out the storm.*

"Still don't want a safe word?"

My chest fought to expand over my next breath. I took another quickly and shook my head, casting my eyes down again. Stupidly, I assured myself that committing myself to one would give him license to make me want to use it.

He brushed his fingertips over my lips, sending a tingle over them.

"He kissed you. Did you kiss him back?"

I sucked in a breath through my now quivering lips.

"In case you haven't noticed, I'm not in the mood to repeat myself tonight. Did you kiss him back?"

"Yes, I...I kissed him back." The words left a sour taste in my mouth. Why? Why had I let myself wander so damn far? A tinge of nausea hit my stomach at the thought I could lose Blake over that one stupid moment.

"Was he in your mouth?"

I waited a second and nodded again, the sickness reeling through me now. His touch feathered down to my breasts, cupping the heavy weight of one.

"What about his hands? How could he resist these perfect tits when his tongue was in your mouth? Did he touch you here?"

He gave my nipple a tug, eliciting a whimper.

"I don't know. No."

Lowering, his palm skimmed over my belly until he was between my parted legs. He grazed the lips of my pussy, barely touching me.

"Here?"

"*No*," I insisted.

"Did you want him to?"

"No."

He slapped my pussy, a sharp motion that sent a shock of pain and unexpected pleasure through me.

"Truth, Erica," he snapped.

"I wanted it to be you," I rushed. "If any part of me wanted those things, that was why. But I'm telling you the truth when I say I didn't feel *anything*."

"You mean to tell me that he held you in a kiss long enough for Risa to see, with his goddamn tongue in your mouth, and you didn't feel a thing?"

I closed my eyes, hating all of this. Everything was confused, as mixed up as I had felt when I let James too close that day. My throat constricted with emotion.

"Blake. Please believe me. Everything happened so fast. He caught me off guard, and maybe for a split second, yes, I thought I wanted him. But then I couldn't stand it. Even believing you were gone, that I'd never have you again, I didn't want him. I wanted you, but he's *not* you. He'll *never* be you. Even if you hate me and punish me, that will never change."

My voice was watery as I uttered the last words, the truth that would haunt me to the day I died if he ever left me. God forbid, he'd ruin me forever.

"Why didn't you tell me? Why the fuck did I have to find out this way?"

I bowed my head. "I didn't want to hurt you, Blake," I said, but it was too late for that.

"Do you have any idea how furious I am right now?" His voice was lower, dangerously low.

I chanced a look in his eyes. They were blurry through the wetness in my own. The lack of sympathy chilled me further. "I'm sorry. I'm so sorry ..." My voice wavered, but I was desperate for him to know it.

"Are you? And will you show me how sorry you are?"

"I'll do whatever you want." I reached for him, but he stilled me, holding my wrists away from him.

"What makes you think I want you after what you did?"

He could have pushed a dagger straight into my heart the way the words hit me. But his eyes told a different story. I saw fury there, but hurt too. Not enough to weaken the hard lines of his features, but enough to give me the smallest of hopes.

"You're the only one I'll ever want. Please don't hate me. Blake, I was stupid and scared. I hate that it happened, that I gave up on us before we could find our way back to each other. I love you. Please ... let me show you."

He paused a moment before releasing my wrists. He rose and crossed the short distance to the couch. The swift rejection gave weight to the already heavy sickness in my belly. My breath left me at the whoosh of his belt leaving his pants. He held it in his hand a moment, a knowing look leveling me. My chest tightened, heaving under my now anxious breathing. Unexpectedly, he let it drop to the floor before settling himself onto the couch.

He unzipped his pants and freed his erection. He began slow strokes up and down the hard length. A different kind of tension rolled off him then, one I could release for him, if he'd let me. Several moments passed as he worked himself up, his gaze never leaving me. I pressed my fingernails into the tops of my thighs. I wanted badly to go to him, but he'd punish me if I moved without his permission. I didn't dare speak it.

"Come here," he rasped.

Relieved, I moved to stand.

But he cut me off. "Crawl. I want you on your hands and knees until I tell you otherwise."

I hesitated a moment, and then began to move. The carpet pressed into my palms and stung my knees as I crossed the distance between us. My cheeks heated with embarrassment. This position delivered all the humiliation he could have wanted to deliver.

Nothing could diminish my wanting him, though. I sat on my heels between his legs, as willing as I'd been a moment ago. The engorged head of his large cock disappeared under his palm and reappeared as his hand slid to the base. The tip glistened with moisture. Licking my lips, I could nearly taste him. Suddenly I wanted nothing more than him in my mouth. I could take away this frustration, ease this ache that burned inside both of us.

"You want this?" Strain weakened his words as his pace quickened.

"Yes." I lifted off my heels, my hands resting on his knees.

"You don't deserve this. The satisfaction it would give you."

The dagger he'd already lodged in my heart twisted. Like a wounded animal, I lowered.

"Please. Let me," I pleaded softly.

His breath hissed through his teeth. I bit my lip, my own frustration mounting with the rise of his orgasm. The words seemed lost. Would he ignore me until he came? I slid my hands up his thighs and back down. I licked my lips, imagining his taste on them, the push of his desire between them.

"Let me please you, baby. I love you. I want to."

His eyelids fell closed, his muscles hardening beneath my touch. "Fuck," he groaned. His head fell back with a shaky breath.

Emboldened, I placed a hand over his, holding down his rapid movement. A second later he was deep in the wetness of my mouth. I circled his head rapidly with my tongue. My cheeks hollowed with a hard suck, and I took him as far as I could. I shifted and moaned, my thighs brushing together as I positioned myself so I could take him as deeply as I could.

That quickly he was at the edge. A few urgent shoves against the back of my throat, and he shuddered with a pained groan. He caught me by the hair and held me to him until he'd emptied himself completely, his cock twitching and throbbing through the aftershocks.

The ache of kneeling and the discomfort of the way he moved me for his pleasure faded into the background as I tasted him, breathed in his scent. From base to tip, I licked him clean. My lover, my beautiful tortured lover. I wanted to be this for him. I wanted to worship him, to serve him. I wanted to be everything for him, even in these dark moments when nothing made sense but the demands of our flesh.

He slipped from my mouth, and the sounds of our breathing filled the silence. My breasts were tight and heavy. Moisture pooled between my legs. I wanted him now, as angry as he'd been moments ago. But I fought the urge to show him, to ask for more. I let my hands slip back to my knees, breathing through the desire that surged.

He raised his head. His face had softened in the

aftermath of his orgasm, but his jaw was resolute. "Touch yourself."

Without another thought I reached between my legs. Pulling the moisture of my arousal over my clit, I began a rhythm. My eyes closed. A soft moan left my lips when I thought of his fingers there, pleasuring me.

"Wish it were me touching you?"

"Yes."

"Want me to sink my cock into that wet pussy of yours?"

"Yes," I gasped. My belly tightened and heat prickled across my skin. My core pulsed and clenched, wanting to be filled with him. All of him, until all of this madness went away and it was just us, together.

"Go ahead and work yourself up."

A flash of fear shot through me as I felt him move away from me. If he was willing to shun me earlier, what would stop him from teasing me to the edge and leaving me there just to spite me? My fingers worked feverishly over my clit. My orgasm built, and I chased it. Eyes squeezed tight, I blocked everything else out. Suddenly I was convinced he'd leave me unsatisfied if I didn't get there myself.

"Blake," I moaned. His name left my lips like a desperate prayer. He wasn't inside me, but he was still with me. Invading my thoughts, deeply embedded in any fantasy that would bring me to climax. I kept him close as I clawed at the now empty couch, my hips lifting into my own chase.

"I'm right here."

My eyes flew open at the sound of his voice at my neck. Before I could focus, he linked his arm through both of mine at the elbow, pulling my shoulders back. My breasts jutted out. My clit throbbed for attention. I shifted restlessly, too eager to finish or be finished. His free hand came to my throat, his grasp both gentle and possessive. His thumb rested on the heavy pulse point that beat stronger as he circled the column of my neck.

"I want to show your body who it belongs to, but I want to hear you say it," he whispered, pulling my earlobe into his mouth. He sucked, bit down hard.

I jerked as much as his restraint allowed me. I was wound too tight.

He soothed the sting with his tongue. Hot openmouthed kisses down my neck had me breathless and squirming. I pushed my hips back into his erection, silently begging him to fuck me. He leaned me forward, so my chest rested against the couch. His hand left my throat and curved around my front. He slipped into my wet heat, his fingers teasing the hard nub of my clit. I tensed at the contact, the leisurely pace of his touch driving me to the brink of madness.

"I own you, Erica. Your heart, the blood that beats through it when I hold you down this way. Your body, the way it moves for me, comes for me. It's all mine. Say it. Tell me I own you, baby."

I shifted into his touch, ignoring his demand.

"Say it."

I winced, the fight stirring in me anew. "No one owns me."

"What?"

Challenge laced his question. Somehow the fire of my

desire fed my anger too. I needed to come, to be free of this tension, all of it.

"No one owns me," I snapped, helpless and frustrated all over again.

His fingertips left my clit. Gripping my hips tightly, he pushed me back against him, his hard cock shoving against my ass. I gasped, my anger fizzling in the tornado of my need to be fucked.

"You're wrong. The second I slid that ring on your finger, I owned you. Don't play dumb and pretend you didn't know it either. You promised me no one would touch you again. Do you remember? I punished you then, and I'm going to punish your ass again and again until I hear the fucking words."

He pulled back and moved sideways, and the next thing I felt was the lash of his belt across my thighs. The cry that emerged muffled into the couch when another landed.

"Blake!"

"We can do this as long as you want. Watching your ass turn red just gets me hard."

"We weren't together." My voice, full of every emotion that he seemed to lack, broke as he unleashed another searing slap against my ass.

"Who's fucking fault was that?" he barked.

Mine. The burning heat of my skin doubled when another strike landed in the same spot. I cried out, tensing and shifting away, but he held me too tight. He wasn't spacing them out. He wanted me to feel this in a way I hadn't fully before.

I own you.

The words wrote themselves across my brain as I took one after the next, tensing until I thought my muscles might cramp. Every one delivered a measure of pain that made pleasure look like a faraway place. Each one seemed harder than the last until I went numb. Tears fell, and the only place I could feel the pain was in my heart, the place where I'd wounded us both.

I barely registered relief when he stopped. My view of the room from the cushion of the couch was blurred with tears. He nudged my knees apart, and I jolted when his palms grazed the sensitive skin that had taken the brunt of his punishment. His fingers slid down the crack of my ass down into my wet sex and plunged deeply. I whimpered, overwhelmed by everything. My body was a live wire, numb and overcharged all at once. Despite all the punishing, I was soaked for him.

He withdrew and pressed a wet fingertip just inside the tight ring of my ass. "I should fuck you here. You deserve it," he murmured.

I shook my head. I'd made it through the pain, but I couldn't take any more. I didn't think I could anyway. I didn't know if he'd let me come at all, but even that maddening fate seemed better than what he was threatening now.

"Please don't."

A second finger entered me, stretching me.

My breath caught, and my brain came back to life out of the fog. My head came up off the couch and I tensed everywhere. "No! I'm begging you, Blake. Please don't. I can't."

He stilled behind me and withdrew without a word. The relief came down on me like a hammer.

"Maybe not tonight, but I'll have your ass. You can count on it. Do you know why?" He lowered, his lips grazing my ear. "Because I own you," he whispered.

My jaw clamped down, some small thread of fight lingering in me. The tightness in my throat signaled the torrent of emotions surging its way to my eyes. Anticipation, pain, love. However many minutes or hours had passed had brought on a violent string of emotions shooting through me like a lightning storm.

"I'm going to fuck you, and God help me, you will *not* come until you say the words."

With a grip on my hip, he slid his cock against the pulsing entrance of my pussy and pushed in hard. An almost feral groan filled the air, and I realized it was my own. A desperate kind of pleasure filled me. It slid through my veins like the most addictive drug, taking me straight out of my mind where the only thing on earth that mattered was his body in mine. He kneed my legs farther apart so I felt every thrust deep in my core.

"Mine." He pounded into me. "You will never forget it again, Erica."

His possession consumed me, took me someplace else. I needed it, I needed him. This. And I *was* his.

Mine. You're mine. I'm yours. Forever. Mindless, I repeated the words like a mantra until they lost meaning. *You own me. You own me. You always have.*

"That's right. I own you, baby."

My eyes shot open. I'd said the words aloud. All of them. In the blind rush of wanting him.

"And goddamnit, you own *me.*"

His confession interrupted my scattered thoughts. Then

he shoved into me so hard I screamed. His fingers went back to my clit, building me up again. Every muscle tensed, but he held my arms firmly. He trapped me in the pleasure, restraining me so all I could feel were his rough movements, the impossible friction inside me. The need to come burned through me like fire in my veins.

"Blake...Oh my God, please let me come. I love you. I'm yours...please...please. I can't stop."

"You want to come?"

"Please!"

"Then come," he said.

On command, the storm in my body exploded. I clenched down hard, pulling him into me. Every muscle tensed, a seemingly endless heightened state of satisfaction. I sobbed with the pleasure, my sounds muffled against the cushions beneath me. Everything released, leaving me weak and trembling. Leveraging himself with a hand on the couch, he took his pleasure, claiming my body with the same passion and vigor as he'd claimed my heart. All of me. I took it all, wanting his possession to reach the soul of me.

He buried inside me with a final thrust, tense and silent.

Sweat cooled my skin. He covered my back with his body, enveloping me with his heat. My whole body seemed to sigh, weak as it had ever been. He finally released a shuddery breath and wrapped his arm around my rib cage. An embrace. Warm, and I wanted to believe it was loving. I flexed my fingers against his stomach, wanting to hold him to me, keep him close. But I was still held captive, and he didn't release me.

"I love you," I said.

As the words left me, I prayed he'd say them back. *For-*

give me. Bring us past all of this. But that quickly, he slipped out of me. Then I couldn't feel him at all. Freed, I turned around. He disappeared into the bathroom. The door shut, loud in the quiet of the room.

Empty and cold, I sat on the floor and wrapped my arms around myself. After a few minutes of listening to the shower I moved to the bed. My legs could barely make the journey. I collapsed onto the cool sheets and pulled the duvet over me, wishing the heavy blanket were Blake's arms around me.

I let the tears fall. Wave after wave, until sleep turned everything to black.

CHAPTER EIGHT

"Erica...wake up."

I jolted awake, eyes wide as the now bright room came into focus. My heart was beating too fast, as if some latent panic still lingered with me. Blake was standing beside me, sipping coffee. He was fully dressed in slacks and a freshly pressed shirt. I relaxed a little, grateful he was there at all.

"We're meeting Alex for lunch. He texted me that he was running late, but you should get ready."

I sat up slowly and pulled the covers up to hide my nakedness. I rubbed my eyes, waiting for the sleepiness to ebb. I glanced at the clock. I'd slept for nearly twelve hours, but my body felt drugged, exhausted to the bone. Slowly I began to remember the night. I hadn't had a drop of alcohol, but somehow I felt hung over. As promised, Blake had given my ass the beating of a lifetime last night. I searched for anger, but my heart just ached with sadness and regret.

When I sought his gaze, he walked away and turned his attention to his phone. "You should get cleaned up."

I rested back against the pillows. My hand went to the mess of my hair, and my thoughts went to how our night had ended. Alone. So far apart. Cringing, I found the strength to get on my feet. My movements were far from spry as I walked to the bathroom. My muscles were stiff, and a dull headache throbbed behind my eyes.

I lingered in the shower, escaping under the hot spray

as if somehow the water could wash away the lingering hurt that filled me. Thoughts of James and the mistake I'd made that both of us were paying for shuttered through my tired brain. Blake was fiercely jealous, but I could see the pain I'd caused him last night.

He'd walked away from me, leaving me alone with the intensity of what we'd done without so much as a word. We'd had intense nights before. He'd pushed me to the edge, and we'd crashed over together. For better or worse, we'd ended those nights together. Not last night, and when he left me alone, we'd crossed a line. He'd breached some new invisible boundary I'd never known was there. Perhaps I'd crossed a line too, with what I'd done to set him off. But the empty feeling he'd left me with wasn't like anything I'd ever felt with him before. That emptiness cast a shadow on all the pain and punishment he'd doled out, making it all that much darker.

The heat of the shower was making me weak and tired all over again. I turned it off and stepped out to towel myself dry, acutely aware that Blake was on the other side of that door with my heart in his hands. We had to talk about what went down at some point, but it wasn't going to be an easy conversation. My head wasn't in the right place to pitch Alex right now either, but somehow that didn't matter as much as it should have.

Blake worked at his laptop while I dressed for the meeting. We didn't speak. As if compelled by some magnetic force, my gaze kept drifting his way. If he sensed it, he didn't show it, his focus seemingly undeterred.

If he had wanted to talk, what would I have said anyway? Instead, I fell into step behind him as we entered the restaurant downstairs and took our table. I tried to mask a wince as I lowered into my seat. I couldn't ignore the discomfort of my rather bruised ass, but I didn't want to give Blake the satisfaction of knowing it bothered me.

When Alex arrived, he greeted me. I smiled weakly and kept up with niceties. Something about leaving the party early because I didn't feel well. True enough, I hadn't. He wanted to know more details, work out the logistics with Clozpin. I nodded, but the fire that might have taken over and pulled me through the conversation wasn't there. I simply stared at my lunch, not hungry in the least. My thoughts circled around what had gone down between Blake and me. What else mattered when things weren't right between us?

An awkward silence fell, but the part of me that might have cared simply didn't. Blake's hand went to my knee under the table and squeezed me gently. I glanced up. My heart pulsed against my chest at the contact, as if it had only started beating again in that moment. He frowned slightly, questioning me, but when I went to speak, tears filled my eyes.

"Alex, we'll be right back," he said quickly.

In a blur, we left the table and found some privacy at the other side of the restaurant. The darkness wrapped around us. His body came close, seeming to force the air from my lungs. I waited for him to touch me. I needed him to touch me or I was going to break.

Gently, he brought his hands up and framed my face. I sighed, my earlier fatigue taking hold again. He tilted my head up, bringing us eye to eye. Those eyes that undid me, that stormed with darkness and passion—everything I had come to love about the man—stared down at me.

I love you. I wanted to tell him. I wanted to let the words spill out again and again until he said it back.

"Blake…"

"Are you okay?"

He thumbed my cheek. More contact, every touch overwhelmed me. My eyes brimmed with tears that began to fall now. My hands went to his chest, wanting to feel his heat, his strength.

"I can't do this, Blake. Not right now. I'm sorry…I just can't."

He hushed me and brushed away the tears. "I can take care of it, okay?"

"No, I can't mess this up. I need to be there."

"You aren't messing anything up. It's fine. I'll talk to Alex. Go up and rest." He gripped my shoulders and skimmed down my arms, resting there only a moment before he left. Before I could call him back, he was out of sight, and I was alone again.

I walked quickly to the elevators, my head down to hide the mess of my face. I brushed away my tears but they kept coming. What the hell was wrong with me?

Back upstairs, I scanned the empty room. Empty, like my hollow, painful heart. I wanted Blake here. I hated that he wasn't, but I was in no condition to face Alex and talk business right now. Ironic, since that was the entire purpose for the trip.

Without undressing, I fell back into the unmade bed. I'd woken without his touch and here I was, barely surviving without it. I began to drift off, ready for home, praying that somehow I could wake up and start all over.

★ ★ ★

I took a seat at the head of the conference table and waited for the rest of the team to settle around me. After sleeping away most of the afternoon in the hotel room and on the red-eye home, I should have been rested. Some of the heavy emotional fog had lifted. Enough that when Blake eventually briefed me on his meeting with Alex, my brain reluctantly shifted back into business mode. The terms they'd agreed to were good, better than I would have pushed for or even asked for. I wanted to be surprised, but with Blake behind the wheel, I shouldn't have expected anything less. All I needed to do was seize the opportunity while it was there and act now so we could stay ahead.

"How was San Francisco?"

Alli's voice interrupted my wandering thoughts. She'd settled into the seat beside me. I met her brown eyes, wishing that somehow I could explain all of this to her. My sweet, loving friend. I didn't know where to begin. How would I broach the topic of being punished by my future husband because I'd been caught in a lip lock with one of my employees when Blake and I had been broken up? God, my current dilemma sounded all kinds of fucked up.

"Good," I lied.

My whole body ached, from the sex, sure, but hours had gone by without any real emotion between Blake and me. On the trip home, everything had been matter-of-fact between us. But I could sense his hesitation, the strain that came through with the short delivery of every word, the careful avoidance of my stares as I silently begged him for more. A look, a touch, anything to let me know we were okay.

Too wiped out to push him, I simply went through the motions. It was a remembered feeling, one I had brought on myself not so long ago when we'd been separated under very different circumstances. All of it wore on me now. I hated not knowing what he was thinking, and a part of me was afraid of what he'd say if I dared ask. I needed to believe that we'd get through this, that there was a light at the end of this tunnel. If I thought for a second that we couldn't—that we wouldn't—I wasn't sure I could go on.

Gradually people pulled up their chairs, and I jotted down some last minute notes. I pushed down all the fears, silently refusing to let the events of the weekend derail my entire day. Despite everything, we had work to do, and I had to push on.

James dropped into the seat opposite Blake. The air grew thick around me, filling the space between them. It crackled with their distaste for one another. The clarity I was grasping scattered when I caught Blake's stare. James shifted in his seat as Blake leveled a look so venomous, I wouldn't have been surprised to find them at each other's throats, literally, in a matter of seconds.

I cursed inwardly, questioning how Blake had convinced me to let him drive this meeting knowing James would be there too, right in the thick of it. I might have guessed that Blake would be looking for an opportunity to meet him head on, to start something that he could finish.

I hurried to speak and shift their attention to the matters at hand.

"This weekend Blake and I met with a prospective partner, Alex Hutchinson, who's given us the go-ahead to refer ecommerce sales to his site, in return for increased exposure and commissions for us. We're still working out the finer details, but this is a huge break for our growth, to expand beyond what we've been doing and broaden our reach. We'll need to make some adjustments to our platform to maximize this opportunity."

"Any updates with advertisers?" James asked, tempering my good news with the cold reality of the hit we'd already taken as a result of the competing site's endeavors.

Alli chimed in. "No one else has pulled their account since last week, so maybe Risa's grabbed all the low-hanging fruit, so to speak. Hopefully the rest remain loyal through this expansion."

I masked a grimace. I had a few other choice monikers for Risa I would have rather used.

"What's the timeline?" Chris, our resident Hawaiian shirt-wearing developer, spoke up.

"As soon as possible. I know it'll be tricky to build this out while maintaining what we have. But I figure with what we've been through with the hacking attempts, we can multi-task easily on this. Sid, can you start looking into their API?"

Blake offered him a stack of papers. "I have the documentation for you. Alex and I went through it. Should be pretty straightforward to implement."

Sid reached for it, his eyes wide. I cracked a small smile, not quite ready to celebrate but grateful at least to have Sid's interest. Seeing the plan moving forward was a little scary. I was wandering into uncharted waters, but this was what we had to do. Sink or swim, and I was determined that we would survive. This opportunity with Alex promised to be the lifeline we needed.

The rest of the meeting went well as I divvied up tasks among everyone. In the process I began to feel more grounded than I had been. I'd only been away the weekend, but I'd returned completely off kilter. Being with the team again had grounded me, and I was eager to dig into this new work. The tension rolling off Blake had eased, so maybe the same was true for him. Still, James sent me a few concerning looks. As always, he knew something was up, that I was off. Except I had no idea how I'd ever tell him why. A weary sigh left me. What I wouldn't give to turn back time.

The meeting ended and people began to disperse. I gathered my notes, preparing to return to my desk and dive into my day.

"We need to talk."

Blake's voice was low, the threatening tone unmistakable. I looked up to find him fixed on James.

James sat unmoving behind a mask of supposed indifference. "About?"

Blake rose slowly. "I think it's better discussed in private. Shall we?" He gestured toward the door.

James casually shoved out of his chair and led the way. My heart was beating wildly as I scanned the office. No one seemed the wiser. Hurriedly I followed. They'd moved a few feet down the hallway by the time I'd joined them, closing the door behind me.

Blake stood across from James, his stance wide and his arms across his chest. "I wanted to be the one to tell you that you'll be giving your notice. Preferably this week."

"Excuse me?" James's posture tensed. "Erica's my boss, not you."

"That's not the point. You'll be leaving."

Blake's tone left no doubt. Anger and confusion whipped through me. I wanted Blake to know how sorry I was, how desperate I was to make this right between us. But he was attacking me where I felt it most. My business. My livelihood. The safe place that was mine and only mine, and he was casting a shadow over it all with these demands.

"Blake, what are you doing? Stop this." I took a step closer, hoping no one in the office could hear us.

He turned to me, his eyes colored with all the hurt I'd caused, compounded with the rage he'd focused onto James. "He's leaving, Erica. It's that simple. Unless you'd like me to leave instead."

"You don't mean that." I stared hard at him, almost too tired to test his resolve.

James's soft chuckle broke our standoff. His cool blue stare fixed on Blake, his hands fisted tightly by his sides. "You really let success get to your head don't you, Landon? You think you can march around here and bark orders. What kind of smug bastard does that? And you have the balls to lay a hand on her. I should beat the hell out of you so you know what it feels like."

Blake snapped to face James again, his jaw twitching. "What the fuck are you talking about? I've never hit her."

I took a tentative step forward, not entirely comfortable with physically coming between them right now. With all the emotions flying around, I didn't trust that I wouldn't get hurt in the fray.

"James, no. You don't understand."

"You told him I hit you?"

I met Blake's imploring look full of confusion, maybe

even a hint of guilt. But he had it all wrong. My heart fell, tears threatening.

"No. God, just stop, both of you."

James took a careful step toward me, his voice softer. "You don't need this shit, Erica. Say the word, and I'll have him out of here."

"Like hell you will."

Blake shoved James then, his slightly shorter frame hitting the wall. James reacted immediately, throwing a punch that Blake narrowly avoided. The two men skirmished. They pushed and pulled until I was certain they'd tear each other apart if I stood idly by. I was desperate to make them stop.

"It was Daniel," I yelled, no longer clinging to that secret truth if it meant they'd stop this madness.

Blake shoved James off, and for the moment he kept a distance, as they both heaved for air, eyes wild with fury.

A look of confusion softened James's anger slightly. "Who?"

"He's—it's not important. But the day you saw me that way, I'd just seen him. We had a fight, and…" I sighed, the weight of the past forty-eight hours crashing down on me in an instant. "He hit me."

Silence fell. No words, no fists. Neither man moved.

The look on Blake's face gutted me. As if learning about James hadn't been enough, these words cast a shade of betrayal across his features that made me want to go to him then. To hold him to me and say sorry all over again. For all of it.

"First this," Blake said, pointing to James, "and now you're telling me that Daniel hit you. What the hell is going on, Erica? Is there anything else you want to tell me? Let's just get it all out."

My lip quivered, tears threatening again. Too wrapped up in his own anger, he wouldn't feel my remorse today. I was alone with it. Alone and scrambling to keep some semblance of peace between my personal and professional life. A lost cause if I'd ever seen one.

"You should go. Both of you. Just leave." The last words caught in my throat, lacking conviction and reflecting my frayed nerves.

James cursed and left us alone, his footsteps disappearing down the stairwell. The door slammed shut below, the sound echoing up to us. Blake stood motionless, his stare burning into me. The silence was painful, my own thoughts reeling and loud amidst it.

I could almost hear his too. More questions of why. *Why had I been so stupid? So stubborn?* When I looked up into his wounded eyes, they confirmed it. The effort to restrain his anger, the culmination of all the hurt, was evident in his posture. The muscles of his arms were taut and coiled, no doubt still primed to punch James into next week.

I would have apologized, tried to bring him back to me, if I weren't so goddamn angry at myself now. I knew he was jealous, but he'd taken it too far. He had no right to confront James and step into my business that way. No matter what had happened.

"I don't even know what to say to you," he finally said.

"Then don't say anything at all. Blake ...I'm exhausted, I'm sore, and I'm ready to seriously lose it. I don't need you berating me, making this all my fault." My voice wavered as

I brushed away a tear that had broken free. "Maybe it is, but I can't bear you telling me that right now. I can't take it."

He hesitated a moment, that heavy silence filling the space between us again. Then, without another word, he left.

Out of my world again. I watched his retreat, relieved of the pressure of his resentment, yet infinitely more miserable than I'd been before.

CHAPTER NINE

I hesitated in the hallway, my hand resting on the door. Alli's laughter with others carried beyond the walls of their new apartment. I wanted to celebrate and be happy for Alli and Heath, but I was on the other side of that emotion as long as Blake was keeping me at arm's length.

He'd taken my request to not say anything at all and to leave too literally. A couple days had gone by. He'd worked late again last night, arriving after I'd fallen asleep and rising before I had. The only proof of his being there was an empty coffee mug in the sink. He always seemed just beyond my grasp, and though I was angry too, the distance was tearing me up inside.

I took a breath and pushed open the door, not remotely prepared for all the love that rushed around me whenever I was around Blake's family. All of it was infectious too though, so I held some hope that they could pull me, and maybe even Blake too, out of this funk.

As if in perfect reflection of Alli and Heath's energy, the apartment hummed with laughter, the buzz of conversation, and Alli's loud whoop when the cork popped off the champagne.

"Erica!"

Blake's younger sister, Fiona, ran over to hug me as I stepped into the main area. Catherine was right behind her, coming for a warm embrace as soon as Fiona stepped away.

"How are you, honey? You look wonderful."

"I'm good. Thanks." I gave a weak smile, self-consciously glancing down at the outfit I'd thrown together. I was surprised I wasn't wearing two different shoes for how focused my brain had been lately. Black skirt, top, and ballet flats. That was hard to screw up.

When I met Catherine's gaze again, a line of worry marked her forehead. I brightened instantly and plastered on a happy face. No matter what, I didn't want my problems with Blake to upset Alli's party. This was an important moment for her and Heath, and I was already worried about stealing her thunder with all this wedding madness that she reassured me we had to cover tonight.

Alli joined us, grabbed my hand, and pulled me farther in. "Let me give you the tour."

"Sure." I gave Heath and Greg a small wave before they disappeared out of view.

Alli took me room by room, through the space. The apartment lacked for nothing, on par with what I would expect from any Landon property. Warm colors, spacious rooms, and tasteful design. Some rooms were still cluttered with boxes, but for the most part, it already felt like a home, theirs.

"It's beautiful, Alli."

Her shoulders crept higher as she smiled. "Thanks. I love it. I'm so excited to make it ours. Heath has been working a lot, but hopefully soon we can do a little more to it."

I smiled too, appreciating how far she and Heath had come. He'd only been out of rehab a couple weeks but they were now well on their way to better, to a normal life together. Alli was hard at work re-immersing in my business and Heath was doing the same with Blake's. Blake wanted him more involved, and from everything I'd heard, he was taking the bull by the horns, investing himself more heavily than he ever had before.

Deep down I was happy for them, so very happy. But I couldn't help but draw parallels to Blake and me. Even sharing an apartment, we felt farther apart than when I'd lived a floor below. Moving in together had been easy, too easy almost. I was hesitant at first, but at Blake's insistence, my overstuffed trash bags that I'd moved a couple months earlier from the Harvard dorms took another trip up a flight of stairs. In less than twenty-four hours, my life had melded even more firmly into the organized wealth of his. While I enjoyed sharing the space, the apartment never really felt like mine, not the way Alli felt about this place now.

"I'm so happy for you," I said, trying to keep my voice steady as Alli looked to me for reassurance, for my support as her best friend.

She smiled, content, and hooked her arm in mine. "Thanks, hon. I am happy. Now let's go get extra happy and drink some champagne. We need to talk wedding details and work out the last stuff for the party with Fiona."

"The party?"

Her eyes shot up, her hand going to her mouth. "Oh shit."

"What?"

"Oh shit shit shit. Just forget I said it."

I stopped our exit from the room. "Seriously, Alli. Just spill it."

Her shoulders slumped. "It was supposed to be a surprise. Catherine wants to throw you two a little engagement party."

I lifted my eyebrows. "Does Blake know?"

"Of course."

"Why didn't anyone tell me?"

"We thought it would be fun to make it a surprise. I know you've been stressed with everything that's going down with the business right now. We didn't want to add one more thing to your plate. And it's no big deal, really. Just a small party at their house with some friends of the family who wanted to meet you and catch up with everyone."

On cue, my stomach rolled. I couldn't imagine who *friends of the family* entailed, but considering how tense things were between Blake and me, I could very well be flying solo for much of the event. That thought was far from comforting.

"Are you okay with that?"

"I'm fine," I insisted. "It sounds like fun. If I can help with anything let me know."

"Don't worry about it. I think Catherine's got everything covered. All you two need to do is show up and be yourselves."

She grabbed my hand and gave me a reassuring squeeze as we reemerged into the main living area. Fiona was filling the flutes, getting as close to the rim as she could without the foam spilling over.

"Where'd the guys go?" I asked.

Fiona sat back onto the couch with her glass. "Upstairs. There's a rooftop deck. Really nice after the sun goes down on nights like this."

I wondered if Blake had arrived and was already up there

with his dad and brother, but I was embarrassed to admit that I had almost no idea where he'd been for the past day and night. I wanted to believe today might be different. The company of his family always seemed to make Blake seem more human, less godlike in a way. Maybe around them we could let down this wall between us so we could talk, really talk. Newly engaged, we were supposed to be in love, stable, wanting to be with each other. Right now we could barely share a room without palpable tension between us.

Alli and I sat down on the large sectional across from Fiona. I admired the open space and light that filled it through a bay window at the front.

"I think we should toast. To the move." Fiona tipped her glass to Alli. "And of course to Blake and Erica's engagement."

"Cheers," we sang in unison.

I relaxed back, taking a sip. Maybe this is what I needed while Blake cooled off. A little champagne and girl time.

Alli wasted no time rummaging through her purse on the floor.

"Speaking of engagements."

She pulled out a sizeable stack of wedding magazines adorned with colorful bookmarks. My eagerness for girl time came to a skidding halt.

"Obviously the most important thing is picking out your dress, Erica, but we need to decide on colors tonight, because it's driving me nuts not knowing, and I'm selfish like that."

I laughed softly. I hadn't given it a single thought. At least not since middle school when pink and purple were on the top of every little girl's list.

Fiona repositioned herself on the other side of Alli. "Oh, I love this one. But maybe in navy." She pointed to one of the models.

Alli pursed her lips. "I don't know. If we're doing beachside, there might not be enough contrast. What about mauve, or something really bright, like fuchsia?"

Fiona laughed. "Making Blake and Heath wear pink vests and ties would be amazing."

Alli joined her laughter. Before long their brainstorming had degraded to pink glittering cummerbunds and they were nearly falling off the couch with giggles. I was willing to give them the go ahead if it meant talking about anything else. Then I heard some clatter in the kitchen and remembered Catherine was prepping dinner for our whole group on her own. The men were still nowhere in sight.

"I'm going to go check on dinner. I'll be back in a minute."

I disappeared into the kitchen and found Catherine stirring something in a large steaming pot. Dinner smelled Italian and delicious. I was suddenly hungry though I hadn't had much of an appetite today.

"Hey, honey. Can I get you something?"

"Oh, no. I'm fine. I was just wondering if you needed help with anything."

Catherine smiled. "I think I've got it covered. Go hang out with the girls."

I surveyed the large designer kitchen, wishing I could find a mess to clean. Anything to give me an excuse not to go for a few more minutes. Back to the bridesmaid's den.

What the hell was wrong with me? Didn't every woman on the planet want to get caught up in this whole process?

How could I run a fashion start-up and lack the slightest interest in the finer details of what was shaping up to be a wedding far beyond anything I would have ever imagined? "Big white wedding" was being given new meaning with each passing moment as Alli and Fiona vied for confirmation of their opinions.

I bit my lip and searched my brain for an excuse to stay. "You okay?"

"Yeah, I'm fine." I nodded. *I wouldn't mind disappearing into the floor right now though.* "I just needed a break I guess. They're..."

She lifted the corner of her mouth, quiet understanding in her eyes. "Driving you nuts?"

I laughed. "Maybe a little."

New peals of laughter echoed from the living room and we shared a knowing look.

"Alli accidentally let it slip about the engagement party. Thank you. You didn't have to do that."

"Oh! Nonsense. I want to. You have no idea how excited our family is about the news. They can't wait to meet you. Honestly, they can't wait to see Blake either. He can be a little reclusive when it comes to making appearances for extended family."

"Well, thank you, again. I feel bad because I should probably be thinking of things like that. I should probably be doing a dozen things that haven't even occurred to me lately."

Everything was moving too fast. Work. Wedding plans. As if that weren't enough, this clash with Blake was threatening to throw everything else completely off kilter.

"Blake's a take charge kind of guy, but I don't suppose he's much help with wedding planning."

I shook my head. "I guess not."

I glanced around the room nervously, my gaze landing anywhere but her face. When she grew silent, I chanced a look. Her eyebrows wrinkled. She stepped closer and covered my hand with hers.

"Is everything okay between you two?" she asked gently. "I hope you don't mind me saying this, but you don't look like a girl who's happily engaged at the moment."

I swallowed over the knot in my throat. "It's nothing to worry about."

"Did he upset you?"

My heart twisted, and I squeezed my eyes closed. How could I begin to put into words what had happened between us these past few days? I simply nodded, unable to hide the hurt. "We upset each other. We were both wrong. And things have been tense. It's been difficult to talk lately."

I stared down, scuffing my toe against the slate tile floor. "Sometimes he's just completely overwhelming. Maddening, really."

She laughed softly. "I could have told you that. Try raising him."

I gave her a weak smile. "I can't imagine."

"He's a difficult young man. He always has been. He's my son, and I will love him no matter what, but he's about as stubborn as they come. But somehow I knew from the moment I met you that you were good for him. I pray every day that he's good for you too. He's changed, in so many good ways. I've never seen him as tender as he is with you, Erica. Something is different. It's little things, but I see it."

Tears burned in my eyes. Before I could say anything or find an excuse to leave, she pulled me to her. I hugged her back.

"Don't give up on him," she whispered. "If anyone can get through to him and break through those walls, it's you."

I pulled back slightly and brushed away the tears that had fallen. "I just wish I didn't feel so far away from him right now."

Blake's voice carried through the apartment, mingled with Heath's and his father's. My heart leapt with sudden anticipation. He was here.

"Blake!" Catherine called out in the direction the living room, releasing me from her embrace.

I wiped my eyes again, hoping to hide any signs of my upset. A few seconds later, Blake had joined us. He held his ground a few steps inside the doorway, his hands unmoving in the pockets of his jeans. My heart stopped at how drop-dead gorgeous he could look with so little effort. All mine, I reassured myself, yet that's not entirely how I felt lately. His green-eyed gaze passed between us, pausing on me. I looked away, wanting to hide my recent vulnerability, but I knew I'd given myself away the second he saw me.

"Blake." Catherine's tone hardened. "You need to speak to Erica. Everyone here is celebrating and making a fuss and this poor child is in tears over you. You need to start talking."

He stared at her a moment, his expression unchanged. "Mom, I'm not talking to you about this."

She grimaced. "Aren't you the genius of the family? Good heavens, I don't expect you to talk to *me* about it.

Speak to your fiancée, soon to be your wife. You fix whatever you broke here, and that's all I have to say on the matter."

She gave him a hard stare and then softened when she faced me again. She gave my hand a reassuring squeeze.

Without a word Blake turned. He passed through the kitchen and disappeared into the hallway beyond. I followed him until we were alone in one of the nearly empty rooms I'd seen earlier. This would be their home office. Two desks lined the wall, already cluttered with a stack of papers.

Blake stood in the middle of the room, his back to me. I closed the door behind me and leaned against it.

The sudden privacy also meant silence, an awkward empty silence between us. I searched for words, for something that could possibly bring us back to where we'd been before San Francisco. But I didn't know what to say to him now. He'd be angry with me for breaking down in front of his mother, not that I'd ever dream of telling her what had happened between us.

"I'm guessing you want to talk," he said quietly, turning to face me.

I nodded and swallowed over the knot in my throat. I didn't want to talk here, but who knew when I would have his attention again. "I didn't want to do this here, but you've been gone. She started asking about us, and I just lost it. I'm sorry."

"I'm here now."

His voice was quieter as he took a step closer. He paused a few feet in front of me, his hands still casually nested in his pockets. Usually I enjoyed the posture, that *could give a shit* attitude that rolled off him sometimes, usually when it came to work. I remembered then how he'd looked when he dropped into the seat in front of me at the Angelcom boardroom, seemingly unaffected. I was as annoyed as I was painfully attracted to him. Today I knew better. I knew he cared, but I was no less conflicted about how I felt about our situation right now.

"Blake ... you hurt me."

His jaw tightened and several empty seconds passed.

"I warned you that if you opened the door to that part of me—"

"I'm not talking about physical pain," I said. "I know we'll be angry sometimes, and we'll hurt each other. That's inevitable. I know that we'll take it out on each other in different ways. I'll admit the other night was difficult for me, not because that's anything we haven't done before, but because in the end, all I could feel was your anger. That wounded me far worse than anything physical could have, because I felt like you hated me, and that you wanted to hurt me. Maybe it made you feel better—"

"It didn't, trust me." A grimace pinched his features.

"Then why? You left me there like it meant nothing to you. It's like you're shutting me out to punish me even more. When is it going to end? How many different ways do I have to say that I'm sorry, that I made a stupid mistake I wish I could take back?"

He turned away slightly, raking his fingers through his hair. The dark brown strands stuck every which way.

"It should have never happened."

I sagged against the door. "I know that. I wish it hadn't."

He faced me again. "No, I don't think you fully understand. The things that happened when we were apart ... all of that happened because you didn't trust me to handle Daniel threatening you."

"That's not true."

"It is true, Erica. If you had, we would have never been apart. James would have never had a chance to get that close to you when you were vulnerable."

"I thought Daniel was going to kill you. Do you understand that? I was falling apart missing you, wishing I could find a way to save our relationship, but when I saw you with Sophia that night, and then Risa, something in me just gave up. I knew we were over, that I'd lost you. It had nothing to do with wanting James. It had everything to do with feeling so goddamn empty inside without you that I let him get too close."

"Do you really think I would have let Daniel hurt me or you? Do you think for a second I wouldn't have moved hell and earth to make sure you were safe from that maniac? Instead you fucking ripped my heart out."

The hurt inflected with the words was real. I knew, because I'd lived that torture too. In fear of Daniel's threats, I'd put us both through weeks of hell.

"This isn't just about James, though I'm not happy it happened, believe me. But this was another ugly reminder of that entire situation. You'd been through a lot with Daniel, and I didn't want to put you through any more. But the reality of it is that you put us both in more danger because you wouldn't come to me for help. How am I supposed to be your husband when you won't let me protect you? Goddamnit, Erica, I've gone against every instinct giving you the space you need, and where has it gotten us?"

My lips trembled as I absorbed the fierceness of his

words. "I made a mistake. I was scared, and all that mattered at the time was knowing you were safe."

"How many more times are you going to put us through this, because you're too goddamn stubborn to trust me?"

"You're punishing me for choices I already made, things I can't undo. Things are different now."

He shook his head. "Are they? Can you tell me that you wouldn't make the exact same choices? Because I can tell you right now, if you'd known, intrinsically and without a doubt to come to me when Daniel threatened you, all of that would have played out differently. And all this time I warned you about James. I knew it. I fucking *knew* he was getting too close to you, and you kept him around. What's more, you're still doing it, even though you know it's making me crazy. I want to tear the motherfucker apart for having his hands on you. Do you understand what it does to me, Erica?"

I blinked away tears at this onslaught. Days with nothing, and now this. "Blake…"

"I want control, Erica. But I'm not going to take it from you. You have to give it to me. You opened the door. Now you have to walk through it. You've tried to draw this hard line between us, with work and our relationship, where you keep the amount of control you think you need. It ends now."

My stomach tightened with that familiar urge to run, to push him away. I didn't know if I could ever give him the kind of control he wanted. What if I couldn't, ever?

"What are you saying?"

"I'm saying that you've said you want me, all of me. And

this is who I am. The shit that went down with Daniel…and now James. Nothing like that can happen ever again."

"I don't want it to," I insisted.

"And I'll guarantee that it doesn't."

My jaw fell open a fraction, the words lost in what he was saying. He had to know how impossible it was, what he was asking of me. Why couldn't dominating me in the bedroom be enough?

"Is this about me being your submissive? You want me to play some Dom/sub game with you? That's fine, Blake. I'll beg, I'll kneel, but I'm not letting it trickle into my professional life. I have boundaries, and you need to understand that."

"This isn't a game for me. And that way of thinking is exactly the problem."

He took a step closer, leveling me with his eyes. Defensively, I leaned back, now pressed firmly against the door. He rested his hands on either side of me, our bodies nearly touching, not giving me an inch. I couldn't think straight this way, this close. He held me in his steady gaze, no shred of doubt to be found there. His voice was low when he spoke again.

"How does it feel, Erica, when you give me control?"

That was a loaded question, but I could tell we were no longer talking about Daniel or James. His countenance had softened, the hard intensity there morphing into something else. Something sexual. No less intense, the energy was palpable. It resonated between us, lighting sparks over my skin everywhere he touched. A fingertip over the bow of my mouth, his thumb on the racing pulse at my neck. God, I wanted his hands everywhere now.

"You let everything go, and it feels good, doesn't it? To know I'm taking care of you, of us. That no matter what, I'll get us there."

He grazed his hand lower, his palm skimming over my breast and down my torso, as if he were marking all the places that were his domain. On my body, the places were many.

"Have I ever left you unsatisfied? Has there ever been a time between us, no matter how far I've pushed you, when you haven't begged for more? When you haven't come hard screaming my name? Tell me if you haven't."

My breath left me and I struggled to replace it. I shook my head, knowing the answer as well as he did. Heat prickled under my skin and pulsed between my legs at the reminder of what he could do to my body, the power he wielded so easily. That kind of domination I could embrace. In fact I didn't want that part of him to change, ever.

He leaned in. The smallest brush of his mouth teased my lips. I arched up to meet him fully but he pulled back, leaving me wanting, dizzy with it. I drew in a shaky breath, trying to get sober from this spell he'd put me under. With promises of the control I was already a slave to, he was luring me into something that meant far more.

"What are you doing to me?"

"Showing you what you want, what we need."

"You know that's not what this is about. I know I can give you anything and you'll be there for me. But you can't…you can't hold me down, stake your claim over me, and expect me to let you *own* me."

His eyebrows shot up. "Is that so? That's not what you said the other night. I heard the words, loud and clear."

"As if you gave me any choice. Dangle me on the edge of an orgasm like that and I'll tell you you're the emperor of Rome."

"You don't want to be owned? You don't want to belong to me as much as I want to belong to you, is that right?"

A dull ache began in my chest at the words. I couldn't resolve what he was saying with the fears I couldn't seem to shake about someone else controlling my life.

"I've never had to rely on anyone, answer to anyone. You know this, and you keep trying to change me, as if somehow I can turn that off."

"If you marry me, that *is* going to change. Permanently."

"What does that mean?"

"It means you come to me before you even *begin* to consider making a rash decision. It means you involve me so I can make sure you do, which includes removing James from your business. It means you ask me for help when you need it, and you don't keep secrets from me, *ever*. And when a situation arises that makes more sense for me to manage, you let me. No matter what."

He leaned in close again, his serious gaze flickering over my features, tracing a soft line down my jawline. When he spoke again, his voice was a whisper.

"It means that every waking breath you take, every step you take, you don't just take to move your own life forward, but ours. You take it knowing I'm right there with you, irrevocably tied to every decision you make."

My chest ached with the effort to fill my lungs with a full breath. One after the next as I grappled with what he was saying. He wasn't giving me room to run, to fight, nothing.

"I—I feel like you're giving me an ultimatum."

My eyes were wide as I questioned him, hoping I was reading this all wrong. The serious look in his eye answered me before he could.

"I want it all, Erica. I won't accept any less. Wrap your head around it, or—"

I tried to still the tremble that worked its way through me. How could he ask me this? Threaten me with our relationship? I felt like a caged animal who'd been backed into a corner.

"Or what?" The words came out sharp, laced with challenge.

His hold on my waist tightened, mimicking the restless working of his jaw. Before I could gauge how pissed he was at my challenge, his lips crashed down onto mine. Now hard and demanding, he sought entrance. I opened for him, barely prepared for the devouring passion of his tongue. Curses rumbled through his chest, muffled in the wild merging of our mouths. The onslaught of his fervency shot through me, revving all my instincts to return his passion.

I kissed him back, fisting my hands in his shirt to urge us together. Tongues tangling, teeth biting, we melded hotly into each other. Pinned by his hips, I felt the unmistakable stirring of his erection pressed against me. He palmed my thigh, raising the hem of my skirt high, making no mistake about what he wanted from me. I sucked in a sharp breath, stifling the loud moan that wanted to burst from my lips when I exhaled.

He slipped his hand between my legs, rubbing me through my panties, making me crazy for him. A small moan escaped, pleasure overwhelming the rational part of my brain that knew we were in the wrong place for this. My body didn't care when I was in his clutches.

"Why, Erica? Why do you fucking fight me?"

My hips churned, bucking against his hand. My panties were soaked and I was ready to have him here. When it came to having his hands on me, he'd win every time. Fighting him was a lost cause, and now that I'd been deprived of his touch for so long, I was ready to crawl up his body if it meant ending this distance.

My hands traveled under his shirt, over his naked torso.

"I want you...right now."

His breath rushed out, and he massaged his fingers against my throbbing sex through the flimsy fabric of my underwear. Curling my fingers, I trailed my nails down his sides, blind with all the ways I wanted him.

Then another loud pop sounded from the living room. The sound was followed by the familiar voices of his family and Alli's calling my name, a sobering reminder that we weren't nearly alone enough to follow through on what we'd started here.

We broke apart, breathless.

"Christ." Blake stepped back unsteadily and readjusted himself.

Even through his jeans I could see that he was painfully hard, fully ready to fuck me on any surface he could find. In this room, that might have been Heath's desk. That would have been bad. So very good, but very bad.

I swallowed hard, trying like hell to drive my thoughts back to reality. I let my head fall back. My chest heaved even as I hopelessly tried to tame the rush of sexual tension that flowed through me. *Fuck*. This had to be worse than the seventh circle of hell. He'd taken several steps away, a crushing distance considering how intimately he'd just held me.

"Blake, I don't want to fight. Please, let's go home and just put this all behind us."

After a moment, he turned back to me, sending my heart flying again. But I didn't see resignation in his eyes. Far from it, he seemed to have gathered his resolve in that short moment as I was putting my brain cells back to work.

"I told you I was sorry, and I meant it," I pleaded.

"I know you are. But it's not enough this time. What I'm asking for…this isn't what I *want*. This is what I *need*. It's what *we* need."

He held me in his gaze, the tension arcing between us. I opened my mouth, but he spoke before I could.

"The choice is yours, Erica."

The simple words. The finality in his voice when he said them. The expectation in his eyes as he waited for me to…to what? To submit? To give everything to him? Every last tiny little piece of myself that was ever worth hanging on to, he expected me to deliver along with my love and trust and future.

I wanted to crack. I wanted to cry, because I knew I couldn't give him the answer he needed. Could I? I couldn't imagine it.

As I went to war with myself, he closed the distance between us. He kissed me, a quick soft press of his lips to mine. The sweet gesture scattered my thoughts again as he looked deep into my eyes.

"I love you, Erica. But if you can't give this to me…" He didn't finish, only shaking his head, eyes a tornado of emotion that seemed to reflect.

But…what was he saying? This was it? Before I could question him, he reached for the door and I moved to let him pass. Head down, his hands stuffed back into his pockets, he disappeared down the hallway toward the noise of the party.

I stood there, paralyzed by what had happened. For all my wanting to talk, I was in disbelief that this is what had been brewing inside Blake all this time.

All the emotions I'd pushed down to go on about my life the past couple days had crept up to the surface tonight, and I'd passed the point of being able to be here with his family and pretend everything was fine. One look at Blake, knowing our relationship was now very much on the line, would have me in tears.

Even if sorry was enough, I couldn't say it any more than I had, and my heart couldn't take any more of this. I couldn't take another minute of knowing that everything I'd given him still wasn't enough.

Without giving Blake's mother any indication of how our talk had gone, I slipped through the kitchen past her and into the living room. The friendly chatter quieted when I entered. Ignoring the others, for fear I'd break down if I made eye contact with anyone, especially Blake, I found Alli. She was standing by the couch, drink in hand. I grabbed my purse and gave her a quick hug.

"I'm sorry," I whispered and found my way out.

CHAPTER TEN

The apartment was dark and quiet. Too quiet.

I'd returned home alone and tried in vain to sleep. Inside I was battling with the enormity of what Blake had said, what he'd asked of me—the proposal *after* the proposal. Except this one hadn't come with a glittering band of diamonds, but the very real threat of having nothing at all. I wanted to believe he was bluffing, that I could talk him out of this way of thinking. But what if he wasn't? What if nothing I could say would sway this position he'd put me in?

I'd texted Alli just before midnight, wondering if he'd stayed the night there. No, he'd left. She didn't know where. Sleep finally took me in the early hours of the morning.

The morning was muggier than usual after an evening of light showers. I stepped outside and found Clay waiting outside with the Escalade, ready to take me to work. Even when he didn't drive me on other days, he was always nearby. Evidently Blake wasn't going to take any more chances with my safety, and I didn't suppose there was much I could say to change his mind on the matter.

I relished the cool dry air of the SUV and let him guide us through the city streets. My mind drifted to Blake and where he was spending his nights. Before my imagination began to run wild again, I looked to Clay.

"Do you know where Blake was last night?"

His gaze lifted meeting me in the rearview mirror. "I

couldn't say for sure, Miss Hathaway. He asked me to stay available for you this week. I haven't heard from him since then."

"Does someone else stay with him?"

"No, ma'am. Just you."

He wasn't worried about himself it would seem, but I was. The streets sped by until we slowed in front of the office. I said goodbye to Clay and walked briskly toward the entrance to the building.

My body desperately needed more coffee to get me through the day, but I'd decided to skip my usual morning routine of stopping at Mocha. I'd been avoiding Simone. I didn't know how much James had shared with her about Blake confronting him. I was already emotionally maxed out with what had transpired between Blake and me the previous night. If I had to face one more emotionally draining situation, I was going to snap.

"Erica."

Pausing at the door leading up the office stairwell, I spun to find a familiar face. Dressed professionally in gray slacks and a light V-neck shirt, Isaac Perry stood before me. *Fucking great.*

"What are you doing here?"

I could barely mask my annoyance. Of all the days to show up uninvited, he had to pick today. He had the decency to look a little uneasy.

"I emailed you. I didn't hear back from you, so I thought I'd swing by since I was in town."

"You could have called and given me a heads up."

"I know, sorry. Was a bit of a last minute decision."

He worked his jaw a bit. He didn't look like the man

who'd groped me months ago. He looked like the man with a boyish smile who'd talked me into a private dinner that started it all.

"I know you have things to do. I won't take much of your time," he said.

"If Blake knows you came here…" I was thankful for once that I didn't have to worry about Blake stopping in on me today. At least I didn't think he would. After last night, I figured we were destined for some more time apart.

He winced slightly, looking down to his expensive loafers. "I know. I realize he's not my biggest fan. I was hoping you'd take mercy on me and give me a chance to explain though."

I took a step away from the door, folding my arms around my chest. We were in public, but the last time I'd seen him, he'd had his unwelcome hands all over me. I couldn't and wouldn't trust him.

"I'm not sure there is anything we really need to discuss, Isaac."

He exhaled, looking more human and less tentative than he had before. "I'm sorry, Erica. I really am. Please, let me buy you a coffee. It's all I'm asking for. Five minutes."

His soft blue eyes pleaded with me, and I remembered the Isaac Perry who'd been charming. Also, he was promising coffee.

"Fine."

His eyes lit up, but I was less than excited. I cringed inwardly as I pushed through the doors of Mocha with him behind me, hoping for a miracle that Simone wouldn't be working this morning. That would have been asking a lot since I'd not once graced the establishment without the vivacious red haired barista greeting me.

She was helping another customer as we settled into our seats. I sat back, tracing the edge of the table. Isaac was going to press me about the advertising, and I still hadn't decided what to do. Blake would be furious, of course, but maybe I'd be an idiot for turning down an account like Isaac's if it meant moving the business forward quicker. With so many emotions tainting the situation, I wasn't any closer to deciding how to approach his offer.

Lost momentarily in thought, I almost jumped when Simone greeted us.

"Hey," she said with a soft smile. "I haven't seen you in a while."

"Hey, Simone. Um, yeah. Sorry," I said. Worlds collided, and I couldn't get into it with her right now. I should probably just tell her what happened with James and be done with it.

"The usual?" she asked, jarring my thoughts back to the present.

"Sure."

Her gaze slid to Isaac, who seemed to be casually appreciating her figure the way most men did.

"Make it two," he said with a polite smile.

I sighed, all too ready for my next shot of caffeine. "So…what did you want to talk about?"

"I wanted to explain—"

"What is there to explain, Isaac? Really. I'm not a fan of men groping me, or touching me in any way without my explicit permission."

"I took things too far, I realize that."

"Way too far. And it's a little hard for me to look past that and jump into wanting to do business with you. Hopefully you can understand that."

His lips went tight. "I do. I made a mistake. My behavior was beyond reproach."

The simple confession settled over me, and just as I considered forgiving him, he spoke again.

"I shouldn't have been drinking."

I frowned, unwilling to accept his excuse. "Are you kidding? We shared a bottle of wine."

"I was on meds. Meds that severely impair my judgment when mixed with alcohol. You couldn't have known that, and it's not an excuse."

"You're right, it's not."

He stared at the table.

"I want you to understand that's not who I am. I'd be lying if I said I wasn't attracted to you, but if I'd been in my right mind, I wouldn't have approached you that way."

I studied him carefully, wondering where all this was going. His need to seek my forgiveness seemed sudden, and I couldn't help but be suspicious.

"What do you want from me, Isaac?"

He sighed and straightened. "It's a small world. We have several mutual connections. I know Blake's written me off, but it's likely that our paths will cross again at some point. Despite all this," he said, gesturing between us, "I was hoping we could work together still. Call it a peace offering."

"A binding financial arrangement is an odd kind of peace offering."

He barely suppressed a smile. "Perhaps, but I figured you'd see more value in that than flowers and chocolates."

"I'm engaged. You'd be wasting your money."

His eyes stilled, narrowing slightly. "I didn't realize that. Congratulations."

"Thanks," I said dryly.

"In any case, I do genuinely want to work with you. Before the alcohol got the best of me, I was intrigued with what you proposed. I'd love to give it a try if you think we can get past my epic fuck up."

I shook my head. If he only knew what I'd been through. "I don't know…"

He sat back in his seat and lowered his head.

"It's okay. I understand, Erica. No hard feelings. I just thought it was worth a try. For what it's worth, I am exceedingly sorry. I'm appalled at my behavior. The more I thought about it, the more I knew I had to see you and apologize. I hope if we see each other again, and I expect we will, we can at least be cordial."

I sighed, wishing I didn't feel sorry for him. I tried to read his body language for signs that he was bullshitting me, but he was as disarming as he'd been the day we met.

"I'll think about it, okay?"

He smiled. "That's all I'm asking for." He rose quickly. "Listen, thanks for meeting. I didn't mean to take you off guard, but some things are better said face to face."

"I can appreciate that." It would have been much easier to rebuff his attempt at a truce via email. Despite Blake's fervent hatred for the man, I now found myself considering this bridge between our companies.

Simone swung by with our coffee, already conveniently steaming from to-go cups. He handed her a bill and thanked her before turning to leave.

"Who was that?" Simone asked.

"A prospective advertiser." Was he? Was I seriously considering this truce bridge between our companies? I wasn't totally convinced that his intentions were all bad, though I wasn't exactly inclined to forgive him either.

"Looks like a good prospect. He tipped me like forty bucks."

I managed a laugh. She sidled up to the seat that he'd occupied. "What's going on? Are you avoiding me?"

I took a sip of my coffee, too tired to paint on a face that wasn't mine. Her eyes narrowed.

"Simone, at the risk of pissing you off and creating tension between you and James, I need to tell you something."

"James kissed you. I know."

My eyes went wide. "You know?"

"Yeah, he told me the other day. Said Blake went nutso on him, telling him to give his notice."

"Fuck," I muttered, as much in reflection of that afternoon as to the fact that she knew about it.

"Listen, you need to figure this out with James. This is kind of what I was worried about with the love triangle stuff, but ..."

"But what?"

"Erica, I care about James. I mean, we've been hanging out for a while, and I know he cares about you. He assures me that he's over any romantic hang up he had with you, but he still very much considers you a friend. I don't know if he and Blake can get past this, but you're in the driver's seat here. It's your call."

I groaned. "I hate this. All of it. Blake has me in an awful position right now. I don't want to fire James, and I'm furious with Blake for confronting him. He did *not* have my blessing to do that. He's obviously very jealous and can't stand the idea of me working every day with someone who made a pass at me."

She upturned her red lips.

"I'll talk to James. And for what it's worth, I'm sorry all this is affecting you. I think you and James are great together. I really do. I consider you both my friends, and the last thing I want to do is come between you over this. Unfortunately, Blake's jealousy is a persistent reminder of an indiscretion that I'm sure both James and I would rather forget. I know we both want to move on, and I hope we can."

"It's not an easy situation. This doesn't affect our friendship though, no matter what. I'm still your girl. Bitches first, okay?"

I laughed, and she held out her hand for a fist pump. I met it, and she slid off her seat.

"Go fix your crazy life, and I'm going to serve up some more rocket fuel to the addicts here, all right?"

"Sounds like a plan. Thanks."

She smirked before sauntering off. I grabbed my coffee and left the café feeling just a little bit lighter. At least that was one fire I didn't need to put out.

At the office, I spent the morning catching up on emails before Alli popped in to brief me on advertising progress. She'd picked up two more accounts, which was a strong start in making up for the lost revenue we'd incurred. I was tallying some quick figures when she interrupted me.

"So what's going on with you and Blake?"

I looked up to her worried eyes. I sighed and dropped my pen. I'd need to spill at some point. After running out on her party, she was bound to wonder what had gone down between Blake and me to make me leave.

"Nothing to worry about. Bumps in the road, I guess."

"I'm *going* to worry about you. Especially when Blake is at my place late, holed up with Heath having some sort of brotherly heart-to-heart til midnight."

I fidgeted in my seat. "I didn't realize he'd stayed that long."

"He didn't come home?"

I shook my head.

"Where do you think he went?"

I clicked my pen nervously. "I honestly have no idea."

"What happened between you two? You've been acting strange since you got back from San Francisco. I thought things went well."

"They did, on the business front. But we ran into Risa there. Listen, I can't talk about this here. Do you want to grab a drink tonight after work? I can try to explain it all...somehow."

I suppressed a groan. That conversation was going to be all kinds of fucked up.

"Okay. I'm going to step out to pick up some lunch. Do you want anything?"

"Sure, just get me whatever you're having."

She left me alone then, and a minute later James took her place in the chair behind my desk.

"You have a minute?"

"Sure."

I shuffled some papers around on my desk, for no reason at all other than to delay whatever he was going to say. But Simone was right. We needed to talk. We needed to get to the bottom of this. I let my forehead fall into my hands. We hadn't even said anything and I was losing my shit. I took in a deep breath. "We should talk."

He leaned back into his chair, eying me. "You're not going to fire me, are you?"

"No." I sulked back into the chair. No amount of coffee was going to make this conversation bearable. "I'm so sorry about all of this. Honestly, I don't know where this all went wrong, but I'm desperate to fix it. I'm just lost about how to do it in a way that everyone can live with."

"Landon's the only one with his panties in a twist about it. The rest of us are being adults. I don't see why you need to cater to his temper tantrums unless he's financially threatening you."

"He would never do that. And ... I don't know, James. I put him in a difficult situation that's kind of impossible for me to explain to you."

"Something to do with this Daniel guy, I'm guessing?"

"It's more complicated than you can possibly understand. Not because you're not capable of understanding it ... but some things are better kept private. And yes. Daniel had a big part in me and Blake not being together. Everything kind of became more and more fucked up after that until we found our way back together again. When he realized what happened between you and me ..." I sighed, closing my eyes. "I guess you could say it was the last straw, and now I'm sort of grappling with how to make things right between us."

He hesitated a moment. "I care about you, Erica. I care about this job too, but if you're going to stay with Blake and as a result, my being here is making your life unnecessarily difficult, I should go. I don't like this tension any more than you do."

"But I don't want you to go. You're important to the company, and to me. Despite everything that's happened, you're still a friend. And I'm not going to fire a friend."

He chewed his lip, tapping his thumb on the edge of the chair looking lost in thought. "Would it help if I wasn't here?"

"What do you mean? I just told you—"

"I mean, in the office. Would it be easier if I wasn't here in the office every day? I could work from home. I mean, it's a technicality, but if it means keeping my job and staying with the company, it's something worth considering."

I did just that. "You'd be willing to do that?"

"Sure. And if eventually you want someone else in house, I can transition out. Maybe go out on my own. Free-lance or whatever."

I wrinkled my nose, not liking that part of the proposal. "I hate this."

"I do too, but it's not your fault. I'm not sure what Blake is making you believe, but I should have backed off as soon as I knew you were coming out of a relationship. You needed a friend, and I failed you in that regard."

"You didn't fail."

"I jumped to conclusions. About a lot of things. This is my doing too, and if I have to make sacrifices for it, so be it."

"I appreciate the offer. But let's not make any hasty decisions."

"I don't think it's hasty, honestly. It's more like a long time in the making. I can see you're stressed. You haven't been yourself all week, and I hate to see you this way. I don't want to be the cause of that. I never have been and I never will. But if we can make this change, at least for now, and that gives you some relief or room to fix things with him, we should do it."

"I'm hoping he'll cool down a little. Maybe I can try to reason with him." That was a big maybe.

He leaned forward, resting his forearms on his knees. "You want to marry Blake, right?"

I paused. "Yes."

"Personally, I can't stand the guy, but obviously he's important to you. Important enough that you said yes when he proposed. I don't want to be the person who fucks that up for you. We made a mess with this workplace relation-ship thing, and now we both need to clean it up."

I offered a slight nod, wishing there wasn't so much truth in what he was saying. "Maybe you're right."

"It's not what either of us wants, but maybe it's the right thing."

CHAPTER ELEVEN

The rest of the day sped by. Maybe not all hope was lost in the landscape of my life. New accounts were coming in, I was at peace with Simone, and at least for now, James and I had a plan on how to move forward. I couldn't deny that the thought of him leaving the company broke my heart a little though. He'd become part of the team, as well as a friend. I would miss seeing him every day, and I couldn't help but resent that Blake was putting me in a position to make him go. As I dwelled on that thought, Alli popped in to remind me of our after-dinner date.

I pulled my things together to leave. A few minutes later, Clay dropped us at a trendy sushi spot on a busy street. Alli and I ordered Mai Tais. I sucked the sweet drink down and politely asked the waitress for another when she delivered our assorted rolls. Today was simply one of those days. If nothing else, maybe the alcohol would put me to sleep when I went home to our empty bed again.

"So James is going to be working from home for a while." I finally blurted it out, knowing that Alli's tense silence was filled with her unspoken questions about what the hell was going on.

Alli frowned. "Why?"

I took a deep breath. "When Blake and I weren't together, James and I started to hang out more, as friends.

I tried to keep things professional, but he started to want more. Eventually he made a pass at me, and …"

Alli's dropped her jaw. "You didn't …"

"We kissed. It was brief, and I wanted it to end about three seconds after it started. Apparently Risa saw the whole thing, and this weekend at the awards event, she told Blake about it. I'm guessing she wanted to get back at me and mess with our relationship. Unfortunately, it worked. Blake was beside himself. We fought. He wanted James gone … or else."

I shoved a piece of sushi in my mouth, hating that he'd won. That I'd given him what he wanted.

Alli stared, unmoving with wide eyes. "I wasn't expecting all of that."

"Well that's why I never told you. It was a mistake, and I wanted it to go away, but it hasn't, so now I'm paying for it."

"So is everything okay between you now that James isn't going to be in the office?"

"I have no idea. We haven't really talked."

I mangled one of my rolls as I thought about the awful distance that had come between us in the past few days. As angry as I was with Blake, I hated every minute when we fought. Nothing was right when we weren't together, and I could only hope all that would change now.

"Anyway, how are things going with Heath? Give me some hope. Things seem to be perfect with you two right now."

She shrugged and placed a slice of ginger on one of her rolls. "I wouldn't say perfect."

I lifted an eyebrow. "Trouble in paradise?"

She laughed, but her smile quickly faded. "I don't know. I worry about him."

"That's understandable, but has he given you a reason to?"

"That's the thing. Not really. But I can't help but worry. He finished the program, and ever since it's like I haven't been able to shake this feeling that he's going to slip up again."

"But he has you. He has Blake and work and his family. It seems like he's on the right track. Everything is going so well, isn't it?"

"I know. On the surface everything is great. The apartment, our jobs. But it seems like whenever I check in with him, he tells me I'm hovering. He reminds me that Blake hovers and his family hovers. Understandably so, but he says he doesn't need one more person studying his every move. I just care about him too damn much to lose what we have."

I contemplated what she was telling me for a moment. I hadn't known the Heath that used as well as I knew the new, sober Heath, but I'd seen enough to recognize how different he'd been. I believed that his relationship with Alli and being deprived of it when he went back to rehab was what sobered him on an entirely different level. Blake believed it too, which is what prompted him to bring him back home early and unexpectedly.

"It sounds like you're waiting for him to fail, Alli," I finally said.

Her shoulders slumped and sadness flickered behind her eyes. "I'm scared. I don't want to go through what we went through again. I was a mess. I mean, you saw me. I *need* Heath—like I'm wildly in love with him and I can't imagine being without him. But for this to work, I need him to stay healthy. I'll do anything I can to make sure that happens."

"I remember you were a mess, but he was too. I think you both need each other, but maybe what he needs more than anything is for you to have faith in him. We all know how Blake is, and parents are parents. He wants you to love him and believe in him, not mother him."

She sighed. "It's hard, because when we were in New York, we spent every spare minute together. We only had to work around my schedule then, but now that he's working with Blake, we have even less time."

"Just because you aren't spending every waking minute together doesn't mean he's in peril. Working with Blake and taking those responsibilities more seriously is good for him. Even if it's time that he can't spend with you."

She nodded. "You're right. I just wish we didn't have to live with this invisible demon threatening to come between us. Every day is an opportunity for things to go wrong."

I caught her hand and gave it a squeeze. "Alli."

She lifted her gaze to mine.

"Stop waiting for something bad to happen. The best thing you can do is love him, show him you care, and make the most out of every minute you have. Stop trying to control what you can't control."

* * *

I hurried under the awning of the building as the rain started to come down harder. Scanning the street, I saw no sign of Blake's Tesla. My heart sank, and the prospect of spending another night without him gnawed at me. Earlier I'd considered calling to tell him about my conversation with James, but something—maybe pride—held me back.

He'd find out…but I wasn't entirely ready to let him know he'd won this round yet.

As I climbed the stairs, I met Cady just outside the door of the apartment Sid and I once shared.

"Hey." She beamed, keys in hand.

"Have you seen Blake?" I asked, my enthusiasm obviously far dimmer than hers.

"He was at the office when I left. Why?"

I hesitated, debating whether to tell her more. "He didn't come home last night, that's all."

"Oh." Concern painted her features. "I think he probably stayed at work last night then. He looked tired, and…well, he hasn't exactly been in a chipper mood today. That might explain why."

I sighed, relief washing over me. Still, knowing he was staying at work wasn't bringing him any closer to home. I thanked her and climbed the stairs to our apartment. I dropped my things on the island and went to our bedroom. The bed was a mess, the sheets an unmade tangle, for all the wrong reasons. I hadn't slept much, and likely, neither had he.

I took a quick shower and emerged. The apartment was as silent as it had been when I'd arrived. Securing the towel around my chest, I went to the dresser where I kept my clothes. My jewelry rested in a shallow box on top of it. I slipped my ring back on, and the diamonds of the matching bracelets caught my eye. I picked them up. The weight of the bracelets rested heavily in my palm. The expensive bands sparkled in the dim light of the bedroom. They were beautiful, but their meaning meant more. I fingered the small medallions. The platinum roulette wheel clinked against its mate, the heart…Blake's heart.

Looking up, I caught my reflection in the mirror. All I could see now were my tired eyes filled with the kind of sadness that only being away from Blake could bring. Fighting this fight with him seemed fruitless and damaging, when my answer would always be yes. When the only future I could envision was one with him.

I wanted him back, at any cost, even my pride. To think I could stand my ground against someone like him—a man who saw what he wanted and stopped at nothing to have it—was delusional at best. But damn, he pushed me. Trusting him with my body and my heart wasn't enough, yet somehow I'd always known that would be true. A part of me knew that one day our relationship would come to this, that he'd push me for all I could give. He'd been controlling and maddening from day one. I'd been a fool to expect any of that to change.

But he was right. I'd fought like hell to maintain that line between our worlds. I'd let him in, bit by bit, but always held him a safe distance from certain aspects of my life. Because I'd given him more than I'd ever given anyone else, I wanted to think that was enough. But it wasn't. That much was clear now.

I didn't want to fight, and I didn't want our relationship to be a battlefield. Perhaps that was why he wasn't giving me any other options now. We both were hurting and unhappy as a result of my fuck up, and now, he was making me pay for it, or change for it.

I clasped the bracelets around my wrist, admiring them. Always I'd worn them with pride. I wanted the world to know I wore them for him, even if no one knew what they meant to us. Our promise. Like the one on my finger.

Blake could own me, he could hold something deep in me, but I'd captured something precious in him too. Something he'd never given anyone else.

I glanced back to the bed, the sharp ache of missing him too painful to ignore.

★ ★ ★

The downpour of rain had me nearly soaked by the time I stepped through the doors of the Landon Group offices. A sliver of light cast across the floor where Blake's door was ajar. I knocked quietly before entering, hoping not to greet him with a heart attack.

Inside he was sitting lazily at his desk, feet propped up, his focus on the televisions across the room before shifting to me.

"Working hard?" I walked around his desk and propped myself on the edge.

"What are you doing here?" Blake asked.

"I should ask you that. How long are you going to camp out here and pout?"

His jaw shifted, and he lifted a tumbler of scotch to his lips. His throat worked on a swallow. "I'm not pouting." He set the glass down, his eyes traveling the length of me, all the way down to my strappy black heels. "You're wet."

I raised my eyebrows and looked out the windows of his office. They were covered with blinds, blocking him from the view of the world outside.

"If you ever left your cave, you might notice that it's raining buckets out there."

He frowned. "You walked?"

I rolled my eyes. "No, Clay drove me. Relax." I glanced over his desk and lit on a stack of documents with a familiar logo.

"What are these?" I asked, picking them up.

He sighed, seeming annoyed. "Financials for Sophia's modeling agency." He pulled them from my grasp and tossed them to the other side of the desk beyond my reach.

I narrowed my eyes at him. "Has she been in town?"

He took another drink. "Why, do you think she hand delivered them?"

I stared at him, unwilling to let it drop.

"No, Sophia has not been in town, at least that I know of. You can put your claws back."

Relieved, I shot him a grin. "Can't blame me for asking, can you?"

"Suppose not," he mumbled.

I took a deep breath and decided to dive in. As much as I wanted to tease him to resolution, we'd probably only get there by talking seriously. Even though the last time hadn't gone so well.

"I've thought a lot about what you said last night."

"And," he said dryly.

"I understand that you're upset, and I understand why. I have held back, especially with the business. It's been my safe place in a way. The part of my life I can go to, no matter what happens between us, and know that it's mine. That every success and every failure is mine. It's everything I've worked for, and it scares me to share it with you. It always has. But I'm willing to change and involve you more."

His gaze held me steadily. "Why would you do that, after all this time?"

"Well, for starters, if we're getting married…" I lingered on that thought a moment, trying not to derail with the possibility that we wouldn't, that he wouldn't want that anymore. "I suppose what's yours is mine in that regard. If I can't trust my husband-to-be with it, who can I trust?"

He set down his glass. He folded his hands on his lap, seeming to study me. "Okay," he said simply. "So James is leaving, I take it?"

I searched his eyes for any sign that he might relent on that point. "Has it occurred to you that you're being a little unreasonable when it comes to me keeping James with the company?"

"If I'm being unreasonable, it's in response to unreasonable behavior, and in that case, I'll call it purely justified. I told you where I stand on this issue. Nothing's changed."

"What if I said that starting today, you can have all the control in the business you want, except for that one tiny piece." I illustrated the tiny piece with my thumb and forefinger, as if that might help.

"You should go, Erica. No point in both of us sleeping here tonight." He lowered his feet to the floor and swiveled to face the computer screens.

Christ was he stubborn. I could almost see his heels digging in.

God love him, Blake fought dirty. He was putting the survival of our relationship on the line to get what he wanted—what he said he needed. I wouldn't be reasoning with him tonight. Not unless I fought dirty too.

"Suit yourself," I said and slid off the desk. Slowly, I fingered the top button of my raincoat. One by one, I released them. Blake's attention turned back to me. His gaze fixed on the front as the jacket parted, giving him a sliver of vision into what I was wearing underneath. It wasn't much.

"You're not going to ply me with sex."

I canted my head. "No?" I challenged, secretly knowing I'd already given in to his demands.

I smiled and shrugged out of the jacket I'd traveled here in. Tossing it away, I stood near naked in just enough black lace to cover the bare necessities. Trails of water from my rain-soaked hair trickled down my body over my already damp skin. I had been worried about the weather hampering my look, but based on the way Blake's lips parted, the effect might have worked in my favor.

"I think I might be able to change your mind."

"You can't. I'm sick of this shit, Erica."

If I'd been blindfolded, I might have believed him, that he couldn't be swayed. But his eyes gave him away, leveled at my chest as I reached for the clasp at the front of my bra.

"I seem to recall you have a weakness for lace," I teased.

"You're my only weakness," he murmured.

The words hit my heart. The playful smile I wore faded. I wanted to be his weakness, but not if he resented it, the way it sounded like he did now. Turning, I walked slowly away. My boldness had taken a hit, and now I only felt embarrassed and hurt. I wanted him to want me, to meet me not even close to the middle, but to consider this one concession.

"Where the hell are you going?"

I lifted my lips again at that small sign of hope. I slowed in front of the couch on the other side of the office and unclasped my bra. I let it slip over my shoulders and down my arms, depriving him of the view of my naked chest. Hooking my thumbs over the barely there panties, I pulled them down, leaving me completely naked, save my jewelry.

"You won't win this way, you know."

I spun, and he was there in front of me instantly, eyes blazing.

"I'm not trying to win anymore." All teasing was lost from my voice with that concession.

"Then what are you doing?"

I ran my hands up his chest. "I'm letting *you* win."

He winced. "You're playing games. I'm not interested in games."

"I'm not playing. I'm giving you what you want. I'm giving you all of me." I reached up and curled my arms around his neck. My breasts brushed against his clothed chest. I could feel his heart beating quickly, matching the wild rhythm of my own.

"This doesn't work. Being apart destroys us. I can't live without you, Blake. I can barely survive a night without you. How am I supposed to risk losing you for a lifetime? If you won't give me this one thing, then I have no choice in the matter, do I? So I'm letting you win. I'm trusting you with everything I have, body, soul, and business. Take what you want, be wherever you need to be."

I met his eyes, wanting him to believe every word.

"And James."

I drew in a breath, resigning myself to the choice I had to make. "He's leaving. It's done."

CHAPTER TWELVE

He regarded me silently. I held myself to him, but he hadn't touched me in any other way. Still holding back. Yet the way his muscles coiled tight under his skin, I couldn't help but feel that could change at any moment. I'd become the hunted, and this chase would turn on its head in an instant. The anticipation had my heart racing.

"That's what you want, isn't it?" My voice caught when he licked his lips.

"That's not all I want."

Lust filled his eyes, mixing with the quiet determination I'd seen grow in him over the past several days. Heat bloomed across my skin under his traveling gaze.

"I'm giving you everything," I whispered.

"I'd like to believe it, but you've done nothing but fight me. How do I know anything has changed?"

How could I show him?

Love wasn't enough. Words, meaning every one I uttered, weren't enough. I was here, naked and vulnerable, chest-to-chest with the man who was demanding I give him every piece of myself. I lowered back onto my heels and let my hands fall down. How much was enough? I'd finally acquiesced to his demands, and now I was scrambling with how I could prove it to him.

I twisted my fingers nervously between us. My fingertip traced the small band of diamonds above my knuckle.

A thought struck me. Nerves tightened my stomach and adrenaline pulsed through me. I closed my eyes.

Fuck. I was about to give him everything. And I was petrified.

I exhaled a shaky breath, hoping the release would loosen the knot in my throat. Opening my eyes, I braced myself for what I had to do. I looked up into Blake's eyes, a tornado of want and worry.

"Blake, I love you so much. And I trust you. I really do." I kept my voice steady, not wanting to give him any reason to doubt me. "So please understand this for what it is...everything...*everything* that I have. Please don't make me regret it."

I closed my eyes a second and dropped slowly to my knees. The only sound in the room was metal against metal, the clink of the bracelets as I positioned my hands on my thighs.

I waited for him. To believe me, to come to me and be the one to bring us back together.

A minute that felt like forever passed. No movement, no words. Only the echo of what I'd done and the anticipation of where it would take us. Slowly he lowered in front of me. I kept my focus on the floor and then the dark fabric of his jeans stretching over his knees. He tipped my chin to meet his eyes. His lips were parted, his breath rushing out in soft pants that met my own ragged breathing.

He drew a line across my quivering lips. "This *is* what I want, if it's what you want," he finally said.

My heart hammered in my chest, a loud reminder of how much he meant to me. "I want you. I can't promise I'll be perfect, but I'll try to be what you want, everything you need."

He slid his palm over my cheek and into my hair, urging me up. I lifted to my knees and steadied myself with my palms against his chest. The hard muscles rippled under my hands. He held me that way, our lips a breath apart, his eyes scorching with emotion.

His breath whispered over my lips. "All I've ever wanted, since the day we met, was your trust. I want to be there for you, to help you, protect you. I can't do any of that the way I need to when you fight me and push me back."

"I won't anymore, I promise."

His eyes softened. He wrapped an arm around my waist, pulling me closer to him. "And I promise that I will *never* let you regret that choice."

A warm feeling expanded in my chest, dispelling the nerves and the doubt. My love for this man shot through me, sending a tremble down every limb. Lust and desire lit up on its path, and I had to have him now. His name on my lips, I kissed him feverishly, as if I'd never have another chance. Hands in his hair, I clung to him, wanting our bodies as close as they could be. He answered the silent wish, bringing both hands to my ass. A quick thrust of his hips showed me how badly he wanted me too.

I gasped for air, breathless from the kiss and the electricity in the air. "Take me now. Take what's yours, Blake."

He lifted me quickly to the couch so I lay on my back. As we kissed, an all consuming kiss, he caught my wrists and held them above me. I arched my back off the couch, restless and eager to feel him against me again. He loosened his hold and I went to reach for him, only to find my wrists bound in the bracelets. They were the most expensive handcuffs I'd ever wear, and their beauty kept me captive in a way nothing else ever had.

"You've given me what I want, Erica. Now I'm going to give you everything you want. You'll lack for nothing tonight, baby."

My fingers itched to touch him, to rake through his hair, down his back. I groaned, the now hopeless desire to move and take hold of him shooting through me. "Then fuck me and don't make me wait anymore."

He moved down my body, kissing a wet path down my torso. A lick into my navel, a soft graze of his teeth over my hipbone.

"Blake," I whimpered.

"I will, baby. Trust me, I will. I want a little taste of you first."

He pushed one of my legs to the floor. Grabbing the other at the knee, he held it firmly against the back of the couch, exposing me to him completely. I lay there, full of need and on display for the man who never failed to reduce me to a shameless harlot with a few well-timed words.

Warmth snaked through me. My heart thundered, sexual anticipation now rushing in over my love for him. I clenched my fists, remembering my bonds. The cool metal tight at my skin where I strained reminded me who owned this moment. I closed my eyes and sighed, going limp into the soft give of the couch.

"That's a good girl. Lay back and I'm going to make you see stars," he murmured.

He brushed his lips down my thigh. Every time his tongue slipped out and made contact with my skin, my eyes rolled back. My fingers curled tightly over the armrest of the couch, steadfast where he'd placed them earlier. Heat flowed through me like molten lava. I swore I'd never been so damn needy and yet so patient and trusting that he'd sate those needs.

Warm, sure hands slid from my knees to the center of my body where Blake spread me farther with his fingers. When his mouth made contact with the sensitive flesh between my legs, I began to tremble. His grip on my thighs stiffened, ready to keep me still. The soft press of the intimate kiss gave way to his tongue, drawing a full velvet lick up my clit. I cried out and my patience took a serious hit as he continued to massage the taut bundle of nerves, sucking and licking, moaning curses against it.

"You taste like heaven." The words blew air onto my throbbing sex, cool under the warm bliss of his mouth. Christ, his mouth. His tongue traveled the same path, up and down, sucking and devouring. Nothing was teasing about how he ate me. I was perilously close to coming now, rocking into his motions wantonly.

"Do you want to come with me inside you, baby? You want something to crush down on when I push you over?" He slid a single finger inside me, just enough to remind me what I was missing.

I nodded quickly, my voice effectively replaced by the breathing I could no longer control. I wanted that. I wanted every intensely erotic moment his beautiful mind could think up. Without another word, he stood. He tugged off his shirt and unfastened his belt.

The sound it made slipping through the loops sent a fiery tingle over my skin. I bit my lip and arched slightly. The corner of his mouth lifted in a smirk as he undid his jeans and pushed them down his thighs with his boxers, revealing his hard, gorgeous, and very ready cock.

"Admit it."

I shifted my focus to his face, as breathtaking as every other part of him. I frowned.

"Admit that you like the belt."

My teeth dug into my lower lip a little harder. The pain, the sweet edge of desire.

"I know you do." He laughed. "Your pussy gets impossibly wet every time. You don't really have to admit it, because I already know. Your body gives you away. But I'd love to hear the words come out of your mouth."

The memory of the leather smarting my skin elicited a physical response beyond anything I could comprehend. For all the fears I'd faced, through little fault of my own, I did like the things we'd done. I couldn't think of a single thing I hadn't liked, or hadn't fucking loved for that matter. I wanted to be pushed. I wanted that edge. Maybe that was twisted, and maybe nothing about it made sense to the rest of the world, but he was right. I liked it, and it was useless to deny it. My lips twisted into a small smile. "I do."

He stood above me, grinning devilishly. "I think I caught myself a little deviant. A smart and beautiful little deviant. I knew you were perfect for me, and you keep proving me right."

I widened my smile. "I like your hand better though. I like when you can feel the sting too, and when you stop to grab me and touch me there."

He groaned and palmed his erection, pumping the rigid length. "I wasn't planning on spanking you tonight, but you're making me want to bend you over my desk right now."

"That could be arranged." I gazed at him through

hooded eyes. I was getting ready to beg for it when he lowered between my legs. When he came over me, the silk contact of our warm bodies sliding over each other was almost too much. I sucked in a breath, and he caught the lower lip I had trapped earlier. Sucking it into his mouth, he traced his tongue over the swollen flesh.

"I don't want to punish you, baby. I want to reward you. I want to spend hours making you come for me. Again"—he lowered his lips to my neck —"and again"—sucking a path down to my shoulder—"and again, until you beg me to stop."

I clenched, all too aware of how close to the edge he'd already taken me.

"I'm begging you right now... to start. Let me come, Blake, please."

"I will. How do you want it? Slow?"

I arched into his mouth as he lowered to my breast. Circling the taut point with his tongue, he sucked and pulled.

He gazed up at me. I shook my head.

"Fast?" Turning his attention to the other, he lavished the same treatment until I thought I'd lose my mind.

"Yeah," I breathed.

"Rough?"

He caught the tip between his teeth and his fingers found my wet heat again. He slipped two fingers in, twisting slowly. He bit down gently on my nipple, and I shuddered and clenched.

"Oh, fuck," I gasped.

He released me and moved up my body again. "Your body tells me everything I need to know, baby. Now I'm going to give you everything you want."

When the hot crown of his head pressed into me, I thought I might die from the sweet overwhelming relief of it. He pushed in easily, and my breath left me with a groan. I was losing my grip on reality far too quickly. Rooted there, he churned his hips. The possessive motion did little for my sanity. Then he kissed me everywhere, my face, my shoulders, my neck.

"Blake, please, let me touch you. I need to."

His body deeply seated in mine, I recognized the vulnerability in his eyes when he nodded. I brought my hands down, the muscles in my shoulders aching from the posture. He unclasped the bracelets, freeing me quickly. The second he did, I shoved a hand through his hair and pulled him down to my mouth for a heated kiss.

As if that one gesture were a green light to fuck me out of my mind, he caught my hip and drove into me. Deep, powerful thrusts that pushed me up the couch until his other hand pressed again the armrest. The leverage allowed him to fuck me even harder, claim me ever deeper.

"This what you want, beautiful?"

"Yes," I whimpered. "God, yes." I raked my nails down his sides, wanting to mark him. I gripped his hips between my thighs, hastening his movements over me. I needed to feel him, us together, everything disappearing in the blissful way it could this way.

"I never thought I could love anyone the way I love you…Erica…God, you have no idea what you do to me."

I trembled, the depth of his penetration sending waves of pleasure like electricity through my body. I was lost in the sensation. I gripped his hair by the roots, my sex crushing down around him. Everything crashed down. Every wall, all my pride. Nothing mattered except this…

Without warning he rose up on his knees. He caught my ankles, placed them on his shoulders. With his next thrust, I went into orbit. He was so deep.

He slipped his hand between us and teased tight circles over my clit. Colors flew behind my eyes. I started to slip. The orgasm so close I could taste it. I could feel it down to my fingertips and all the way to my toes.

"Blake." His name flew out of my mouth like a plea.

"Tell me what you want."

"Hard!" I screamed, the climax already ripping through me. My back bowed off the couch completely, my muscles spasming beyond my control.

With a fierce growl, he dug into the flesh of my hips. With both hands, he shoved me down onto his cock and fucked me harder than I had ever been fucked in my life. His cock lengthened inside me, hitting my core in the delicious way that it always did seconds before he came.

He cursed, pulsing into me. Eyes to the sky, he caught his breath. He looked as destroyed as I felt. Slipping out of me, he fell back onto the couch. Hands on his head, he blew out a slow unsteady breath.

"Why?"

He turned his head to look at me, confusion mingling with the utter wreckage on his face. "Why what?"

"Why on earth would you deprive us of that?"

He laughed, and I smiled too, too wasted for anything else but levity. Then his smile faded. He brought his hand to my knee, and stroked my leg gently. Several empty minutes passed.

"Don't leave me again, Blake," I said softly.

Our eyes locked. "I didn't leave you."

"You left our bed, and I didn't know where you were."

"I didn't want to stay away. I never want to be away from you. You're all I think about. You're the only person I ever want to be with."

"Then why did you leave?"

He sighed. "If I came home, I was going to fuck you senseless."

I laughed again, despite the seriousness I was trying to convey. "When did that become a crime?"

"Not nearly a crime, but as amazing as this is—and believe me, it was amazing—fucking you wasn't going to get me what I wanted. If anything, it would only complicate matters and confuse the issue. We both know sex isn't the issue here. But I was hoping you'd come around, sooner rather than later. I was prepared to jerk off until you gave in to my demands, but I can't say I was looking forward to it."

I shook my head in disbelief. "And now that I have?"

He slid his hand down farther, catching mine and threading our fingers together. "Now I want to take you home and show you how grateful I am until the sun comes up."

★ ★ ★

I dressed for work and joined Blake in the kitchen. Seeing him there pouring coffee made me realize even more how terrible the brief distance had been. I wanted Blake in my life, every morning, every night, and every minute we could steal in between. Married life, I figured, would cater to that pretty well. A little flutter of excitement went through me at that sentiment.

I navigated around the island for my coffee, and he snagged me close for a kiss. I melted into it. His lips lingered and his tongue teased. Memories from last night whirled through my mind. Every touch, every toe-curling moment. Now I wished we had time for more. Still, the weekend was close, and we could spend at least some of it in bed. I wanted Blake by my side, but I also wanted to catch up on some much needed sleep. I hadn't really slept since the trip to San Francisco, and the fatigue was catching up with me.

"I'm exhausted." I slipped out of his embrace and lifted myself onto a seat at the island with my coffee.

"Makes two of us. Why don't you stay home?"

"Some of us have to work, dear."

A comfortable silence fell as we drank our coffee.

"When does James leave?"

I tightened my jaw, lingering bitterness at James leaving seeping in "I wanted to talk to you about that, actually."

He set his cup down with a thud. His eyebrows went up with a challenge.

"It's not what you think," I reassured him.

"What is it then?"

"Asking James to leave wasn't something I wanted to do, but I did it for you."

"For us," he said.

I exhaled heavily. "Whatever. It's difficult for me to not draw parallels to your situation with Sophia, though."

He leveled an expressionless stare at me before turning to refill his cup. "She lives in New York."

"You've also slept with her. You have a history with her.

You had a sexual and romantic relationship. Even if I didn't despise her personally, it would bother me that you still see her…sporadically or not."

He turned and leaned against the counter. The pose was casual, but I could sense the tension rippling below his clothes. I resented what this woman's name brought into the room. I also resented his clothes. These conversations seemed to go better when we were both naked.

"The only reason I ever see her is on business. I've told you this. Why do you keep pressing the issue?"

"Because I'm human, and like you, I'm jealous of anyone who wants what's mine. You're mine, and neither of us can deny that she wants you. You can claim you're *just friends* all day long, but I could say the same about James and me, and the words would fall on deaf ears."

"What do you want me to do about it?"

I traced the rim of my cup, suddenly scared to the death that I was dancing on the edge of disaster with Blake again and so soon after we'd come to terms.

"How long have you been invested in her business?"

He knitted his brows. "Four years."

I nodded. "That's a long time."

"What are you getting at, Erica? Spit it out."

"I'd like it if you would consider removing yourself from her business. I'm not saying I want her business to suffer, but I can't help but feel like keeping that connection with you is like a lifeline for her. Like she'll always have a chance to try to get you back."

"She has zero chance of getting me back."

"Did you tell her we were getting married?"

His jaw tensed. He pushed off the counter and dumped

the remains of his coffee cup into the sink. "You're a pain in the ass, Erica. Do you realize that?"

I laughed, relieved to have a little comic relief. "Do what you want, Blake. I'm just letting you know how I feel. You want me to be honest with you, so I am. I made a sacrifice for the health of our relationship, and those sacrifices are more easily made when there isn't a double standard."

He circled the island and stood in front of me. Staring down, his eyes glimmered with humor. Something had changed in him, and already I loved it.

"I'll take it into consideration."

"Thank you," I murmured, arching up to kiss his lips.

"Does that make you happy?"

I smiled. "You make me happy, so yes. The less of you I have to share, the better."

He hummed and lowered again to kiss me, tracing his tongue over my lip. "How about we make you happy one more time before work."

CHAPTER THIRTEEN

I worked busily through my tasks all morning. For the most part, everything was on track. Blake and I were good, James and I had an understanding, and I was ready to move on with my life. After lunch Daniel texted me, reminding me of the meeting we'd scheduled for the afternoon.

I cursed myself for forgetting. Stepping outside, I caught a cab to Daniel's campaign headquarters. As much as I didn't need a second job, meeting Daniel's assistant campaign manager's frazzled energy made me sorry for him. Without delay, he led me through the hustle and bustle of the headquarters office that always put me on edge.

"Great to see you again, Erica." Will shut the door behind us. Running a hand over his dark blond and generally untamed hair, he settled down behind his desk.

I sat across from him and pulled out my notebook. "You too. How has everything been going?"

"Well, as I'm sure you know, we're in the midst of the debates." He threw his hands up.

I twisted my lips up. "No, I didn't. Is that good?"

He raised his eyebrows. He still thought this was an important job for me, not a situation that Daniel had coerced me into, which would explain my total lack of knowledge about the campaign as it currently stood. If I wanted information, I knew how to seek it, but nothing about the Massachusetts governor's race appealed to me, even with my biological father as a prominent candidate.

"So far, yes, it's good. Mr. Fitzgerald is winning most of them. We have a strong position in the race, and with only a month of campaigning left to do, we want this last push to be what solidifies the win."

"Of course." I was still uncertain how I felt about Daniel winning or losing. He was my father, and even though he was a murdering sociopath, part of me wanted to root for him. I shook the strange thought from my head and pressed Will to fill me in more. I hadn't been in the loop for weeks. Thank goodness, Daniel had given me some space, but I had a feeling that wouldn't last much longer.

Will spent the next hour bringing me up to speed. We strategized and bounced ideas around. Somehow I was able to draw some parallels between my own venture and Daniel's marketing goals, and by the time I left, I'd armed Will with some new initiatives to carry through until our next meeting in a week.

The constant hum of the area beyond Will's small office seemed to grow in volume. Sensing a change, I shifted my focus from Will. Through the glass windows of the office, a few people gathered near the entrance where Daniel now stood. He looked imposing as ever in an impeccable suit, but his stance was casual. His lips moved silently. Then his blue eyes met mine and his smile seemed to broaden a bit. A few seconds later, he joined us in Will's office.

I stood awkwardly. Should I shake his hand?

"Will, one of the interns out there had questions about some press releases that were going out today. Quotes and what not. Can you take care of it? Give me a moment to speak with Erica."

"Of course. Take your time." Will stood quickly, gathering up his phone and papers.

As unsettling as Daniel's presence could sometimes be, I relaxed when Will's brand of stress left the room. Daniel sat back, legs crossed, drumming his fingers on his knee.

"How are you doing?"

"I'm good."

"How's Blake?"

I shot a concerned look his way. He laughed quietly. His mood seemed light, but out of habit, I approached any direct communication with him, especially on the topic of Blake, with caution. Maybe I was still a little shell shocked from some of our other less civilized meetings.

"I'm just asking. Last time we spoke you said you were engaged. Any news on that front?"

I inhaled a breath, relief tempering the worry that he still harbored a serious grudge toward my fiancé.

"Um, no. Not really. How's Margo?" I asked, hoping to change the subject.

Daniel shifted his gaze from me.

"She's coming to terms. The election has been a saving grace for her, given her something to focus her energies on, thank God."

"That's good, I suppose."

"She actually asked about you the other day."

I hadn't seen Margo in weeks, since before Mark's death. No part of me wanted to face the woman who'd mothered my rapist knowing that our unfortunate connection was what had ultimately led to his death. I couldn't see the sorrow in her eyes and share it. And I couldn't pretend I didn't know my father was the reason she was now childless.

"Does she know I'm working with you on the campaign?"

He nodded. "She knows. You and Will worked out the details?"

"Yes, I think we came up with a good plan for your next steps. If things continue to go well outside of the online outreach, it seems our efforts could put you over the edge. I mean, I haven't done this before in terms of politics, but it's promising, I'd say."

"Excellent. That's what I want to hear. I'm glad we could figure this out, one way or the other."

I doodled into my notebook. He was glad now, but he'd put me through hell to get me here when he could have simply asked nicely. Without the murder and violence and death threats that I hoped were all now safely in the past.

"Erica."

I lifted my chin at his more demanding tone.

"Would it help if I said I was sorry? For everything that happened?"

"I'm here now. Isn't that enough? Do I have to be happy about it too?"

"I'd feel a little better if you were. If we win, there will be plenty to be happy about."

I tried to imagine that for a moment. I wasn't sure my vision of victory lined up with his. "Do you really believe that winning this election will bring you happiness?"

A deep frown marked his brow, and he stood. "I have a full day. Need to go over some things with Will before I go, but it was good to see you."

I collected my bag quickly, stuffing my notebook into it as I rose. "I'll see you later then."

I stepped past him, reaching for the door. He placed a hand at my elbow and I jerked away. My heart sped up at the memory of the last time he'd touched me, shaking me with rage.

I looked over my shoulder. Our eyes locked.

"Even if it means nothing to you, if you aren't necessarily happy to be here, I want you to know that I'm glad that you're a part of this."

I gave a short nod and moved forward.

I waved Will a goodbye and left as quickly as I could. As I did, I caught Daniel's figure watching my departure, his expression stoic.

★ ★ ★

I stepped into the apartment to the savory smell of dinner, quiet jazz playing in the surround sound. Blake was in the kitchen, a look of concentration on his face as he put the finishing touches on two plates.

"What is all this?" I tossed my bag down and leaned against the island to watch him.

"If I did everything right, it should look and taste like beef wellington. Julia Child would be proud, I think."

I smirked, enamored by the gesture and a little proud too. Not surprisingly, Blake was amazing at anything he put his mind to.

"If I knew getting on my knees was going to result in home cooked meals every night, I would have done it sooner. You know food is the way to my heart."

He grinned. "Watch that mouth. I might have to punish it later."

I hummed with a giggle. "Sounds intriguing. I hope you put it to good use."

He flashed me a dark look. "Don't mistake my culinary prowess for weakness, sweetheart."

"I wouldn't dare. Nothing you do is anything less than perfectly dominant. Just don't make me call you Master while we eat, okay?"

I came up behind him and circled his chest with my arms, giving him a hug as he placed tiny springs of herbs on top our plates.

"Fair enough. Come on, let's eat," he said.

I let go, and we walked to the table. My cheeks heated at the memory of being tied down to the very thing, having come home to a far less amiable Blake.

"What are you thinking about?"

I widened my eyes as if I'd been caught in the very act. "Um…the table."

He laughed and popped a bite of steak into his mouth. "You're trying to rush us through a gourmet meal so I can tie you up, baby?"

"No. I like to unwind a bit before you start practicing your rope work. What has you so chipper anyway?"

He leaned back in his chair. "Max is out."

My eyebrows shot up. "Out of Angelcom? That's amazing. How did you do it?"

"Unfortunately, my chat with Michael was pretty fruitless. He said exactly what I thought he'd say. Always wants us to work it out between us, not get involved. So I worked it out."

"How did you do it?"

"I was talking to Heath about pulling our investment from Sophia's business. He's invested too, you know. I'm not sure it can be done without—"

"Wait, what does this have to do with Max?"

"Basically, I looked into every investment I shared with the dissenting board members and figured out the absolute worst move I could make on each of them. A few short conversations later, I had consent."

"Wow. You fight dirty."

"This surprises you?"

"No," I admitted.

He shrugged. "I could have hacked their bank accounts and bled them dry. I was being nice."

"Did you tell Max?"

He shook his head, the undercurrent of contentment still glittering in his eyes. I hated Max, sure. But I loved seeing Blake finally happy after what he'd put him through.

"I had one of the admins send him a copy of our minutes with our sincerest apologies. He'll get the message."

I chewed in silence for a moment, trying to imagine Max's reaction to the news. I wondered if he cared as much about getting kicked out as Blake did about getting him out. If nothing else, Angelcom was a major channel into Blake's affairs that gave Max opportunities to hurt him again in the future. Without access to that, Blake was safer. *We* were safer.

"You must be relieved."

"I am. And I'm hopeful too, because while we were voting on board positions, I had them add someone new."

"Who?"

"The future Mrs. Blake Landon, of course."

I stared at him in shock and searched for words.

"I think some of the trust issues that we have maybe root from the fact that I've been involved with your work, and you have virtually no involvement in mine. I'm happy that you came to me, Erica. I can't tell you what a relief it's already been. But I don't want you to think that you have no power in our relationship, that you have no say. And I don't want to discourage your growth as an entrepreneur. It's that spirit that attracted me to you after all, so the last thing I want to do is dampen that flame in you. I've thought about it, and I think a position on the board would be the perfect place for you to participate with your experience as a startup."

I set down my fork and swallowed over the tightness in my throat. The words and the gesture were almost too much for me to process right away. Everything that I was so scared of having taken away from me felt that much safer in Blake's hands. In his control. Maybe all I had to do was give up a little control to have it come back to me in a different way.

"Thank you. I'm flattered that you would even consider it. But are you sure? I mean, I already feel like I'm in over my head at any of these industry events. I can't imagine sitting on the board and holding my own. Involving me at that level is a huge decision."

"Deciding to marry you was a huge decision. Adding you to the board was easy. You'll have these guys won over in no time. You're smart and beautiful, sassy as hell. They won't know what to do with you, the same way I don't half the time. I can't wait to sit back and watch, frankly."

"Aren't they all investors, though? I'm not an investor. What place do I have?"

"You're my wife, or you will be. And this is what I do. I find new projects to invest in. When I decide to drop one or five million into a new project, you'll be a part of that decision process now."

I toyed with my napkin on my lap. "I have no wish to ruin this amazing night, but maybe this is a good time to talk about that. I mean, I'm assuming you want a pre-nup, right?"

We hadn't talked about ownership of assets, or any of those things since he'd asked me to be his wife. I wasn't sure I'd ever be able to shake the inequity between us when it came to money. As much as he reassured me that it meant nothing, I wanted to earn my way, make my own contribution to our lives.

The warmth in his eyes faded a little, a seriousness coming over him. "Make no mistake, what's yours is mine. I don't need a legal document to make me feel any safer in our marriage. If you decide to divorce me and rake me over the coals, I'm not sure any amount of money would ease the pain of losing you. It's a non-issue for me."

"That seems rash. You've spent half your life amassing your wealth, and you want to risk it all now?"

"Are you a risk? Usually when you leave me, you just take my heart. That's the biggest risk of all, I'd say."

I tossed my napkin onto the table and looked past him, hating the fresh reminder of how I'd hurt him. Before I could slip much further into my pout, he caught my hand and pulled me up and onto his lap.

"I don't want to talk about the what-ifs of not being together, in any capacity. I love you. I want to marry you. Nothing's as important as making that happen. That bond, that promise, is the only paperwork I'm interested in having between us."

I sighed. I wasn't going to win this argument. I rested a hand on his chest, feeling the slow rise and fall of his breathing. His heart beat there, feeding the flesh and blood of the man who I loved so much it hurt. "I hope you know I would never—"

He lifted a finger to my lips. "I trust you, and believe me when I say I'm not worried about it. About Angelcom, is it something you want to do? I mean, I wanted to vote you in while I had them all by the balls, but if you really don't want to do it, you don't have to."

"I think it would be fun. And I agree it would be nice to have some more insight into everything you do. It's scary of course, but it would be a good experience for me. You've taught me so much already."

"Good." He threaded his hand through my hair and pulled me down for a kiss. My mind reeled a bit as I reveled in the softness of his lips. His firm but loving hold around me, anchoring me against him. Amidst the sweet moment between us, I stumbled over all this…progress. That part of me that had wanted to hold back and protect myself for so long now seemed very small, almost childish. Giving Blake my trust, all of it, had already changed things between us more than I could imagine. In a very good way.

This shift reminded me of something less positive. I pulled back, searching his eyes.

He reached up and brushed a strand of hair back from my face. "Everything okay?"

"There's something I wanted to talk to you about."

I went to move, but he held me there.

"Tell me."

I hesitated a moment. "Isaac came to the office yesterday."

"Did he."

The displeasure that left his lips was less of a question and more of a threat. I toyed with the fabric of his shirt. I wasn't so sure I liked talking about people he despised in such close proximity.

"He reached out to me a couple weeks ago. I ignored him at first, not knowing how I wanted to handle dealing with him in light of what he did."

"You didn't mention it."

"I didn't, but I am now." I looked into his eyes, trying to convey that this too was progress, even if it was packaged in news that he didn't like. "I didn't want to upset you, and I wanted to think through it a little on my own also. He wants to advertise with us. It wouldn't be a small account either. It would span all the publications relevant to our market, which would be an enormous coup for us."

"You can't bring him on as an advertiser." His voice was flat, without a shred of doubt.

"I had a feeling you'd say that, and I understand your reasons. Obviously I share them. For what it's worth, he seemed genuinely sorry. Outside of that incident, he seems fairly harmless."

"Anyone with that much money and power is far from harmless."

"Then with all your money and power, what makes you any different?"

He lifted his eyebrows. "Do I come across as harmless to you? Because I'm in love with you doesn't mean I'd hesitate dismantling someone who threatened you, me, or either of our businesses."

"True enough. It would help us bridge the revenue gap while we roll out these changes with Alex, but I suppose it's not a risk worth taking."

"You'd pay for it later, I can guarantee it. Everything comes with a price."

I studied him a moment. "What's between you two?"

"As if trying to force himself onto you isn't enough of a reason to hate the man?"

I slanted my head, a silent call for his honesty. "I know there's more. You knew him before we met, and you didn't like him much then."

He sighed and released his hold on me. He patted my ass in a way that said, *Shoo*.

I frowned. "No. You can tell me right here while I'm on your lap."

His expression didn't change for a moment, and I worried he might not agree. Finally he blew out a breath and began to speak.

"As long as I knew Sophia, Isaac had been in her circle of friends. She modeled for his shoots and they'd known each other for a while. When I ended things with her, he came to her rescue. He played the hero, and oh, did he play the part. I'm certain he only wanted to fuck her, and who knows, maybe he did. When we broke up, he made a point to demonize me to her and others. I didn't really care what everyone else thought. I cared more that she felt like I abandoned her."

"But you didn't abandon her."

"I told you before, she didn't take it well. She was clean

when we broke up, and she couldn't understand. It took a lot of willpower for me to not go back to her if only to see her stop hurting. But it wasn't just the drugs. In reality it was the last straw. The distance when she was in rehab just polarized how different we were. How it would have never worked."

"Did you love her?"

He drew his lips drew together. "I don't know. We said it, but I can't tell you if what I felt then was love. I wanted to take care of her, and she thrived on being taken care of. It worked for a while, but I can't say that was love. It wasn't anything close to what we have, Erica."

I chewed my lip, trying like hell to ignore the jealousy that coursed through me.

"I've thought about what you said, about exiting from her agency. Financially, it could be damaging for her if I did. I own more stake in it than anyone. I invested heavily when she started to help get her off the ground. Beyond that, Heath is also invested. I'm not sure what his thoughts are on the matter, but he seems hesitant. Their relationship is different. They have more of a friendship, a connection that she and I didn't. Maybe because they went through a dif-ficult time in their lives together and have come out of it. I don't know, but a part of me doesn't want to push Heath on it if I don't have to."

I looked past him, trying to hide my disappointment. Making James work from home wasn't exactly convenient for me either. I tightened my lips into a firm line as resent-ment set in. Blake slid his palm over my cheek and turned me slightly, regaining my attention.

"I understand why it bothers you, so I'm going to see

what I can do. Maybe it can be done more gradually so it doesn't impact her business so dramatically."

"You baby her still."

He tensed slightly. "Maybe. Old habits die hard."

"She's not as helpless as she seems. If you'd seen how she spoke to me…she can be truly vicious. If she uses that personality in her business life, she'll do fine."

"Jealousy can turn people into very ugly versions of themselves."

My thoughts swirled around the sentiment. I'd been forced to expel James from our office to satisfy Blake's own jealousy. I pushed off of him abruptly, despite his effort to keep me there.

By the time I reached the kitchen with every intention of cleaning until I wasn't so pissed anymore, he was behind me. He spun me and pushed me back to the counter.

"Stop."

"Stop what?" I snapped.

"What do you want me to do? Destroy her business?"

"You're smart, Blake. I think you can figure it out. Put her on a payment plan. Make her take out a loan. Maybe she can start selling what I imagine is a sizeable designer shoe collection. But I don't want her claws in you, *at all, in any way*."

He rolled his eyes. "Her claws are not in me. Yours are. Like, right this fucking minute."

I gave him a hard stare. I didn't care what he said. His assurances were a waste of air if whenever I crossed paths with Sophia, the look on her face told a different story. Until he'd severed their connection, she'd always dangle it in front of me.

"You're mine, and the next time I see her face, I want her to know it. Call me jealous, and if that makes me ugly, then so be it."

He pushed my hair back behind my ear. "I like that you're protective. It doesn't make you ugly."

"Then end it with her. Please." I softened in his arms, wishing he'd just do the right thing.

A long moment passed between us. My resentment melted into a pile of disappointment.

"Okay."

I lifted my gaze, but before I could say anything, his lips were on me, silencing me, giving me everything I wanted.

CHAPTER FOURTEEN

Marie stood behind me, curling small sections of my hair. Alli had a concentrated look on her face as she brushed some color onto my cheeks.

"You're fussing too much, Alli. This is an engagement party, not the big day. I'm fine."

She stood back, head cocked to the side. "You are now. You look perfect. Also, you should get used to it. Getting married is like prom on steroids."

My lips lifted with a smile. "That's what I'm afraid of. You keep saying things like that, I'm going to take Blake up on his offer to elope."

Fiona looked up from her seat, another bridal magazine in her lap. "You wouldn't!"

"No," I relented. "You're the only friends I have, and if I deprived you of this wedding, I'm sure neither of you would ever speak to me again."

"Nonsense." Alli fluffed a spiral of hair that Marie had just released. "We should go dress shopping soon though. I think that's the key to getting you into wedding mode."

I sighed. "You could be right. Maybe I should start looking at those magazines for ideas. I don't even know where to start."

"Well, don't look too hard, because Alli and I have picked just about everything out for you already," Fiona chimed in, her eyes glittering with humor.

I laughed. "Okay."

"Satin and strapless." Fiona opened it to a page, showing me a photo of a beautiful model bride.

"Hmm, pretty. What about lace?"

Alli widened her eyes a bit. "Is that what you want?"

"I don't know, maybe. I think Blake likes lace."

"Must run in the family," Alli quipped, her eyes alight.

I laughed, trying to keep myself still so Marie wouldn't inadvertently catch me with the hot iron.

Fiona did little to mask her look of disgust. "Oh my God, this conversation has to end. Please. You'll give me nightmares."

Alli and I laughed, sharing a look.

The door opened then, and Heath poked his head in. "Mom wanted me to tell you guys that people are starting to show up, so come out whenever you're ready. Don't make them wait too long to meet our guest of honor." He winked.

"Go away, Heath. You're going to make her nervous," Fiona said.

"It's fine. I have my liquid charisma right here." I lifted my nearly empty champagne flute.

Marie loosened the last curl. "You don't need liquid charisma. Everyone will love you."

I warmed at her words. Of all the people here, Marie was my only family, though the more I thought of it, the more that line between Blake's family and mine began to blur. Alli lived in both worlds right along with me, and I was far from an outsider in the Landons' lives. They were a warm and welcoming family that I was belonging to a little more each day. The absence of my own relatives mattered less, and the times when I mourned not having a more normal family were fewer.

"We'll be out soon. As soon as we're beautiful." Alli ran her fingers through her already perfectly straight hair.

"You're already beautiful, gorgeous." Heath smirked, his eyes fixed on Alli.

She blushed, pretending to ignore him.

"Gross, get out." Fiona tossed a throw pillow at the door, missing her target as she closed the door shut, his laughter audible from the other side.

Marie curled the last piece of my hair. "You're all set, baby girl."

I stood, taking in my appearance once more. I wasn't as concerned about how I looked as I was about holding my own in front of all of the Landons' friends and family. This was going to be family overload, but I was as ready as I ever would be.

Alli hooked her arm through mine and gave me a little nudge. "Let's go charm the hell out of the Landon family tree."

"I'm ready. Let's go."

Blake met us as we left the spare room where the girls and I had stationed ourselves to get ready. He looked delectable in dark jeans and a pin-striped collared shirt rolled up at the sleeves and loose at the waist. He'd look good in a burlap sack, a toga, basically anything. While everyone else meandered farther into the house, I stayed back to steal a moment with him.

"You look stunning. I can't wait to show you off," he said, his eyes darkening.

"You like it?" I glanced down at the cream-colored

strapless dress I wore. Covered lace at the top met sheer layers of the skirt that fell just below my knees.

"Love it. Very bridal. But of course, I love you more."

He caught me up to his body and leaned down for a kiss, gentle and filled with devotion. That awareness, the ever-present arc of energy, crackled between us. His lips brushed against mine almost reverently. I closed my eyes and sank into the embrace. He traced the seam of my lips with his tongue. I sighed and opened to him, welcoming the sweet taste of him.

His tongue lashed deeper, seeking and nibbling. I moaned softly, pressing myself up to my toes. He pulled away slightly, shaking his head.

"Let's go before I decide to steal you away from here and make love to you instead."

I wouldn't argue one bit, if I hadn't known his parents were expecting us and had already put so much time into planning the party.

"Alli spent at least twenty minutes on my makeup. She'd kill me. Not to mention your parents and everyone else."

He paused. "Are you nervous?"

I shrugged. "Maybe a little. I won't know most of the people."

"You will soon. They're mostly my parents' friends from when I was growing up. They'll love you." He clasped our hands together, lacing our fingers. Chest to chest, we made no effort to move. I could stay this way, hiding away in his arms all day. As if the rest of the world didn't exist.

"I love you, Blake. We say it all the time, but sometimes I wish I could show you more. Nothing seems to do the words justice."

He lifted my hand and pressed his lips to the band that adorned my ring finger. "You do show me. Every day, by being with me. And if that's not enough, you have the rest of our lives to prove it to me."

I smiled warmly. "Sounds like a good plan."

"Come on. Let's go."

Blake led me into the large open living area that joined with the Landons' designer kitchen and an impressive dining area. The combined rooms looked out onto the ocean through a wall of windows. The already expansive room had begun to fill with mingling guests. Before I could think of introducing myself, Catherine ushered over the first group of friends. Recognition lit up Blake's face, and I steeled myself for the first of what would be many introductions tonight.

Hours passed as we went from one group to the next. The members of Blake's extended family were as sweet and lovable as the immediate. To them, Blake was still a young man, a boy even. I could see it in their eyes and the way they interacted with him so casually. No longer the intimidating, dominating man who fought tooth and nail for what he wanted, Blake joked and even reddened a few times as people shared stories of his youth.

I repeated the story of how we'd met in the Angelcom boardroom, reliving the moments. The attraction that charged our initial interest in each other had only grown since that time.

On the outside, Blake was perfection. Beautiful, wildly successful, rich beyond anything I could fathom, and he was charming to boot. So few people knew his heart, though. The darkness that lived there sometimes, and the passion that had deepened our bond. In the picture he painted of his youth, I saw a highly intelligent man searching for answers in our convoluted world. And in that seeking, he'd lost a friend.

Though he refused to talk about it with any depth, I knew he carried the weight of Cooper's suicide with him. I'd guessed too that something had altered in him when it happened. A commitment to the control he so needed had been born. A fervent determination to never go through that kind of terrible experience again combined with the opportunity that Pope, his mentor, had given him to succeed with the software venture made control possible for him. He now had more control than any average person could ever hope to have.

I was lost in my own thoughts for a moment when Blake's countenance turned stony. I followed the path of his gaze and stopped abruptly. Max stood casually next to the man I recognized from photos online to be his father, Michael. Dressed in khakis and a dark V-neck, Max carried his usual charming smile into the room. The two men were the same height and build, and Michael was no less attractive for being an older man. His skin was darkened by the sun, his hair white with the hint of blond that had faded out with age.

When Max's gaze lit on us, he stilled a moment. Michael proceeded toward us. Without a word, he pulled Blake into a casual hug. The small gesture spoke to how their relationship went beyond the professional world. Max pivoted away and merged with another group of people in the party.

"It's great to see you, Blake. And of course, many congratulations."

When Michael pulled back, his eyes smiled. For a magnate, he possessed more warmth than I would have expected.

"I wasn't convinced you'd ever get around to it, but I am very pleasantly surprised."

His gaze slid over to me, with no less warmth or appreciation. "You must be the lovely Erica I've heard so much about. Catherine kept me on the phone for nearly an hour last week. I think she wanted to make sure I made the trip, but of course I would have anyway. I'm Michael, by the way."

I shook his hand. "I'm so glad you did. It's wonderful to finally meet you."

Blake's posture had relaxed only slightly. "You didn't mention that Max was coming with you."

Michael glanced back in the direction of the door where they'd entered. "To be honest, I didn't know he would be. I let him know I'd be in town, and he already knew about the party, so I assumed your mother extended an invitation."

Michael's expression cooled slightly while Blake's nostrils flared.

"Michael, Erica, if you would excuse me a moment, I'll be right back." His smile was tight, but the tone of his voice betrayed the anger that now simmered below the surface.

Michael sighed heavily. "I'll die a happy man if that rivalry will settle itself one of these days. In the meantime, they're taking years off my life."

"I'm sure you're not the only one who'd like to see it end."

"Without a doubt. It's unfortunate that two people with so much intelligence can devote so much time to trying to outdo each other."

I couldn't disagree entirely, yet I knew that of the two, Max was the aggressor. I bit my tongue though. Michael seemed mercifully in the dark about the finer details of Max's tactics, or perhaps he simply ignored them. A man of his professional stature might not have much choice. He had empires to run while his son and protégé had it out over affairs that likely were not worth his time.

Blake and Catherine stepped out of sight. I felt for them both. Max shouldn't have come, but now that he was here, worry knotted in my gut. He couldn't be pleased with Blake removing him from the board, and I could only hope that an argument didn't erupt and ruin the night.

Michael's expression was thoughtful. "Perhaps you could be the one to make them see the absurdity of it all, Erica. They know you, respect you. Men can be awfully short-sighted sometimes. Reactionary. I'm sure you know this from experience. Maybe all they need is some guidance from an intelligent, compelling woman to make them see what a waste of time all this is."

I felt myself flush. The man barely knew me. Besides, what power did I have over either of them? Max had gone to such great lengths to upset my company's success. I was the last person who could bring them peace. I'd become a third party, inextricably involved in the whole terrible mess.

"I appreciate the vote of confidence, but I think stepping between them would be dangerous."

He nodded. "Perhaps. Max is my son, and Blake is very much like a son to me. Neither of them listen worth a damn to anything I say, sadly. You've certainly captured Blake's attention though. Now if only Max would do the same, maybe we'd have some progress. It's hard to care about much else when you have a beautiful woman in your arms."

He smiled, and I warmed despite myself. I wanted to say more and try to enlighten this idealistic albeit sweet man with the truth. But it would do no good. Michael, Max, and Blake were like gods at war with one another, having no perspective on the potential impact of all those involved. Except Max knew exactly what his impact would be on me. The health of my business might have been a passing interest at the time, but it had considerably more importance as soon as Max realized he could hurt Blake through it.

Still, I hadn't spoken to either Risa or Max since their site went up. As much as I wanted to tell them exactly what I thought of them, I'd chosen to stay silent.

"You look like you could use a drink."

I spun to find Max extending a glass of champagne to me. I hesitated, but sensing Michael's eyes on me, I took it, if only in the momentary spirit of peace. I masked the disgust for the younger man, painting on a tight-lipped smile.

Max nodded to his father. "Dad, Greg was asking about you."

"Was he? I'll go find him then." Michael scanned the room and then turned back to me. "Erica, it was lovely to meet you finally. We'll chat again before I go, but if not, perhaps you can convince Blake to come to Dallas for a proper visit. It's been too long."

"Of course. I'll see what I can do."

He kissed me on the cheek and winked before leaving me with Max. Being alone with him made me instantly uncomfortable. This was supposed to be a happy day, but I had nothing nice to say to Max. No matter Michael's optimistic thoughts about everyone getting along, Max had wounded me and attacked my business in a way that was unforgiveable.

"Why are you here?"

He scoffed, feigning offense. "You'd think you might be happier to see me. I was a few signatures away from giving you two million dollars. Or did Blake's four mil trump that whole thing?"

"No, but your propensity to shit on everything he does certainly colored that choice."

"Was it a choice? Or did he back you into a corner? That's how he works, you know. He manipulates and positions himself to the point where you can't make any other decision but the one he wants. Is that the kind of man you want to marry?"

"What do you want Max? Or did you just come here to upset everyone?"

"I was hoping I could speak with you, actually."

I shrugged, taking a sip of the champagne. "Here I am."

"I'd like to discuss business, and I'd rather not do it in front of parents and childhood friends. Could we speak alone?"

He eyed me steadily. Looking around the room, I couldn't see Blake, but the thought that he would intervene if he saw us speaking seemed likely.

"Blake doesn't want you here. You should really leave. His parents put a lot into this party, and I'd rather not see it ruined because you two can't get along."

"Agreed. I'll be on my way as soon as I can have a moment of your time."

I sighed, my aggravation growing the longer I stayed in this holding pattern with him. As much as I wasn't in the mood for any kind of powwow with Max, I also didn't want Blake to cause a scene. I'd let Max say what he needed to say and hopefully get him to leave so the rest of the night could carry on as planned.

"Fine. Five minutes, and then you need to leave."

"Fair enough."

Reluctantly, I led him from where we stood down a hallway that led to Greg's den. The room was cool and quiet.

I walked in and turned at Greg's large desk, leaning against it.

The door closed behind Max with a click.

"That's better isn't it?" He walked closer, something hidden in his guarded expression.

"Say what you have to say."

He stopped a few feet away, a distance I assured myself was safe. My stomach tensed. An uncomfortable sensation prickled under my skin.

Lifting his glass, he smirked. "How about a toast?"

I rolled my eyes. "What would we possibly toast to, Max?"

"To Blake."

I canted my head, waiting for him to continue.

"For winning the girl, driving me out of Angelcom, and managing to turn my old man's eye from his own family for the better part of fifteen years. How's that for a toast?"

Resentment laced every word. But when I considered what he'd done to both of us, I couldn't muster an ounce of sympathy for him. I was glad he was losing his battle with Blake, and I could certainly toast to that.

"Cheers." I lifted my glass to him and let the champagne slide down, the liquid welcome to my mouth now parched from the hours of introductions and conversations.

A smile lifted his lips. "So tell me, how's business?"

I laughed. "Wouldn't you like to know? You lost your inside connection. I suppose you'll have to guess and hope for the best now."

"You sound bitter, Erica. Why? I told you I was interested in the concept. You chose not to let me invest in it. Shouldn't it show my commitment that I was willing to make it happen with or without you?"

"It speaks volumes to your commitment to chase after Blake's ventures trying to carve out something that could rival anything he's created. You had access to privileged information about my company and used it against me. Below the belt, I'd say."

His eyes narrowed slightly. I didn't care. I wanted him to feel any dig I sent his way.

"We didn't exchange a non-disclosure. I was well within my rights."

"You were well within your rights to be a deceitful, unethical bastard. Unfortunately there's no law against that."

He laughed quietly. "Thank goodness. Lucky for you, there's no law for fucking your way to the top either."

I closed my eyes. I set my glass down, suddenly too exhausted to want the relief of a drink.

"Get out." My voice lacked the force I'd meant to deliver with the demand.

When I opened my eyes, he'd come closer, facing me.

"I'm just saying, if you wanted to fuck someone for your funding, I was right there. You know that's what everyone thinks, right? You don't need me to ruin your reputation. You did that all by yourself, sweetheart."

I winced. "You're lying."

"Am I? People love to talk. A little bit of industry gossip can spread quickly if started in the right circles. Pretty girl like you, taken under the wing of someone like Landon. He's got a reputation of his own, you know. You're the last in a long line, so don't go feeling special just because he's going to marry you."

"You don't know anything about who he really is. He loves me—" I stopped myself, confused by how slow the words were leaving me. How tired my body suddenly felt. I shook my head, but the movement only made me dizzier. I was drunk, suddenly more drunk than I could remember being in a long time. *Shit.*

I stared down at my glass, and amidst the rising bubbles, barely visible granules floated near the well of the glass. I looked up, my vision blurring. When Max came into focus, his perfect white teeth gleamed through a deviant smile. He was a demon in disguise, if I'd ever met one.

"We'll see if he loves you after tonight."

A surge of panic powered my legs to carry me toward the door, but he blocked my passage catching me by the upper arms

"Going so soon? Stay a while."

He shuffled me backwards and shoved me back onto the couch. A new wave of fatigue hit me with the impact. I struggled to hold myself upright. Every muscle sagged, weighted with this new and sudden weakness. I'd underestimated him before, and now again. Confusion swirled through me as I tried to think my way through what was happening. My mind was moving too slow, my attention scattering until he was beside me, catching my jaw painfully so I faced him.

"Best case scenario, I thought you'd look like a fall down drunk in front of Blake's family. But this is so much better. Now I'll get a little taste and maybe...just maybe we can ruin Blake's happily ever after when he sees you this way. Drunk, just fucked, like the cunt that you are."

"Max, no." My head felt like a drum barrel, buzzing with a never-ending soundless vibration. I told my limbs to move, but when they did, it was Max pushing me down sideways on the couch.

Then his mouth was on me, forcing his tongue past my lips. Feebly I pushed at him. He answered the weak effort with a snicker, his breath hot on my face.

"That's right, MacLeod said you were a fighter. You get around, don't you? Does Blake know what a little slut you are?"

The mention of Mark's name conjured a memory deep and violent. "Please, no," I slurred. The words melted into the space between us, along with my fading consciousness.

He muffled my weak cries.

"Don't worry. I'll make it quick. I've had a hard on for you for months, Erica. Going to show you what it feels like to get fucked by a real man, not some two-bit hacker riding on my family's success. If we're lucky, you'll remember it too."

I grasped desperately for control, to fight the paralysis that slid like cold molasses through my veins, making everything slow. My lungs struggled for air, the effort to breathe taxed amidst the rising panic and whatever invisible enemy my body was fighting.

"That's a good girl."

Losing my grip, I was vaguely aware of him pressing me roughly through my panties.

No, no, no. God, no.

No one would hear me, but my mind screamed it until my vision went black.

CHAPTER FIFTEEN

My eyes fluttered open, and then fell shut. Every time I reached for consciousness, something knocked me back down. I'd never been this tired in my life. Even as my conscious mind began to grasp details from what happened, my body demanded sleep. I gave in yet fought the unsettling urge. Something wasn't right about it. The weariness weakened my muscles, sank into my tired bones.

As I drifted in and out of sleep, my stomach twisted, sickness brewing in my gut. The potent nausea and the real threat that I'd be sick right where I lay was what finally propelled me out of bed. On my feet, I shoved the bathroom door open and barely made it to the toilet.

Several exhausting minutes later, I sat unmoving on the floor. My head rested on my arm as I caught my breath.

"Baby."

Blake's pained voice came up behind me. Then his arms were cradled around me. He palmed my back, the heat of his touch penetrating the thin nightshirt I wore. The fatigue took root again, weakening me in the security of his arms. I sat back against him and wiped my mouth, determined not to make a bed out of the bathroom floor.

He kissed my shoulder. "Are you okay?"

I nodded. "Better now." Thankfully, being ill had quelled the sick feeling for the time being. I wanted to move, to shake this weight that settled over me. "Help me up? I feel so weak."

"Sure. Just go slow."

I nodded again, the task of lifting to my feet impossible at the moment. He circled my shoulders and then my waist until I was upright. He tucked a loose lock of hair behind my ear, and I caught his reflection in the mirror. His normally expressive eyes hid behind the dark rimmed glasses that he rarely wore.

I let go of the security of his solid body and held myself up at the sink, gathering enough of my strength to wash my face and brush my teeth. He brushed my hair back from my face and neck, allowing the cold sweat to evaporate off my skin.

"Do you want some tea? Can I get you anything?"

"Tea would be good, I think." My voice was so small. I couldn't be sure he'd heard me until he stepped away, kissing me gently on the cheek before he went.

I could have been sleeping on my feet, but I managed to make my way back to our bed. In the whirlwind of this physical onslaught, my mind kept asking what had happened. What had brought this on? This wasn't a hangover. This wasn't any kind of sick I'd ever been, and my brain was too murky to make sense of it. I sank into the bed and the second the blanket covered me, the welcome warmth was just enough to pull me back into the same deep sleep.

The night was black but slowly the details of my surroundings began to register. The grass was wet on my feet. Cool against the warm air. Then he yanked me forward. Ignorant as I was, I still knew where we were going. The same place he'd always led me.

A hundred times maybe, and I went every time. Like the stupid, drunk girl I was, I followed.

Laughter. Everyone was laughing, celebrating. People I knew. I frowned, wondering why they were all here.

The pressure of his grip on my arm increased enough to be painful, and the familiar fear coiled in my gut. It was coming.

The vicious sneer, an expression painted on by his smug satisfaction, his hatred. He hated me. He had to, to do this to me. I'd plead, but he'd pin me down. The same gravel in his voice as he gritted out his plan for me.

Except when I met his eyes they were different. No longer the dark round irises that haunted me. Confused, I searched his features until they solidified and recognition dawned. Max. The face, this body pressing down on me now, belonged to Max.

My heart lurched seconds before the familiar pain. No matter how hard I fought, he'd always find his way in the darkness, taking what he wanted.

Powerless, I couldn't move. I couldn't run. Gasping for air, grasping for reality, I said his name. A questioning plea. Then, realizing I had a voice, even over the noise and the blur of laughter around us, I screamed. I screamed for help.

I shot up in the bed still screaming until I realized I was home, in our bedroom. Air rushed in and out of my lungs, feeding the lightheadedness. My skin crawled, tingling with sweat and imagined trails of another man's hands on me.

I started when Blake barreled through the door. He was shirtless, dressed in his pajama pants. He circled the bed and slowed, sitting on the edge of the bed. My breathing was ragged and uneven. After a minute he spoke, barely a whisper.

"Can I hold you, baby?"

Eyes wide, I held his gaze. I couldn't speak, still too much in the dream. Could I let him? Did I want him to? I couldn't make sense of anything until he reached for me tentatively.

I caught his hands between us, keeping them at a safe distance. The sudden contact shot remembered pain through me. Still, against every instinct, I held them, something in me not wanting to let go. I clenched my jaw down, swallowing hard over the dry knot in my throat. Tears welled, but something inside me fought the reflex to fight. My rational mind reminded me that he was no enemy, that I needed him. Like holding onto an electric fence, I simply waited out the panic and pain.

"Erica...sweetheart. Breathe. It's just me, okay?"

I breathed through it until my body relaxed enough to let me speak. I found my voice again, now hoarse. "I had a dream. I...I'm not sure what happened."

"A nightmare...like the others?"

I nodded quickly. He'd known about the dream and how it crept up on me sometimes, as much as I wished it would disappear forever.

"Kind of, but it was Max. He was Max, somehow."

I recalled his face, the dream version merging with the face my conscious mind knew. Then a rush of visions from the party fluttered through my brain. Marie, Michael, and a blur of people. Then Max, his arrogant smile as he hovered over my powerless body. Bile rose in my throat. I let go of Blake and wrapped my arms around myself, as if that could protect me from what my mind was showing me now.

"Blake, what happened?" I rushed, my eyes now wide

with alarm. "I can't remember, but I know something happened. Just tell me."

The grief in Blake's eyes as he worked his jaw confirmed it. "He didn't hurt you, baby."

Reaching up to touch me, he fisted his hand and lowered it before he could make contact. His complexion was pale save a dark bruise on his cheek that I hadn't noticed before. The muscles in his arms flexed as if he was restraining himself from touching me more. Then I noticed his hand, a thick white bandage wrapped around it.

"You're hurt."

He shook his head, his jaw tight. "He's hurt worse."

I covered my mouth. A new wave of nausea hit me as I tried to string the words together to ask him. I didn't want to know, but I had to. I held Blake's gaze, searching, wishing I didn't need to ask. If I didn't want to hear it, he didn't want to tell me.

The tears poured from my eyes as my body shook. I could only piece together a few details from the night, but somehow I knew something terrible had happened. And heaven help me, it had happened at Max's hand.

"I need to know what he did," I whispered.

He closed his eyes a moment as if to collect his anger. "I walked in on Max ... touching you. He didn't—he didn't have sex with you."

My eyes clenched shut, forcing more tears out. "Oh God."

"You were drugged. It was obvious. You could barely move. You've been sleeping for a couple days."

"Why would he do this? Why?" The words came out in a sob as I struggled to understand why he'd want to hurt me, to put me through the kind of torture that I'd barely survived before.

"He'll never do anything like it again."

"How can you know that?"

His eyes became serious and still in the brief silence. "I rearranged his fucking face, Erica, that's why. We're both lucky I didn't kill him because I had every intention of it. Took three of them to pull me off of him." He flexed his hand, grimacing.

"Everyone saw. I can't imagine what they must think."

He reached for my hand, pulling it away from my face. I licked my dry lips and took a steadying breath. The contact didn't hurt the way it had a moment ago. Something had rearranged in my mind as the dream separated from reality.

"They don't think anything. They know what he did. My mom's been worried sick. Marie's been calling off the hook. Alli, Christ, I've had to turn her away a few times. I haven't had anyone by so you could rest. I knew you'd need some time. No one thinks any less of you. I can guarantee they think a hell of a lot less of him."

"He called me a whore." I winced at the words as they resurfaced in my memory. "Said I'd fucked my way to the top. He wants to ruin us, Blake."

"He's the one who's ruined."

I flashed him a questioning look.

"I've never seen Michael so devastated in my life. I don't know what will happen between them, but this is one fuck up that even Michael might not be able to look past. He pulled me off Max, but I'll never forget the way he looked at him. He didn't even go to him, to help him. He just walked away."

"He was telling me about wanting you two to make peace."

His nostrils flared. "There'll never be peace between us until one of us is dead."

Hatred played out on the hard lines of his features. I reached up and traced the tight muscle at his jaw. He released it, turning into my touch. He pressed a soft kiss against my fingertips. The sweet gesture began to unravel the horror I'd woken with. Blake was here. We were together, both safe. I reminded myself of these truths over and over, even when my mind grappled with the broken memories of what Max had done.

"Are you sure he didn't..."

His eyes widened, sadness lingering there. "I'm positive. I came looking for you before anyone else was there. His intentions were pretty clear, but he didn't get far." As if gentling a frightened child, he skimmed my arm, circling his thumb over my shoulder. "I would have killed him. No one could have stopped me, then or now. His heart would have stopped beating if he'd gone an inch farther than he had."

A strange kind of relief washed over me, as if I'd narrowly escaped death. If Max had raped me, I couldn't begin to grasp what it would have done to me. It would be a kind of death all its own, the same way Mark had killed a part of me when he took my innocence years ago. I pushed down the lingering nausea, all the feelings new and fresh washing over me. A fine mist swept over my skin. He hadn't taken what he wanted, but the threat that he could have haunted me.

I outstretched a shaky hand to Blake's chest. Bringing myself closer to him physically was like pushing through a wall. All my instincts told me stay back where it was safe. He let me come to him, unhurried, his touch a whisper on my skin. Trembling from head to toe, I finally found a place on his lap. He caressed me slowly, carefully, up and down my back until I relaxed fully against him.

"Everything's going to be okay. You're safe now. I've got you, baby."

He hushed me quietly while I broke down in his arms. This new violation compounded with the weight of the old until I thought I'd cried all the tears my body could produce. Through my sobs, he murmured reassurances. Promises of his love, that he'd always protect me and keep me safe, filled the air around us until I believed it, with every ounce of my soul.

★ ★ ★

The relentless fatigue that had weighed me down for days had finally lifted. For the first time since the party, I had energy, but at Blake's insistence, I stayed home from work another day. Unable to be alone with my rambling thoughts, I wasted an afternoon watching movies. Comedies with no emotional depth that couldn't threaten the mental peace I'd been trying like hell to achieve.

I shrieked when the door to the apartment opened. Jumping up from the couch, I beheld Alli's worried face.

"Sorry, I didn't mean to scare you. I brought you lunch." She held up a paper bag.

I lowered my hand from my racing heart. "Okay. Thanks."

She joined me on the couch, setting the bag down

on the coffee table. "Sorry," she said again. "How are you doing? I wanted to see you sooner, but Blake insisted that you needed your rest. Heath told me he was at the office today, so I thought I'd sneak in and see you."

"I'm okay. Better. Whatever Max put in that drink completely took over my system for a while. But I'm finally starting to feel human again. I'm looking forward to getting back to work tomorrow though. Sitting around gives me too much time to overthink everything."

She chewed her lip, her eyes glazing. Before I could say anything she pulled me into a tight hug. I held her back as I too fought tears. She knew. Everyone knew. I couldn't hide from my best friend and pretend that I wasn't hurting.

"I don't even know what to say," she whispered. "I'm still in disbelief. I just can't believe it."

"It's okay, Alli. I'm okay," I reassured her, wanting to believe it too, even as my voice wavered. Maybe I wasn't okay today, but I would be. I would get through this, the same way I got through it before. Except the more I thought about what Max did and the party, the more I questioned if I'd ever *really* gotten over what Mark had done to me.

"It's not okay. He can't get away with this, Erica."

I sat back and brushed my tears away. I didn't want to be breaking down right now. I didn't want to stir it all up again when I'd spent all day trying to forget. In addition to bombarding my brain with mindless television, I had been busy shoving down the memories of the other night that kept popping up, back down to the dark place I kept Mark's memories. I didn't want to think about any of it.

"Erica?"

I looked up.

"You're going to police, aren't you? They'll need you to cooperate with them if they are going to prosecute."

"I think so," I said, betraying the fact that I still wasn't really convinced that I could go through with it.

"You have to. I can't believe he's got the audacity to press charges against Blake after what he did to you. His vengeance seriously has no bounds. The whole thing is so backwards and wrong."

I sat up straighter, making sure I'd heard her right. "He's doing what?"

"Blake didn't tell you? Max is pressing charges against Blake for assault. Obviously he was acting in your behalf. The bastard deserved everything he got."

I let out a breath I'd been holding. I let my forehead fall into my palm. "I can't believe he didn't tell me that. He told me he messed Max up, but I didn't even put it together that he could be in trouble over this. Shit, I can't even think straight. This isn't good."

Alli touched my shoulder gently. "He never wants to worry you. He knows this isn't easy for you, especially with what you went through with Mark. I'm sure Heath would have probably done the same thing in Blake's shoes. Thankfully, the Landons have good lawyers."

"I'm sure the Popes do too. God, he doesn't need to be dealing with this shit too. Now I'm upset all over again."

She sighed quietly. "Are you going to talk to the police? Promise me you will."

I nodded quickly.

I'd been wrestling with the prospect of going to the police. Blake had told me that they'd left cards and would want to speak with me. Something about it scared the hell out of me. Maybe it was the same thing that had kept me from going to the police when Mark raped me. Deep down I'd blamed myself. The blame and the shame of sharing the experience with someone else had kept me silent. I buried it all, so far down that I didn't care about finding my attacker, about having a voice.

But this was different. I knew Max, and no one could question what he'd done, with all the people who had been there. The drugs in my system were proof enough of his intentions. How I'd find the strength to walk into the police station and tell my story though, I'd never know. But if it helped Blake out of this madness, I'd do whatever I needed to do.

"I'll go with you. You won't be alone." Alli reached for my hand.

"Thank you. I don't know what I'd do without you."

"You'll never have to know. I'm always here for you, and I'm not going anywhere. We all are. We're all but family now."

My heart pulsed with gratitude for her friendship.

"Hey, I have an idea." Alli brightened a little and took my hand.

I raised my eyebrows. "What's that?"

"I know this is probably the last thing on your mind, but what do you think about going dress shopping this week? It would take your mind off all of this upset."

I smiled and nodded. "That sounds perfect."

CHAPTER SIXTEEN

"Alli told me about Max pressing charges."

Blake had worked late and he hadn't been home five minutes before I approached him. I could think of little else since Alli left that afternoon. On top of that, I was pissed off that he didn't tell me right away. He tugged off his shirt and stepped out of the bedroom into the adjoining bathroom, effectively ignoring me. I followed him in.

"Blake."

"It doesn't matter."

"Having criminal charges against you matters."

He let out a sigh and turned toward me. I tried to hold my concentration on the matter at hand, but his shirtless body and the way he smelled when he pulled me close the way he did now always seemed to scatter my brain cells. A hand on my hip, he leaned down and pressed a soft kiss on my lips.

"It doesn't worry me, so it shouldn't worry you, okay? You've got enough on your mind."

I stared into his eyes, letting him know that I sure as hell was going to worry. "Will this affect your work? What about Angelcom, or all the other businesses your name is attached to?"

A short laugh escaped him. "Are you talking about my reputation? Money talks, Erica, and thankfully I've got plenty of it. The same reasons the board wanted to keep rubbing up against Max until I put their balls in a jar are the same reasons why none of this is going to matter to any of them. I'm the one holding the cards. Anyway, I could give a shit what anyone else thinks."

I couldn't help the worry that rooted right next to all the hate I now held for Max.

Blake framed my face in his hands. "Listen to me. Do not worry about this. It's nothing I can't handle, and trust me that I'm handling it."

"How?"

He sighed and released me, leaving a few inches of distance between us.

I looped my fingers into his jeans, tugging him back. His eyes widened a fraction.

"I'm going to talk to the police tomorrow. I don't remember everything, but hopefully it'll be enough. If that means testifying or whatever, I'll do whatever I need to do."

He paused. "I'm glad to hear it. Not for my sake, but for yours."

I frowned. "I'm not sure I'd do it if it weren't for your sake. I hate that he's done this to you."

"Why wouldn't you tell the police your story, Erica? He deserves to face what he did, and God knows, you deserve justice. You'll never have it if you don't tell the police what happened. You're the victim, and they need to hear *your* story, not mine."

I dropped my gaze to Blake's waist where my fingers idly tangled in the loops of his jeans. "The thought of going through it all makes me sick, that's why."

He tipped my chin until I met his serious eyes. "There

are times when it makes sense to let go, and there are times when you need to fight, no matter how miserable the idea might seem."

I got lost in his eyes for a second. "And you want me to fight."

"I won't make the decision for you. But if this is any indication," he said, gesturing to the now deep red scabs decorating his knuckles, "you know where I stand on knocking him down to size."

I winced at his injury and how it'd been incurred. I couldn't imagine Max's injuries, but I relished that he was likely still suffering with them. I drew in a deep breath through my nose. I'd spent the past few days trying to push past all of it. I couldn't go down this road again. I wouldn't give Max the satisfaction of breaking me like Mark had.

"I appreciate that you fought for me, but this isn't about revenge."

"You're right. It's about holding Max Pope accountable for the first time in his life. He needs to learn a lesson that he's been working up to for a very long time. That's not revenge. That's justice. That's making a situation right that's been wrong for too long."

I could argue all I wanted, but Blake was right. Max hadn't just threatened me, crossing a line that could never be uncrossed. He'd betrayed my trust, threatened both my business and Blake's. Blake's grievances extended far beyond the experiences we'd shared with Max. Before I'd even met Max, I'd known he was a playboy, a spoiled young man. He skated above the consequences that would have fallen on anyone else. Instead, he'd been shielded by his family's fortress of wealth and prominence. Professor Quinlan had used such a circumstance to his advantage, earning me a meeting with him with the promise that he'd invest in Clozpin.

How long would this go on? How long could he wreak havoc over our lives without consequences, spurred by this mindless jealousy that Blake inspired in him? Maybe Blake was right. Perhaps this was the one strike that couldn't be ignored—by Michael or by the law. Maybe this infraction would finally show him he wasn't immune from consequence.

Blake broke my thoughts with a kiss that was both tender and careful. Pulling back, he studied me. "How was your day? Are you feeling any better?"

"I feel fine. I told you that this morning. I'm going back to work tomorrow, regardless of what you say. If I sit around here lazing around one more day, I'm going to lose my mind."

He smirked. "Well, we can't have that."

Turning away from me, he started the shower. He stripped naked and opened the door, filling the room with a rush of steam. I chewed my lip, following his backside as he stepped in under the stream. The fire that had lain dormant for days lit within me. Apparently the days of being deprived of intimacy had taken its toll, and now that my energy was back, I was having a hard time ignoring it.

I wasn't sure if I was ready, but I missed our closeness. Blake had been careful with me. Exceedingly careful. I hated that what happened had put an invisible wall between us, separating us by our fear of hurting each other when I needed Blake more than ever.

I pushed my jeans past my hips to the floor and tugged off my bra and shirt at once. He turned to watch me, his countenance reflecting the quiet hunger that was simmering through me. I stepped into the shower behind him. He let me pass to share the water. Our bodies brushed close, setting off all the familiar alarms. My nipples grazed the soft hairs on his chest, hardening instantly. I paused my journey there, perfectly content with our proximity, the hot water pulsing down on us.

"I missed you," I said.

"I missed you too, baby."

I placed my hands on his chest, eager to feel every ridge slide under my fingertips, to entwine with him. I grazed lower over the taut muscles of his abs. I wanted to go lower. I wanted to feel his hot flesh in my hands, to know he wanted me as much as I wanted him. After all of this madness, I longed for his touch, for the reassurance that nothing had changed between us. I traced the line of hair that led from his navel downward. He caught my hand, halting my journey.

"Turn around," he said quietly.

I gazed at him from under my lashes, my breath hitching with the simple command. Good things were usually in store when he told me to turn around. I spun and braced my hands on the cool marble of the shower wall. I closed my eyes, imagining his hands on me, while the water ran down my back between us.

I heard a small click, and then his hands were in my hair, massaging and lathering. While it wasn't the touch I expected, I welcomed it all the same. I let my head fall back as he rubbed ten tiny circles over my scalp.

"Feel good?"

I hummed. "Very. Thank you."

"Anytime."

I smiled. He moved the spray to rinse me and cleaned the rest of me from head to toe. He washed my shoulders, massaging the tense muscles as he went. Turning me so we were face to face again, he left no expanse untouched, between my breasts and over my belly. He avoided lingering anywhere I especially wanted him. The whole process was driving me crazy, but he didn't seem to be in a rush, nor did he seem to be enjoying the usual game of sexual torture that we so often played.

He knelt to rub the loofa along the soles of my feet. The sensation tickled, but seeing him crouched at my feet, unable to hide his desire bobbing under its own weight in front of me seemed to cancel that out. Every innocent contact piqued my craving for a more intimate touch. He was hard, and I was burning with need.

When he rose, I took the loofa from him and tossed it to the floor. I caught him by the hair and levered against him, bringing us chest to chest. He groaned and pushed me back against the shower wall. Instinct took over, and in seconds I was climbing him. Thigh over hip, arching into his hard body. He cupped my ass, increasing the contact. We couldn't be close enough.

"I miss you. I want to feel you," I whimpered.

I caught a breath of air, before sealing my mouth over his again. His erection pressed against me, teasing me. The connection sent a tingle of desire through me. But the sensation was tainted. I kissed him harder, drowning the doubt. He moaned, sliding his hand down my thigh. He trailed a slow path between my legs, slowing over my mound before cupping me. I tensed in his arms, not immediately understanding why. My chest heaved, my rapid breathing betraying the battle raging inside me. *Shit.*

"Baby?"

I kissed him fiercely, closing the small separation between us, answering any question he might have. Damn it all, I needed him. No less than I'd ever needed him.

He pulled back and caught my roaming touch, stilling me. "We don't have to do this."

"I want to."

He hesitated. "I know. I want to too, but…give yourself some time."

"I'm fine," I insisted, even as my voice wavered.

Was I? I knew what I wanted, what I craved, but I recognized the tension. On edge, ready to react, I battled with my desire. The battle made me as angry as I was horny, starving for him to love me, to fuck me right through the feeling that I didn't want to face.

He kissed me, a slow chaste kiss that I barely felt through the heat and mist that collected on my skin. The gesture seemed to repeat his words.

"I'm fine, Blake," I repeated. "He didn't do anything. I'm fine. Nothing's changed."

He stared down, concern swimming behind his eyes. "Just because he didn't get a chance to follow through doesn't mean you haven't been through emotional hell. We're not talking about banged up knuckles. You know as well as I do those wounds go deeper than either of us want them to. You need time. We should take some time."

I hated that he was probably right. I hated that I'd

become so flawed and vulnerable in a matter of days. "Maybe I'm stronger than you give me credit for."

He let out an exasperated sigh. "I have no doubts about your strength, Erica. I'm talking about your state of mind, your well-being. You can't brush this whole thing off like it's nothing."

"How about you let me tell you what I can take?"

My embarrassment mingled with the rejection. I left him there alone. In the bedroom I slammed drawers as I collected underwear and a shirt and then went to bed. Huddled onto my side, I tried to ignore his presence when he joined me. A moment passed before he came behind me, wrapping an arm around my waist. Pressing his lips to my shoulder, he caressed down my arm, eliciting a shiver that almost made me forget my irritation.

"I pushed you past your limits before. Let me honor them now, even if you won't."

I closed my eyes at the truth in his words. Truth and love and all the concern that the men who'd lodged this emotional wall between us had none of. I sighed heavily, giving myself over to trusting him.

"Look at me," he whispered.

Reluctantly I turned, positioning my body to face his. A smile softened his features as he traced my jaw, running a sensual line over my lips.

"I love you, even when you're marching around all pissed and indignant."

"I hate this."

His eyes dimmed. "I know you do. I know we both want more, but it's worth waiting for. Tonight, all I want is to taste your sweet lips and hold you. I have the rest of my life to make love to you. Tonight, I just want you in my arms."

Something cracked in me, that need to fight wilting under Blake's gentle insistence. My muscles weakened, and I surrendered.

★ ★ ★

I walked into the office the next morning ready to face the day. Ready to face my life. Alli rose to meet me as I drew near her desk. "You're not going to believe this."

My eyes went wide. There was a whole range of possibilities for things I might not believe. "What?"

"PinDeelz is down. Sid said it's been down since last night."

"Do we know why? It could be anything. Server issues or a surge in traffic."

"I don't think that's why."

She hauled me over to her workstation, and pulled up the site. As bold black and white image branded the screen. I'd seen it before, on our own site. M89. The hacker group's logo had replaced the competing site's home page, but now I was more confused than ever.

"I don't understand. If Trevor and Max have been in cahoots to build this thing, why would Trevor hack it? Moreover, *how* would he hack his own site?"

Alli twisted a strand of hair between her fingertips. "I don't either. Unless somehow things went sour with Trevor, and this is payback. Like he's making a statement or something."

"Just when I thought things couldn't get any stranger."

"The good news is that at least one of their advertisers got back in touch about renewing their ad contract with us. Never mentioned PinDeelz of course, but I'd say we can expect to hear from more of them now."

I chuckled softly. "Unbelievable. We'll see how many come crawling back, I suppose. Or how long the site stays this way."

"Speaking of crawling back, what did you decide about Perry?"

"He seems sorry, but it's not enough. Blake's right. It's a bad idea to get involved with him."

"I'd have to agree." James's deeper voice interrupted us. He seemed to have appeared out of nowhere.

"James, hey," I said, confused about his presence in the office.

"Alli thought it'd be a good idea for me to be in while you were out."

"Right." I nodded quickly, not wanting to think about Blake's potential reaction to this. "Well, I'm glad you're here. Can we catch up for a second?"

I left Alli for the small privacy of my office. James followed me and sank into the chair across from me.

"What's going on? What did I miss, other than an entire week?"

"I talked to your fiancé. That was pretty interesting, but I'm going to stay on in-house for now."

I dropped my jaw and the shock settled over me. Already I was more overwhelmed than I expected to be in my first fifteen minutes back at work. Fear rooted in my stomach. "Are you kidding me?"

He laughed. "It's nothing to worry about. You should probably talk to Landon about it though."

"Okay, fine. In that case, you want to give me an update? I'm behind on everything."

I spent the rest of the morning getting up to speed. After a week away from watching the pot boil, I could fully appreciate the progress that had been made in my absence. We were close to rolling out the changes that would have put us light years ahead of Max's site. While the threat of competition might be in the past, I could see clearly now that the competition had been important motivation to push us forward in an entirely new way.

As lunch approached my phone rang. My heart nearly stopped when I saw Risa's face light up the screen.

I answered, hesitating a moment. "Hello?"

"Erica, it's Risa."

"Yes." *Obviously. What the hell do you want?*

"Listen, I know I'm probably the last person you want to talk to. I just…I really need to talk to you."

"About what?"

"Could we meet for lunch?"

An anxious feeling rolled through me. Risa was associated with Max, and nothing good came of meeting with him to discuss *business*.

"I have nothing to say to you."

"Please, I'm begging you. Please. I know you hate me. And you have every right to. If you don't want to ever see or talk to me again after today, I'll stay out of your life completely."

I stared at the white partition in front of me. She sounded different. She sounded…desperate. I wasn't supposed to care, but I did. I squeezed my eyes shut, trying to imagine how I was going to possibly handle this on my own. Then an idea occurred to me.

"I'll meet you at the corner deli near the office at noon."

"Perfect, thank you."

I hung up before she could say anything else and Skyped Alli to come talk to me.

She popped in a few seconds later. "What's up?"

"By any chance, are you interested in meeting with Risa for lunch? She wants to talk to me. I don't trust her, and I don't trust myself not to strangle her if I go alone."

"Sure. I've got a few words for her myself."

"It's a date."

CHAPTER SEVENTEEN

"Thank you again for meeting me."

Risa looked like a stray puppy sitting across from us. Alli sat back with her arms crossed, giving Risa her best stare down. I didn't think Alli was capable of hating anyone, but she looked pretty convincing right now. Even as pathetic as Risa looked, I struggled to pity her. Her normally pin-straight glossy hair was tossed into a messy bun. Dressed in jeans and a simple black button-up, her face made up, she looked tired and worn. The shrewd and energetic girl who'd left Clozpin and taken my user database with her seemed to have aged in the short time since she'd left. I wanted to tell her she looked like hell, but figured I'd save it.

"I'm still not convinced I should be wasting my time with you, so if you have something to say, say it."

Her eyes glistened as they darted between us. "I'm sorry. I want you to know that."

"It's a little late to be sorry," Alli snapped, taking the words from my mouth.

"I know, and I don't expect forgiveness. I made a mistake. Max…he made me believe leaving was the right choice, the *only* choice if I wanted to make something of myself and push my career forward. He's not who I thought he was."

I clenched my jaw, keeping the words down. He wasn't who I thought he was either. He was so much worse.

"He used me to get to you," she continued, her wounded eyes pleading with me. "He played on all my emotions, my own jealousy and insecurities to get me to leave. But now, I don't even know who he is. He's in trouble, I think, and he's so obsessed with destroying Blake. It has nothing to do with the business I thought we were going to build together. It goes so much deeper than I ever realized."

I leaned forward, studying her. I began to see that she had no idea what had happened between Max and me.

"Risa, Max drugged me and tried to have sex with me last week. That's how much he wants to hurt Blake. Trust me, you have no idea how depraved he is until you've walked in my shoes."

"What?" Her jaw fell open, her eyes fixed on me. "Oh my God. I didn't know. I knew he and Blake fought, but I had no idea."

I tensed against the emotions that threatened. I couldn't lose my shit in front of her, as much as Max's behavior still tore at me. I clung to my anger instead.

"Yes. You should ask him about it. I'm sure he'll spin some story about how I came onto him at my own engagement party. And maybe since you thought it'd be a fun idea to tell Blake about James, you can swap stories about what a whore I am." I clenched my teeth, barely resisting the urge to leave. If nothing else, I'd wanted to meet Risa once more to get my verbal pound of flesh. Who knows when I'd get another chance to tell her what I thought.

"I don't think you're a whore. At one point, in the heat of the moment after you'd fired me, I mentioned that I saw you with James to Max. He's the one who wanted me to tell Blake. I didn't want to, really. Blake looked so angry when I told him that I regretted it immediately. I didn't even know you and Blake were engaged."

I lifted my chin, my lips in a tight line. "And thriving, somehow, despite all this. Despite you and Max trying to ruin my business and our relationship, *me*, we're stronger than we ever were. So what do you want now? He's the one you chose. Now you have to live with that choice."

"I want to leave him. I really do." Her eyes glistened. The napkin in her hand was twisted nearly to shreds. God, she was a legitimate mess.

"Then leave him. It has no bearing on me."

She nodded quickly, her head down. "I want to," she whispered. "I'm afraid he'll ruin me. Whatever happened between you, he's a completely different person. I don't know who he is. I think he's in financial trouble. He said he can't fund the site anymore. Everything we worked for, down the drain. And I've been overhearing conversations with his father. I don't know for sure, but I think he's cutting him off. Everything is so fucked up right now."

"I know, Risa. But I don't really care either."

She released a heavy sigh. "Let me make it up to you. I felt terrible before, but now …I can't believe what he did to you."

I laughed. "I don't want you to make it up to me. I want to move on with my life, and you're not going to be a part of that. It sounds like you fell prey to a horrible person with terrible motives, but I'm not the person to reach out to for help."

Her dark brown eyes looked serious for a moment. "I can help you find Trevor."

I cocked an eyebrow. "He's pretty elusive. I have a hard time imagining he'd let you or even Max get very close."

"I can try to find proof that Max paid him, maybe an address so you could track him down. He's not going to stop. If anyone hates Blake more than Max, it's Trevor."

I narrowed my gaze at her, curiosity burning through me. Would I have a chance to find one enemy through another, or was this just a dangerous step that would bring Risa closer to my world when I wanted anything but?

"I'll admit I'm intrigued, but not enough to take the bait. Trevor isn't a concern of mine right now. Unlike you and your partners, I don't plan my days around revenge and counter attacks. I just want to move on with my life. I have a wedding to plan and a business to run. I'm sorry Max took advantage of you. Maybe I shouldn't have, but I actually cared about you, Risa, and that's hard to forget. I hope if nothing else you learned a lesson from all of this."

"I don't expect you to take me back, but I want to make it right. I'm going to make it up to you somehow."

★ ★ ★

I leaned against the wall in the cool dark hallway outside the office while I considered an early retirement. This had to have been the most emotionally exhausting day back to work in history. I lifted my phone and pulled up Blake's number.

"What's up, baby?"

I sighed, still unable to process all of it. "So…I had lunch with Risa today."

"What?" His concern came through clearly in that one word.

"I brought Alli with me, and Clay drove us. It was fine."

"What did she want?"

"I guess she wants to make it up to me. Says she feels horrible about everything, though not surprisingly, Max didn't tell her what really happened at the party. She just thought you two got into a fistfight."

He snorted.

"But at least for now, she's still with him. She seems worried about him retaliating if she leaves. Honestly I feel sorry for her, even if she's made her own bed."

"They deserve each other," he muttered, the clicking of a keyboard quiet in the background.

"She thinks that Michael is cutting him off."

Silence hung in the air. No clicking, no words, only the faint sound of Blake's breathing.

"Why does she think that?"

"She said she overheard conversations between them. And he told her that he can't fund PinDeelz anymore. I'm not sure, but I'm guessing that might have something to do with the site being down. It says M89 hacked it right now, which makes no sense."

"I hacked the site."

My mouth opened to speak, but the words lodged there for a second. "You hacked their site?"

"Don't act so surprised. He had it coming."

If I weren't so shocked, I might have felt a little sorry for them. "But how … if Trevor built the site?"

"Trevor is a troll, not a developer. And he obviously didn't build their site with the same dedication he has for hacking. I was able to get in and wipe the server with very little effort. He's a shitty programmer."

"But wait, what about the M89 logo?"

"I just did that to fuck with Max's head."

A short laugh escaped me. Blake was devious, but I kind of loved it.

"Maybe it worked. Risa mentioned that Trevor fell off the map. Max can't reach him."

"No doubt because he's not paying him anymore. The business Max was using as a front to pay Trevor was dissolved a few days ago. If Michael is cutting him off, that might be why."

My mind spun as I absorbed these new details. Attacking me would have been the shot that set off this whole chain of events. And if what Risa said was true, Max's world might be imploding. His finances, his family, maybe even his freedom.

"If all this is happening because of Michael, it would make sense why none of your other investors would want to upset him."

"Don't let his charms fool you. Michael's a great guy, but he's not someone to cross."

"But his own son?"

"Max is finally getting what he deserves. I have no sympathy for him, and neither should you."

"I know. Trust me, I don't," I said. My thoughts drifted. I still had to speak with the police, and I was less than thrilled about it.

"I have to run, Erica. I have a call. But I forgot to tell you earlier that Mom wanted to have us for dinner tomorrow night. I told her we'd go, but I wasn't thinking. Are you okay going there and seeing everyone so soon?"

"Of course. Blake, I love your family."

"I know, but after everything that went down...we don't have to go if you don't want to go back there so soon."

"No, it's fine. Really, I'm fine. I have to move on. I can't undo what happened, but I can't dwell on it either. Remember that I've been through worse. Beyond that, it'd be nice to get together with everyone. Most of the time they overwhelm me, but you've been keeping me in isolation long enough. I'm actually looking forward to all the commotion now."

"Okay, I'll let her know we'll be there."

"Sounds good."

"I love you, baby."

I smiled. "Love you too."

★ ★ ★

I focused intently on the magazine on my lap, trying like hell not to feel overwhelmed. Living inside my brain lately was like living inside a three-ring circus. Sid and James had the re-launch plans under control, so Alli and I decided to take the afternoon off to go dress shopping. I was still reeling from the meeting with Risa so I didn't argue when she suggested the break.

"Baby girl."

I lifted my gaze to find Marie walking toward me. She smiled warmly, but I could see the worry in her eyes. I rose from the bridal shop's ornate cream-colored couch, and hugged her when she was close enough.

"You look good, honey. How are you feeling?"

"I'm good," I insisted, swallowing over the rush of

emotions that came with seeing her again. "I feel really good. Back to work and everything."

"I'm glad." She didn't budge, her arms wrapped tightly around my shoulders. The longer we stood that way, the less control I had over the tears burning behind my eyes.

"Marie." I laughed weakly to keep from sobbing. "You're going to make me cry again. I can't cry over this anymore."

She pulled away, her eyes glistening as mine were. "It's okay to cry. What happened was terrible. I can't imagine what you must be going through."

I shook my head and rubbed my eyes. "It's nothing I haven't already survived. I'll be fine."

She frowned and I regretted the words as soon as they slipped from my lips. I had started to take for granted that everyone knew about Max, and most even knew about Mark. Having my past so out in the open wasn't a comfortable feeling, but oddly it had given me a small measure of relief. Sometimes hiding what had happened and pretending like it hadn't become a part of me took more energy than simply owning it.

Over the past few years I had often battled over whether or not to tell Marie about what happened with Mark, but in the end, decided it was better not to burden her with it. I don't know why I said it now, except to take another step toward bringing that scar out into the light. Still, I didn't want to worry her with it today.

She rubbed up and down the tops of my arms slowly. "What do you mean?"

"Nothing. Forget it. This is supposed to be a happy day. Right?" I smiled and sniffed, trying to pull myself back together.

Her lips were tight and then she released a small sigh. "Of course. Thank you for inviting me. I'm not sure how I'm going to keep from balling like a baby when I see you in a white dress though. Have you picked anything out?"

I looked around for Alli. "No, not yet. Alli is with the sales lady picking out dresses for me. She says she knows what I want anyway. She usually does, so I'm going with it." I shrugged.

Then Alli emerged with another young woman. They both had their arms full of more white lace than I'd ever know what to do with.

My stomach fell. *Oh hell, here we go.*

Fifteen minutes later, the sales lady was clipping the back of my dress, cinching the fabric tightly around my bust and waist. Carefully I stepped into the little room the store had reserved for us. Alli and Marie sat on the edge of the couch, eyes wide as I emerged. I turned to face the mirrors.

Marie's hands went to her mouth. Before I could let the waterworks loose, I turned my focus back to the dress. It was beautiful, but the details of its design escaped me when all I could imagine was walking toward Blake in it. To be his wife. To be his, forever.

The reality of that thought hit me like a sledgehammer. I didn't know if I wanted to be sick or pass out or launch into tears. All I knew was up until this moment, the thought of getting married had seemed more abstract. Right now, it was real and staring me in the face, impossible to ignore.

Alli came up beside me with a broad smile. "It's beautiful. I love it. Do you like it?"

"This is really happening," was all I could say.

She laughed and squeezed my shoulders. "Yes! This is happening, and you're going to be so happy."

I laughed a little at how surreal it all felt. "I can't believe I'm doing this. I'm actually getting married."

Marie stood on the other side and took my hand, so much love in her eyes. "You ready for this, honey?"

I stared back at her reflection, frozen as I asked myself the same question. A weight inside me lifted when I heard myself answer.

Yes.

I'd never been more ready.

CHAPTER EIGHTEEN

I stared down at my feet as they sank into the wet sand. Wave after wave lapped against my calves. While we waited for dinner, Blake and I had walked down to the shore, stopping at the edge of his parents' private beach. I took in the salty air, moist on my skin in the warm summer night. I lifted my gaze to the darkening horizon.

"Don't you feel like we're standing at the edge of the world?"

Blake bent to catch a shell rolling up with the tide. "I suppose so." He tossed it back into the restless waters. "You love the ocean, don't you?"

"I do. I'm not sure I can ever be without it again." I laughed quietly. "I guess I like living on the edge."

I met Blake's gaze. His eyes were quiet, contemplative. The fading glow of the sunset cast shadows across his face. The vintage T-shirt he wore ruffled in the breeze blowing off the ocean. Though still damp at the bottom, his jeans were rolled up past his ankles. Blake was perfect in all the ways that mattered to me. Perfect and all mine.

He took my hand and pulled me to him. I went willingly, loving the warmth of his embrace. He circled my waist, bringing us chest to chest. My hands found his hair, mussing the dark brown strands. I smiled, memorizing him and this moment.

"Sometimes I wish I could just sweep you up and take

you away. Run away from all this madness and take a real break. A long break."

I drew in a breath. I couldn't agree more, but I also knew how unrealistic it was. I'd spent a long time wishing I could run away from my life, but not having any idea where or whom to run to. Instead I'd resisted the urge and forged ahead, making life work through the hardest times. Through my mother's death, through the separation from the only father I'd ever known until recently, and then through the hell that Mark had put me through. And here I was— stronger, happier than I'd ever been, enjoying this perfect moment with the man I loved so completely.

"I want to escape with you too. But this is our home, and our lives will always be here waiting for us. Besides, taking more time off would send me into a meltdown. I have a ton of catching up to do from being out so long." I immediately thought of the mountain of work I'd barely put a dent in so far this week. Risa's lunch had thrown me off when my focus should have been on the details surrounding the impending upgrades.

Then I remembered something.

"So what is going on with James? I nearly had a heart attack when I saw him at the office this morning. What happened?"

"Alli wanted him in the office to help while you were out."

"I can't imagine that's the only reason why you let him stay."

"No, we talked."

"He came to you?" I pulled back slightly, in disbelief that James would actually seek Blake out, or vice-versa.

"I think we can both agree that he's fairly protective of you, so when Alli hinted that you'd been hurt, it didn't take long for him to show up at my office wanting to know more."

"And?"

"I think initially he wanted to know that I didn't have anything to do with you being hurt. He seems caught up on this idea that I abuse you."

He winced, and I didn't like the emotions that played out there.

"I don't think it has anything to do with you. His dad was violent. I think it's a sensitive subject for him."

"Maybe that's it. Anyway, after learning that Max attacked you and knowing that Daniel hurt you too, he posed a compelling argument that he stay, for your sake."

"And you agreed?"

"Basically, as much as I would like to, I can't be with you twenty four hours a day. With everything that has happened lately, it makes sense that James be there to make sure that you can be safe at work."

I put more of a separation between us, staring at him in disbelief.

"Let me make sure I have this right. Are you telling me that you're willing to let James stay with the company with the understanding that he act as my in-house bodyguard?"

"Erica." An undercurrent of warning came through as he uttered my name. "If you think I'm taking any chances with your safety, you're crazy."

I tried to step away but he didn't budge. "I can't stand the idea of having all of you hovering around me, waiting for something terrible happen. I want to be trusted to take care of myself, at least a little bit."

"I know, but taking care of you is my job now. Remember?"

True enough. I'd given up the right to fight him on this matter.

"Beyond that, I knew agreeing to remove James from your life wasn't an easy decision for you to make."

"You didn't give me much choice."

"You still had a choice. I'm glad you made it and were willing to make that sacrifice for us. I'm not saying I completely trust that he doesn't still harbor feelings for you—"

"He's seeing Simone. I'm pretty confident he's moved on."

"He made a point to tell me as much. I haven't had much success with getting over you personally, so you'll excuse me for taking his reassurance with a grain of salt. As I was saying, he might still care about you, but as long as he can keep his hands to himself, those feelings can serve to keep you safe and out of danger while you're away from me. Keeping him there seemed like a worthwhile concession."

"Blake Landon making a concession?" I rolled my eyes.

He hauled me back up, slapping my ass through the thin cotton of my dress. I yelped and squirmed.

"Roll those pretty blue eyes at me again, and you'll regret it." He massaged me where he'd made contact, grabbing me gently. "Maybe you could thank me instead."

"Thanks." I meant to sound sarcastic. Instead I was breathless as he pressed me against him, his hands splayed possessively at my back and over my ass.

"That's more like it."

I suppressed a smile. "You're hopeless, you know that?"

"Yes. Hopelessly in love with you. Get used to it. Marriage is forever."

His eyes glittered in a way that made me forget I was annoyed with him.

"On that note, actually. I was hoping we could talk about wedding plans tonight."

I weakened a little. "Yeah?"

He took my hand and we began to walk back toward his parents' house.

"I don't think it's any secret that you can't quite compete with Alli's enthusiasm over all this wedding stuff."

"You picked up on that, did you?"

He laughed. "I'm very observant. But I was thinking maybe we can scrap all this elaborate planning, and just do something small. We can still have my family, your family, but skip trying to put on some big display. I want to be married to you, Erica. I don't want to wait. Put me in a pink cummerbund, and let's just do it."

"Really?"

"Really. What do you think? We could do it here or at the Vineyard. A little ceremony on the beach, get some pictures, and spend a couple weeks at the house there just us. Then I can re-explore every inch of your body with the sweet satisfaction of knowing you're my wife."

I smiled broadly, loving the sound of all of that. Especially the re-exploring my body part.

"Sounds perfect."

He raised an eyebrow.

"All of it. It sounds perfect."

★ ★ ★

Alli nearly overflowed my glass of *Pinot Grigio* laughing over something Heath was saying. I was too busy listening to Fiona vent about her last date gone wrong. A couple empty bottles littered the table as we finished yet another expertly cooked family dinner, courtesy of Greg, who was proving to be a force in the kitchen.

Greg tended to be quiet, as least compared to the rest of the family. But he was approachable. More approachable than Blake was at times, though I could see similarities between the two men. How people became a product of their parents always fascinated me, maybe because it was a perspective I'd largely lacked. Blake was so different from both Heath and Fiona, yet they all shared this common thread that made them a family.

I could not have asked for a better family to become a part of. My heart swelled every time I thought of what a blessing they'd become. Having Blake would have been enough, but becoming a part of their world made the whole prospect of marrying into another family more than I would have ever expected.

Catherine defied all the horror stories I'd ever heard about wretched mothers-in-law, and Fiona was sweet, plain and simple. Heath, as troubled as he'd been, too was becoming a loyal friend. And Greg seemed to be the glue that held everyone together.

A sudden dinging rang out and my gaze fell on the glass that Blake held.

"We have a little announcement."

"Oh! What is it?" Alli clapped her hands together, straightening in her chair.

"You already proposed, Blake. Enough of the fanfare. You're making me look bad," Heath said.

Alli turned a deep shade of red and shoved him. He caught her by the wrist, pulling her back to him and planting a chaste kiss on her lips.

Blake cleared his throat. "Anyway, we wanted to let you know that we've made some decisions about the wedding." He looked to me, silently letting me know I could take the floor if I wanted to.

I inhaled a deep breath and began. "Well, as most of you know, I haven't had a lot of time and energy to devote to wedding planning. I know you all were probably wanting and hoping for something big, which, to be honest, has been a little intimidating."

Catherine shook her head. "Nonsense. We are here to support you and Blake, no matter what you decide. Selfishly of course, I would love to be there to see my son get married, but however you want to do it is entirely up to you. It's your special day."

"I would love to have you there, all of you. You all have already become my family…" I tapped my foot nervously, reminding myself not to start crying. Damn if this wasn't a sensitive subject. Then I felt Blake's hand on my knee, reassuring me. "And my own family being so small and kind of distant, we thought that it would be wonderful to have something small with the few people close to us. For the sake of simplicity maybe, and also because we could do it sooner."

"You're not pregnant, are you?" Heath blurted out.

He was nursing a glass of wine. Alli frowned and hit

him harder on the shoulder. He shot her an apologetic look.

"No, definitely not," I said quickly.

Catherine grabbed the last nearly empty bottle of wine and refilled her glass. "Well, you wouldn't get any arguments from us. We're bored and retired. I need a grandbaby sooner rather than later."

I snapped my jaw shut. *Oh hell*. Blake could barely hide a grin. He gave my knee another small squeeze.

"Dinner was great, Mom. I think that might be our cue to head home."

★ ★ ★

Maybe the white wine and ocean air did something to me, because I couldn't keep my hands off Blake as he drove us back to the city. I crept my hand over his thigh to the bulge in his jeans and kneaded gently. He placed his hand over mine but didn't stop me.

"What do you think you're doing, sweetheart?"

"I want you tonight, Blake. I can't wait anymore." I stroked him, his erection growing under my touch. I wanted every inch of him, and tonight I'd have it. I didn't care what had happened. Blake was my lover, and our bodies were made for everything I wanted to give him tonight. It had been too long and I needed him. Except *need* didn't do justice to the emotions running through me tonight. Something else was at work, and slowly I had begun to put it together.

His hold over me firmed, slowing my movements. He worked his jaw, and I could sense his concern.

"Wait until we get home," he said quietly.

I thumbed over the soft head of his cock and grasping him more firmly.

He sucked in a sharp breath. "Christ."

I hummed with pure female satisfaction, leaning over so more of our bodies made contact. "I don't want to wait," I whispered into his ear. My breasts rubbed against his arm as I reached to unzip his fly.

But he stopped me. "Erica, put your hands on your knees. Right now." His expression hardened as the sharp command left his lips, the earlier vulnerability disappearing.

My heart beat rapidly as I assessed his mood. Was he mad or bossing me around? Regardless, a little rush at being told what to do fluttered through me, settling low in my belly. I eased back into the seat and rested my hands on my knees.

He glanced at me briefly before turning his attention back to the road.

"Lift up your skirt and take your panties off. I want to see you."

I smiled, pleased with where this was going. I obeyed and hiked my skirt up high enough so he could see me naked and ready for him. I wanted nothing more than to straddle him on the highway, but I could live with this until we got home.

"Good. Now touch your breasts."

I hesitated a second, considering his request and how hot it made me. Then I cupped my hands over my breasts, noticing how heavy and tight they'd already become.

"Pinch your nipples, just like I would. Nice and hard."

I did as he asked, and the sensation arrowed to my pussy.

I stifled a tiny moan. My nipples quickly beaded into taut buds begging for his mouth. The way he looked back at me now, his eyes dark and dangerous, melted me on the spot.

"Tell me how that feels."

I closed my eyes and squirmed, the feel of leather on my ass reminding me of my nakedness. I groaned. "I'm warm all over. But I'm frustrated. I want your hands on me."

"I know you do, baby. Soon enough. Do you want me to let you touch yourself some more?"

"Yes. Please."

"How about you slide your fingers into your pussy and tell me how that feels."

I exhaled sharply, my need urgent now. I couldn't possibly last long this way. I moved down to my torso until my fingers traced the seam of my sex. I glided my index finger along my opening, over my sensitive clit, and back down again. I opened my eyes to find Blake's on me again, his tongue wetting his lower lip. Seeing that small sign of his own hunger, I pressed into myself. I arched my back off the seat and moaned, wishing he were filling me now, where I'd wanted him for so long.

He adjusted himself before hitting the gas a little harder. "Talk to me, baby. We're close."

"You could be inside me so easily. I want you here, your mouth and your cock. It's not enough, just me. I have to have you or I'm going to lose my mind, Blake." I grabbed my breast with my free hand, pinching my nipple as he'd told me to before.

"Fuck," he breathed. His grip tightened on the wheel.

"That's what I want. I want you moving inside me,

slamming into me. I want to forget everything except how that feels, how perfect you make it feel every time."

He glanced sideways and caught my thigh with his free hand. He tugged my leg up so my knee rested on the console. I was fully open, exposed and eager for the attention he should have been putting on the road.

"Keep going," he rasped.

"You're the only one who's ever made me feel this way. I love it. I love you. I've been going crazy missing you, needing you. Blake, I need you."

I pumped into my sensitive tissues, my mind reeling with want.

"Blake, please," I moaned, having no care of where we were. I was close and I couldn't wait.

"Don't stop. I want to see you come for me."

I did as he asked, desperate for any relief, even at my own hand. I edged closer to orgasm, the promise of it coiling tight in my muscles. Eyes closed, I had no idea where we were until the car came to a sudden stop and Blake's hands were at my breasts, his mouth hot and wet at my mouth.

"Come, baby. Hurry."

His hand covered mine as I hastened my final strokes. My muscles tensed, my skin burning under the small places where we touched.

"Blake," I breathed his name, over and over.

"I love watching you do this. God, I want you so bad. So fucking bad."

Then I crashed over, just as his teeth sank down into my shoulder. I cried out, shaking with the force of the climax.

I came down slowly, the reality that I was spread

eagle in his car on our not-so-private street slowly dawning. I swallowed over a gasp, gradually pulling myself back together. Blake leaned back, seeming to do the same as he stared through the window.

"Let's go."

CHAPTER NINETEEN

I leaned back against the door of the apartment the minute it shut behind us, only a little sated. My legs were still jelly, but every cell was charged, ready for him.

"Come here."

Blake turned after a few steps, hunger and hesitation at war on his beautiful features. Hunger won as he came back to me, pinning me gently. He kissed me, petal-soft brushes of his lips over mine. I shivered as he traced the skin of my shoulder down my arm, lacing our fingers together. He pulled back a fraction.

"We don't have to do this if you're not ready."

My heart ached at the smallest increase in separation between us, that small recession from where we'd been moments ago. I gripped him by the hip, wishing I could will him back to me, wishing distance were the only obstacle between us.

"I want to."

"I can wait. God knows, I don't want to, but I can."

Strain laced the words as he spoke. I arched into his gentle touch—whispers of skin on skin, quiet declarations of the love between us that had very recently had no outlet. Blake was my lover, and we loved with our bodies.

"I'm ready, Blake. I need this, to be this close to you." I had to find my way through this, so we could find ourselves in each other again.

He cupped my cheek, holding my gaze. "I *will* wait. As long as you need to."

"No more waiting. I'm ..."

I shook my head, not wanting to show him my doubts, but it was too late. He leaned away, his green eyes questioning me.

"I can't take this anymore. I don't know if I'm ready or if I'll freak out somewhere along the way, but we have to try because I can't live like this, without you."

"I'm right here. I'm not going anywhere."

"No, it's not the same. You know it's not. This is who we are, how we love, and sometimes I can't show you any other way."

"You need time to work through this. I can see the hesitation in your eyes. I can feel it when you hold back. It shreds me. I can't stand the idea of being the one who scares you and brings you back to those memories."

"I know ... God, you'll never know how sorry I am, for all of this." I sagged against the door, defeated by what Max had brought between us.

"You don't need to be sorry. I've told you a hundred times. You need to believe me when I say that. None of this is or has ever been your fault."

"I wish I could make it go away. You have no idea how badly I want that ... to have Mark's memory wiped away forever, but even his death couldn't do that. I thought maybe it would, but it didn't. It took away the fear that he could hurt me again, but what he did to me on the inside ... I don't know if I'll ever be free of it. I want to believe it won't haunt me one day, but all of this ... lately ... everything feels so fresh. Sometimes I feel like I'm seeing it again, but with different eyes."

"How do you mean?"

"I know it sounds crazy, but before, with Mark, right after he attacked me and for the years after, I was never really *better*. I was functional and happy enough and moving forward with my life, but in order to be, I put what Mark did to me away. I locked him in a box, threw away the key, and convinced myself I was fine. But I wasn't. Before you came into my life, I hadn't really faced any of it. Maybe out of self-preservation with school, because I couldn't imagine letting the rape ruin me and everything I'd worked so hard for. But I can't block it out anymore. It's like this terrible ugly scar and I'm too exhausted to hide it anymore. You've seen it, and you don't judge me or pity me for it. It's a part of me, and for the first time in years I'm realizing that I'm not all the way healed yet. And that's okay. But I'm better because of you, because of us."

I brought us chest to chest again and kissed him softly. I breathed him in. His scent, his closeness, made me dizzy.

"I'm not going to lie to you, Blake. I'm a little shell-shocked. I hate that I am, and that I reacted the way I did before. And I can't promise that I won't again, in some small way. Physically, there's no question about what I want, but I never know what will trigger my mind. You're right that I need time. But I can't spend that time away from you because you're the one who makes me better. You're the only one who can bring me through this, because I've never trusted someone the way I trust you. I love you so much it hurts sometimes. You have to believe me, that you're the only one who can heal me, Blake."

I held him tightly, letting a tear fall down my cheek.

The emotions running wild inside me were creeping over, one way or the other.

"Baby," he breathed against my lips, his shoulders softened under my hands.

"Please." I kissed him again, more firmly, more demanding.

He pulled away again slightly, worry etched into the lines at his eyes. I reached to him, but before I could seal the plea with another kiss he had lifted me up by the waist. I wrapped my legs around him and let him carry us to the darkness of the bedroom. He lowered me at the foot of the bed, never breaking the contact.

I sifted my hand through his hair, deepening the kiss and melding our bodies together. My tongue found the ridge of his lips, flicking lightly for entrance. He sighed against me, opening. Our hands slid over each other. Even as the tension radiated between us, every move was measured and unrushed as it had never been before. I couldn't remember when we'd taken this much time and care. And even though a part of me was screaming for him to hurry, to take me with all the passion he possessed, somehow this was more important. This slow dance of asking with each touch.

As our clothes fell to the floor, our hands found their way to each other again. I broke our kiss and sat on the edge of the bed. I inched back, unsure how he wanted me or what I could handle. Only the moon lit the room, casting a violet glow on the ruffled sheets beneath me. He stood for a moment, a dedicated love painting his shadowed features.

Catching my foot, he lifted it to his lips and pressed a kiss to the pad of my big toe. I lay back, letting my body relax into the soft comforter as he worked his way up my calf, tracing a decadent path to my knee and up my thigh. Stopping just short of my pussy, he traveled the other side.

The craving I'd been battling for days was now impossible to ignore, impossible to resist. My earlier orgasm had done little to quell it. I wanted to beg, but he'd take his time now regardless of what I said. Nothing would push him past the limits of his control. He followed his path with his hand, and my eyes flew open. I caught his hand mid-thigh, stilling his journey. Breathing through the rapid beating of my heart, I struggled as a different kind of rush worked its way through me.

His eyes widened, every muscle frozen in place. I searched for words as he waited for me to speak.

"Don't use your hands, okay?" My voice was small. I hated what the words implied, but I couldn't *not* tell him and risk this moment between us.

The line of his jaw hardened, the muscle below twitching. I gave his hand a reassuring squeeze.

"It's okay," I said, avoiding the real reasons, reasons he'd likely already deduced. One of the least pleasant memories I'd had lately was of Max's hands on me that night. I wanted to squeeze my eyes shut until the image went away, but instead I focused on Blake.

He'd let my foot fall back to the bed. Now he stood, penetrating me with his stare. He wouldn't miss a trick tonight. Most days, he was more tuned to my body than I was. Knowing what we were up against now, nothing would get past him.

"Erica, I've said this before, but we need a safe word. If you didn't think we needed one before, I need you to have one now."

I rolled my eyes.

"Think of it as giving me peace of mind too."

"I'll tell you when to stop. I always do," I insisted.

"No. It's harder to tell me to stop and explain why. All you need is one word, and that says it all. It tells me to stop. It tells me I'm pushing you too far, that your mind is screaming at you to tell me to stop enough to say it. We need one now, or we shouldn't go any further tonight because I won't risk pushing you. Not tonight."

I sighed, unconvinced that we needed one, but if it meant that much to Blake, I'd relent. "What should it be? Just pick something."

"You have to pick it. It's your safe word. Pick a word that you won't hesitate to say if I'm pushing you past your limits. I don't intend to, but—"

"Limit."

He raised his eyebrows.

"That's it. I'll say *limit* if you're doing anything that I can't handle."

"Okay, that works."

He seemed convinced. He released a breath, and the worry in his eyes subsided. I had no idea that choosing the word would give him so much reassurance, because I'd always thought of it differently. As if saying it meant I couldn't take all he could give me, or that I was fully subscribing to the submissive role that I had slipped further into than I'd ever imagined.

Silence settled over us, an empty expanse that threatened our moment. I hooked my heel behind his thigh and pulled on his hand to coax him over me. Instead of settling between my legs, he lay beside me. I turned into his body, bringing us flush. Both our heads on the pillows, we stared into each other.

"I want this," I whispered. "Please don't let me ruin this or scare you off."

"Tell me exactly what you want."

"I want you to make love to me, Blake, and never stop. For the rest of our lives, I want love in our bed. Nothing can come between us like this again, no matter what."

Before he could respond, I kissed him. It was a kiss full of frustration and determination and more than anything, love. Our love was what could pull us through this. He met my passion, angling me how he wanted me. We breathed each other's air and drank each other until the seconds turned into minutes. Until my lips were tender and swollen. The heat between us had made our skin sweat. My hesitations weren't gone, but they were far in the background. I circled the hard thickness of his erection between us, stroking him to the tip.

He groaned, arching his hips upwards into my grasp. I slid to the base and back to the tip, pumping him gently.

"This is what I want. Come here."

I pulled his hip toward me and rolled to my back. He moved with grace, hovering over me, but we barely touched. Hands on either side of my head, he lowered. The heat of our bodies met. He kissed my shoulder and nuzzled into my neck.

"Put me inside you."

Trembling slightly, I found the hot flesh of his cock again and guided him to me until the head barely penetrated me. I pulled again at his hip and arched, signaling him to push into me. Inch by inch, he slid inside with no hint of resistance from my body.

"Oh my God." My eyes rolled back, a wave of relief and pleasure flooding me. Every cell in my body seemed to sigh, because he was with me again, where he should have been all this time. This unbearable chasm between us had finally been breached, and nothing had ever felt more right.

"Look at me," he whispered.

When I opened my eyes, Blake's were dark, hooded with lust. But the usual intensity that could barely be reined in had somehow been subdued behind his concern for me. He'd rooted in me, nestling there until I spoke.

"You feel amazing, Blake." My voice wavered, thick with emotion. "I feel like I could come already, but I want this to last."

He released his breath, rocking into me gently but not thrusting fully.

"You know I'm not opposed to making you come as much as you want. No need to hold back."

I smiled and wrapped my legs around his waist. Gripping his hips between my thighs, I coaxed him to push into me again. He did, again and again, each movement a little more sure, each press of our bodies unwinding me and washing away every thought that could haunt me in the midst of this perfect moment.

We loved that way, without words, his motions guided only by my own. We were in tune, as if his body heard me. With every surge of our bodies meeting, the fire inside me grew. I rushed my hands over his skin, wishing I could hurry his movements to sate this consuming hunger but loving the slow climb. The flame was no less intense, and the need to come no less potent.

"Tell me when you're going to come. Tell me what you need."

The desperation of his voice, his breath against my neck pushed me to the edge.

"Oh, God. Now ... I'm coming now."

The flash of heat rushed over me as the orgasm took hold. I marked his skin with my nails when I needed more. I crushed down around him, creating an acute friction between us. He drove deeper, pushing me to that oblivion where no one else had ever taken me.

"Erica ..."

Over the pounding in my heart, I heard the question in his voice. He wanted to know I was with him, that we were okay to let go. He didn't need to be so careful. I was mindless now, immune to the terrors when we were this close to rapture.

"I love you. I love you so much," I whimpered, tears forming in the corners of my eyes. Everything was incredibly right now, finally. The words left my lips again and again.

He took my hand in his, pressing it into the bed above my head. With the other, he gripped my hip and lifted me off the bed. He drove hard, and I cried out. The pleasure vibrated through me, soaring right over the climax that already had me breathless and weak.

"No one can take this away from us," he rasped, surging into me. He stole my next breath with a devouring kiss. Tightening his grasp where he held me, he came.

★ ★ ★

I opened an eye to daylight peeking in through the window. Another morning greeted us, and with one glance at the clock, I decided it was time to get moving. Blake's warm body curled behind me. Half the pillows had made their way to the floor. The sheets tangled around us. When I went to rise, he moaned, tugging me back so I was locked against his muscular chest.

"It's getting late. We should get up."

"Don't care," he mumbled, nuzzling into my hair. "You're too pretty to leave."

I smiled. My heart swelled, and I relaxed into his embrace. He caressed a soft path down my arms, down the tops of my thighs, and back up to the jut of my hips. He caught me there and shifted me back. Enough that our bodies were molded together. Enough to feel how hard he was. The fact wasn't surprising, but it did threaten my ability to get to work on time.

We'd had an amazing night, and I couldn't stop thinking about it. Not just the sex, which as always left me nothing short of boneless and satisfied in the most wonderful ways. But we'd broken through a barrier, and we'd done it together. I refused to let my past keep us apart, and we trusted each other enough to rise above the fears it had planted in both of us.

Something had changed between us over these past few weeks. Over all the push and pull, the snags in the road, we were learning to move forward together. Sometimes we were out of step and stumbled, but we were finding a new kind of rhythm. Every time we trusted each other, we moved with a little more grace.

The way Blake had made love to me last night had

embodied that grace, and I couldn't have been any more relieved and fulfilled. I squeezed the arm that hugged around my waist, unable and unwilling to resist.

He made his way to my shoulder, raining kisses over my back and up to my neck. There his tongue darted out, licking and sucking gently at the sensitive skin. I closed my eyes and arched back into him before I even realized what I was doing. Encouraging him, leading us down a path I had no hope of turning away from.

I caught his hand and guided him to my front, down toward the V between my thighs. He stopped before he could touch me where I wanted him to, and I didn't have the strength to push him any further.

"Touch me. It's okay."

"You sure?" His voice was rough from sleep, making it all the more sexy as he released the muscle that was keeping him away.

"I'm sure," I said.

Slowly he lowered his touch until he reached my pussy. With tentative strokes, he teased my clit. I added pressure to his fingers, urging him, even more sure that we were fine and this was absolutely what I wanted. Slowly and then more rapidly he moved over me until I could hear the wet sounds of his motions. A soft moan escaped my lips. Tension rippled through my core, the part of me that wanted to be filled.

Behind me, Blake lifted up to his elbow. He curled my hair around his hand and gave it a soft tug. I arched my neck, exposed as he continued his assault. His breath tickled my sensitive skin as he sucked and licked, and nibbled.

"Blake," I whimpered. I pushed back against the heat of his erection.

"Something you want?" He kissed along the line of my jaw and behind my ear, his diabolical fingers working their magic over my clit.

"Yes."

He left my clit to rub his cock against my entrance, teasing me. Against every instinct, I resisted the urge to push into him, to take him inside me all at once. He'd call me greedy, because I was. I wanted all of him, and I hated to wait for it.

If that wasn't enough, he gripped tightly at my hip, securing me in place, ensuring that I'd move only when he wanted me to. My skin burned under his dominant touch.

"Tell me what I like to hear, and I'll give you what you want."

"Fuck me, Blake. Make me yours."

"Ah, I love your dirty mouth," he murmured before pushing in a bare inch. "Do you have any idea what it does to my cock when you beg me to fuck you?"

I fisted my hand in the sheets. Already my longing was razor-sharp. He thrust in and out that small, maddening amount. Patiently I waited for more. Then he rolled his hips with a short thrust and pressed deeper. I gasped at the sensation of his small reward.

"I love you, Blake. Please ... please."

"You have no idea how much I love hearing you tell me."

Still he took his time, sinking into me inch by inch, driving me wild with the need to be fucked. His grip tightened and released. Then, without warning, he released me. His palm found contact with my ass a second later. I cried out, clenching helplessly around his cock, warmth rocketing through my limbs.

"Fuck, baby. I love watching my dick slide into you. So smooth, like this is where I was meant to be." He rooted with a sharp exhale. "And you're so fucking tight. Takes my breath away."

My moan turned into a strangled cry when he slapped my ass again, harder than before. The responses of my body launched me into orbit as he began a rugged pace, driving deep into me. Our bodies molded tightly together. He banded an arm around my waist and slammed his hips into me from behind.

"Blake," I cried out when he hit the end of me. Again and again, so quickly I was scrambling to the edge. At the brink, his hand slapped again, hard. I shuddered as the climax came down on me, shooting out into every limb. A second later, Blake was there. His cock buried deep with me, he groaned. He held himself there and the warm rush of his release filled me.

We lay there, wasted in the morning light. *What a way to wake up.*

After a moment, Blake slipped from me and rolled over to his back, his chest moving with the effort to catch his breath.

"Shower?" I asked, rolling to face him.

"Go on. I'll join you in a minute." He turned his head, catching my stare. "What?"

I traced a tiny circle over his shoulder. "I was just thinking that I'll never get tired of putting that look on your face."

He grinned. "You'd better get your sweet ass in that

shower, before I make you put that look on my face for the rest of the afternoon."

"You have to work, Mister."

"Trust me. For that, work can wait."

He twisted and reached for me, but I scooted away, barely missing his attempt to pull me back to him. Not that I would have minded much, but I had my own mountain of work waiting for me at the office.

I lingered in the shower, my muscles taxed and tired. I smiled when I thought about all the ways we could make up for lost time over the weekend. Finally, realizing he wasn't coming, I finished up and turned off the shower.

I stepped out, and when he wasn't in the bedroom, I went searching for him. Padding through the apartment, towel wrapped around my chest, I followed the sound of his voice and found him in the kitchen still wonderfully naked. His chest wore a few scratches from our evening adventures, and his just-fucked wayward hair was adorable in a way only I could fully appreciate.

"All right, thanks. Let me know if anything else comes up." He ended the call and dropped the phone down on the counter. I was in his line of sight but he stared ahead.

"Is everything okay?"

He looked to me, but I couldn't tell what was going on in his head.

"Blake?"

He blinked, seeming to jar himself from whatever thoughts were buzzing through his head. "Everything is fine. More than fine actually."

"Who were you talking to on the phone?"

He rubbed his forehead absently. "That was my lawyer.

He wanted to let me know the charges were dropped. So the hearing was canceled."

I lifted my eyebrows. "That's it, just like that?"

He shrugged. "Just like that."

"Why would Max drop the charges against you? He can't possibly hate you any less that he did a week ago."

"He didn't drop them. The prosecutor simply dismissed them. The lawyer thinks maybe it's because of the nature of the situation, with Max being charged for sexual assault. Even with that though, he seemed to think it was a pretty lucky break. But I'll take it."

My chest fell with a sigh of relief. "That's great."

My thoughts immediately shifted to the nagging reminder that I still needed to go to the police station to give a statement. The charges against Blake had been my motivation to actually go through with it.

"You're still going to the police, right?"

He must have read the doubt in my eyes because he came to me. I stood still, paralyzed by the sight of his perfectly sculpted body. He stood before me and skimmed his palms down my arm. I shivered, his touch cool against my skin.

"You need to do this," he said quietly.

"Why? Why do I need to put myself through this?" Tears quickly brimmed my eyes. Apprehension took root in my gut.

"You said it yourself that you still have healing to do. I'm here for you. I always will be. I'm here to love you in every way that you need to be loved. God knows, I can't help myself. But telling me, telling Alli…It's not enough. You need to be strong and stand up to what happened to you. Then and now. Every time I think about what Max did … what he could have done … my blood boils. But I can't do this for you. This is your chance to make things right, and you're the only one who can do it."

I closed my eyes. "I can't. Something about it … I don't want to break down in front of a stranger. To admit how stupid I'd been … how vulnerable he made me. Everyone saw." I choked over the last words.

He hushed me and pulled me close. I melted against him and let the tears fall.

"You weren't stupid. He made you vulnerable, but you don't need to be now. You're strong." He held me a little tighter then. "You can do this."

CHAPTER TWENTY

Officer Bates led me away from her desk to a small private room. She might have been my mother's age, a little heavy set. Her hair was pulled into a tight ponytail. A few short curls had escaped from it, framing a face that was lined.

The chair legs squeaked against the concrete floor, and we sat down at a table across from each other. I twisted my fingers together nervously as she opened a file and shuffled through some of the papers. My heart pounded at the walls of my chest as I waited for her. My meager lunch turned in my stomach a little. My pep talk affirmations were drowned out by the voice in my head that kept reminding me how much I didn't want to do this.

What Max had done was the ultimate trigger threatening to dredge up the past that I wanted to stay in the past. This was part of working through it. But I didn't know this woman. A stranger to me, she seemed as hard and cold as the room we now shared, and I didn't want to be vulnerable now to her, or anyone else for that matter.

She scanned the papers and glanced over at me briefly. "You okay, hon?"

I regained my focus on her face. My breathing had become erratic. I licked my lips. "Yes, I'm fine. Just nervous, I guess."

She pulled out a piece of paper and positioned her pen above it. "No need to be nervous. All you need to do is tell me what happened exactly how you remember it. I'm going to write it down here. I'll read it back to you when we're done. And if everything is accurate, you sign it and then we're done."

I nodded quickly. My mind had invented all of her coldness. In that second, she'd become someone different, someone who maybe wasn't judging me in all the ways I was afraid she and the rest of the world would.

"Okay," I finally said.

"Tell me what happened the night of the assault."

I closed my eyes and let my mind travel back to the night.

Over the next half hour, I relayed to Officer Bates how the evening had unfolded. From talking to guests, and then Michael, to relenting to Max's request to speak privately. I told her all I could remember until everything went black. Over the past week or so, fragments of the night had resurfaced. I would have rather they hadn't, but any information might be helpful to paint a more complete picture of what had happened. The rest had been witnessed by Blake and several others. While she scribbled down the final pieces of my account, I cringed inwardly that anyone else had seen me so helpless.

"Is there anything else you'd like to add?"

I shifted my focus back to her and shook my head, unsettled by how little I actually remembered from the night. As promised, she read it back to me. I signed it, my hand trembling slightly as I did.

Nervousness wasn't making me shake, but a flood of relief. This was over. Finally. She let me know that they would be in touch if they needed anything further and showed me out of the room.

As I left, the concrete block that had taken up residence in my stomach lifted. It was all said and done, literally. I couldn't know if it would mean justice for Max, but it began to mean something more to me. I'd done something I'd never had the chance to do before. I'd overcome my fears and insecurities enough to tell my story. I wanted to believe it was an important step toward healing.

I made my way through the rows of desks and back out to the bank of elevators. I waited there a moment before I heard a man's voice behind me. I turned slightly to see Daniel with another man who I recognized as one of the detectives I'd spoken with.

"Miss Hathaway. You must remember me, Detective Carmody?"

My hand twitched, but he didn't reach out. Instead he maintained a casual stance, almost too casual compared to how shrewdly he was studying me. I forced an impassive look.

"What brings you here?" the detective asked.

My gaze flashed to Daniel. The displeasure in his countenance made my heart stop.

"A private matter," I murmured.

"Fair enough. Well, Mr. Fitzgerald, thanks for your time. I'll leave you two alone." He shifted back to me and lifted his chin slightly. "I'll be in touch."

The elevator opened, and we stepped in together. I retreated to the back of the car, my hands going to the cold metal railing.

"Can't say I was expecting to see you here." Daniel's expression revealed nothing.

Oh, shit. What if he thought I was talking to someone about the still unresolved case of Mark's suicide?

I stuttered over how to begin, not knowing what to say. "It's nothing about Mark."

He glanced up at the numbers descending above the elevator door. "Assuming it has something to do with Max Pope then."

I stared at him stupidly, my brows knitted together. "Yes. But how did you know?"

His gaze fell back down to mine. "I run a law firm, remember? Who do you think he called first?"

My jaw fell open. I startled when the bell dinged, announcing our arrival at the ground floor. He stepped out and I released my death grip on the railing to follow him. We pushed through the heavy doors of the police station and slowed a few steps outside. He pulled out a pack of cigarettes and tapped one out. I wrinkled my nose.

"You should really stop smoking."

He shot me an annoyed look and took in a drag. "Really? I'm at risk of losing a race that I've sunk millions of my own money into. And you're telling me to give up smoking. You've got to be kidding me."

I took a defensive step back. His anger, however fleeting, still had the power to make me take pause.

"Why were you in there?" I asked, assuming whatever the reasons were tied directly to his presently pissy mood.

"Because *someone* is leaking information to the cops."

I froze. None of that sounded good. "What information?"

"Someone leaked a tip that you're my daughter. They know good and goddamn well how damaging it's going to be to my campaign too. Pricks." He grimaced and blew out a smoky breath.

That would have explained why Carmody looked at me that way, like he knew a secret. He did.

"You didn't deny it?"

He laughed. "What's the point? You clearly are, and if there's any doubt, a simple DNA test would confirm it. The two of us drink a cup of coffee in their office and they would have their proof."

"Who would have tipped them off though?"

He shook his head, a bitter smile twisting his lips. "Call me crazy, but I've got your fiancé at the top of that list. Unless you want to start telling me who else knows, because I sure as hell haven't been advertising it."

My stomach plummeted as I mentally ran through the list. Sid, Alli, Marie…maybe even Heath knew now. But none of them would have any reason to benefit from the information being made public.

Blake had his own reasons to out Daniel, but would he do that? Even after I'd made him promise me he wouldn't? Maybe learning that Daniel had hit me would have been enough to nullify that promise. In the context of our new arrangement, maybe his promise meant nothing at all if Blake deemed it in my best interest. Still, that seemed an extreme position to take. The repercussions of this information going public would be damaging for Daniel, but I couldn't see how Blake would want to bring the extra attention to me either. He wouldn't do that to me. Would he?

"Daniel, Blake knows I'm your daughter, yes, but I really don't believe he would leak the information. He assured me he wouldn't do that to you." I hoped he couldn't hear the doubt in my voice, because above all, I wanted to keep us safe. I'd lived under the fear of Daniel's death threats before.

He laughed again, sucking in a long drag on his cigarette.

"He promised me," I insisted.

"I promise Margo about ten things a day. Keeps her happy just to hear me say it even if I don't always deliver. Sorry if I don't put a lot of stock into your hacker's promises. Lot of fucking thanks I get for getting his ass out of a jam too."

I frowned. "What are you talking about?"

"Who do you think got the charges dropped?"

"You did that?" I hesitated as I absorbed this news. "How?"

He looked at me sidelong, an almost bored expression on his face. "Shouldn't surprise you that I have a few prosecutors who owe me favors. Wasn't too much to ask someone to look the other way for someone defending a sexual assault. He tuned Max up pretty good though, I'll say that."

"Then you know what happened."

He nodded, his expression still blank, if a little more tense.

"But if he came to you, isn't your firm defending Max?"

He grimaced then. "Fuck no. Jesus, who do you think I am?"

My eyes went wide, too wide maybe in response to what he was asking. Who was he? One minute he could be tugging at my heart strings, and the next he could be ruthlessly threatening to eliminate the man I loved. I couldn't ever be sure what kind of man Daniel was.

He exhaled sharply. "As much as I may not want the world to know it, you *are* my daughter. And the man drugged you and tried to rape you. I'm probably going straight to hell anyway, but I'm not completely fucking heartless. It's enough I have to live with what Mark did. I may not always follow the rules, but I'm not about to help Max get off scot-free."

My brain spun with all of this new information. I would have never told Daniel about the attack, but a small part of me was glad that he knew, especially if it meant snubbing Max from the protection of one of the most prominent firms in the city.

"What are you going to do now?" I asked quietly.

"I've got to talk to my PR people about damage control. I'd say it's only a matter of days before all this hits the presses."

He studied me a moment. "If you really believe Blake didn't leak the info, then you can tell him to at least help me find out who did." He tossed his cigarette on the ground, and stamped it out. "Because I want to talk to that person."

I believed him, and I had little doubt he had plans to do more than talk.

★ ★ ★

I offered a quick hello to Cady, who looked up from her desk outside Blake's office. Her hair was a bright shade of pink today.

"You can go right in." She motioned toward the door though it went without saying that I could, and I would, whether Blake liked it or not.

"Thanks," I said, and entered.

Blake spun in his chair when I shut the door behind me.

He smiled, and my heart melted a little. So much had happened since I saw him a few hours ago, and there was no one I wanted to see more.

I walked toward him, and he rose to meet me. He pulled me to him and pressed a kiss to my forehead. I leaned in, welcoming the relief of being in his arms, even if my relief might be short-lived after we started talking. He tipped my chin up. His eyebrows drew together.

"You're upset."

I sighed, exhaling the relief in the same breath.

"I saw Daniel today. I went to the police station to give my statement, and he was there. He'd been talking to the same detectives who interviewed me last month."

"Did he say something to you?"

He guided me to the couch on the other side of the room. He sat down beside me, his worried look demanding I tell him everything. I was prepared to tell Blake the truth, but I wasn't sure if I was entirely prepared to hear it. I was giving him more control than I ever had, but he had no right to release this information, no matter how much he hated Daniel.

"The police know that Daniel is my father. Someone tipped them off. Did you tell them? Please just be honest and tell me if you did."

Blake's frown deepened. "No."

I looked into his eyes, studying his expression for any signs that he might be lying.

He flinched slightly. "Erica, have I ever lied to you?"

"No," I admitted finally, sliding back into the smooth leather of the couch. I realized suddenly that learning Blake had done it would have be easier to accept than grasping at the unknown. It was a miracle I could sleep at night for all the people who'd made it their life's mission to tear one of us down.

"Did Daniel threaten you again?" he asked.

"No, thank God. You're his number one suspect though. Obviously, I assured him you wouldn't do this, but he doesn't take much stock in the promises you've made to me. He's pissed, and he can't wait to get his hands on whoever gave the police this information. He says if it's not you, you should find out who it is."

"What if it was an anonymous tip? How the hell am I supposed to trace that? Tell Daniel to fuck off and do his own research."

"Blake." I glared at him.

"What?"

"This is serious. The police know, and I'm pretty sure they'll want to talk to me again soon."

"You should have told them the truth when you had the chance. Now you have to keep up with the lie and risk obstruction of justice."

"I didn't want to see Daniel behind bars."

He cursed, his expression suddenly tight. "Erica, you're maddening sometimes, you know that? The man hit you and threatened to kill me. God knows what else he's done that warrants a lifetime behind bars."

"He's my father, Blake. I'm sorry I don't have a picture perfect family like yours. My mother's dead and my stepfather started over without me. Unfortunately, Daniel's the only parent I've got. I'd rather not live the rest of my life with the knowledge that I put him behind bars for killing the man who nearly destroyed my life."

He shoved a hand through his hair, a gesture that always betrayed his growing frustration, usually with me.

"So what now?"

I sighed. "I don't know. Before, I was just a girl Mark was hitting on the night he died. Now I'm officially his stepsister and the illegitimate daughter of a powerful man with a multi-million dollar campaign on the line. The discovery is bound to raise eyebrows. They'll have more questions without a doubt."

"You definitely told the police that Mark was coming on to you that night?"

"Even if I hadn't, it was obvious in the photos. They had a whole series of shots of us dancing. Him...talking in my ear." I shuddered, the memory creeping over my skin.

Blake stared off in silence a few moments.

"Why would there be so many photos you that night? There were hundreds of people at that event, and I don't remember seeing a ton of press there. You were stunning, obviously. I can't deny that you would have caught anyone's eye that night. But doesn't that strike you as uncanny?"

I couldn't disagree, but I couldn't come up with another answer that made sense. I'd never really thought about the unlucky existence of the photos when the detectives came to the apartment last month asking questions about Mark. I was too nervous about protecting Daniel and sounding natural doing it. But what luck to have so many shots of a man about to die? Of all the people there, the who's who of the city, that someone would take an interest in us, in me…

Then it struck me.

"Oh my God." My hand went to my mouth.

"What?"

My stomach fell, and I thought I might be sick.

"Shit," I whispered, shaking my head in disbelief.

"Erica. Talk to me," he pressed, pulling my hand away and slipping it into his palm.

"Richard." I looked up. "Richard was covering the event that night with a photojournalist. And he knew I was going to be there. I remember, Marie told him to look for me."

Blake and I shared a knowing look.

"What else has she told him?"

BLAKE AND ERICA'S STORY CONTINUES
IN THE HACKER SERIES SEQUEL

HARD LIMIT

HERE'S A SNEAK PEEK…

PROLOGUE

E: Meet me at the club in 10 minutes. Please don't be mad.

I reread Erica's text until my brain caught up to her meaning.

Fucking hell.

The club she was referring to could only be one. My knuckles went white, as if gripping the phone on the brink of crushing it might stop her from doing this. Drawing in a deep breath that did nothing to calm me, I pulled up her number and held the phone to my ear. I listened to the endless ring, biting back the string of curses that would fly if she picked up. I knew she wouldn't.

The warm timbre of her voicemail greeted me. I was stung with missing the woman behind the sound, but I couldn't ignore the infuriating fact that she wasn't picking up the fucking phone. I hung up and grabbed my keys. I flew down the stairs to the Tesla and, wasting no time, pushed my way into the rush hour traffic.

Checking the time, I calculated my journey and how long she'd be there without me. Ten or fifteen minutes if I were lucky. My mind spun over what could go down in that span of time in the exclusive underground establishment I'd known for years as *La Perle*.

She'd be prey.

If I were lurking in the shadows there as I'd done more

times than I cared to admit, that's all I would see in her. A little blond bombshell with just enough fire to make a Dom want to make her his. A man would have to be fucking blind not to want to bring her to her knees.

I hit the gas and swerved, bypassing a cluster of slowing cars that put precious time between us. As worry plagued my thoughts, so did unwanted memories of the club. I hadn't stepped foot in there since I met Erica months ago. I'd had no reason to go back to that life. My jaw clenched as I thought of everything that had played out there, countless meaningless moments that I'd kept coming back for, years after I left Sophia. Everything about the place was charged with the promise of sex, the darkest kind of possibilities hanging in the air between every bated breath and less-than-innocent exchange.

My chest was painfully tight. Anger was there. The teeth-gnashing frustration that only Erica could elicit. But under all of it was love. Love for Erica that set my desire on fire. Though I wanted her far from all of it, my basest desires painted a fantasy of finding her in the club and being the man to tame her—even as I knew how fucking impossible that task was. In the daylight, she never made it easy, but hell if she didn't submit like a dream at night.

I hit the brake at a red light. I closed my eyes, and there she was, gazing up at me with those hooded blue eyes, endless oceans. All that hellfire spirit tempered in the name of the pleasure I would give her. And I always gave her more than she could handle. I never let her rest until she was sated. Until I saw the wonder in her eyes that only I could put there, having pushed her to a place no one had ever taken her. Until the only word she could form was my name.

We were never short on passion. We couldn't keep our hands off of each other. Adrenaline raced over the fatigue that had settled into my bones after another sleepless night. I could fuck the woman until I was blind, and it wouldn't be enough. She'd promised me a lifetime, and I had every intention of loving her well every day this life would give me.

Love was a small word for what I felt for Erica. Maybe it was an obsession, this never-waning determination to make her mine in every way she'd let me. Heath had noticed, even warned me when he saw how she was changing me. He was no stranger to addiction, and no one could deny that she was my vice. The drug I refused to live without, no matter how many times she pushed me away. I'd fought like hell to keep the upper hand between us to protect her, to keep her out of the path of those who would hurt one to destroy the other. I couldn't lose control and risk losing something more important—the one person who'd come into my life and made it worth living.

Yes, she'd changed me, as much as a man with my particular affinities could change. She'd pushed me. She'd walked into my life, five-feet-three inches of fiery independence. Her mere presence challenged me, getting under my skin, making me habitually hard until I could find the unexplainable peace that being inside her supple little body could bring. Even now, I could barely take a full breath, knowing she was beyond my reach. I clutched the steering wheel tighter. My bloodless fingertips tingled with the need to feel her body under them, loving her, claiming her, restraining her.

Fuck.

I adjusted my inconvenient hard on. Pointless when

visions of the night before flooded me now. Her full, swollen lips parting for me and only me. Her nails digging into my thighs as she took all of me in the hot bliss of her mouth.

I released my tense hold, exhaling an uneven breath. My thumb grazed the worn leather of my belt. The hammer of my heart kicked up. The light turned green, and I sped closer to our destination. A flicker of anticipation took over with a rush of blood to my now rock-hard cock.

If nothing else, I'd enjoy punishing her when this was all said and done.

Continue the story now . . .

DISCUSSION QUESTIONS

1. The events of *Hardline* cause Blake and Erica to discover and accept some honest truths about each other and their relationship. What honest truths do they have to accept and how has their relationship evolved to this point?

2. Erica has some significant emotional and physical walls that Blake continues to try to breakdown. Why do you think Blake is able to crack these walls that Erica's spent a lifetime building? What is it about Blake that allows those carefully constructed walls to crumble?

3. Risa and Max both do some pretty significant damage to Blake and Erica's lives in *Hardline*. What do you drives these actions. Going into the book, is this what you expected from these characters?

4. When Blake confronts Erica about what happened with James, you see the events unfold from Erica's perspective. During that highly charged moment, what do you think is going through Blake's mind?

5. Blake asks Erica her to give up control to him in many aspects of her life, which goes against her very nature. What is Erica really giving up when she makes that choice? What is she gaining?

6. In the aftermath of when Blake confronts Erica, they are slow to put the pieces of their relationship back together again. Why do you think it takes as long as it does for Erica to come to Blake, and for them to find a sense of resolution with all that's happened? What do you think is the breaking point for Erica to realize what it is that she really wants and needs?

7. Blake tells Erica she's his only weakness in a moment of true vulnerability. In what ways do you think Erica is his only weakness?

8. Blake has significant issues with James and his friendship with Erica. In turn, Erica can't escape her jealousy over Blake's relationship with Sophia. What parallels can be drawn between these two separate working relationships? Is Blake's jealousy justified? Is Erica's?

9. At a critical time, Erica explains how much she needs Blake in order to heal after all that she's been through. What do you think would have happened to Erica had she not had Blake there to support her? In what moments do you feel this healing the most?

10. Daniel has made many interesting choices in order to protect Erica. Do you think his questionable actions and choices are defensible? Has your perception of Daniel changed based on the newest choices and actions he's made?

11. In the end, Erica makes the choice to report Max's brutal attack on her. What do you think has changed within Erica,

since she decides to report this incident when she wasn't able to do the same after Mark's attack? What allows Erica to make that choice now?

12. *Hardline* ends with a cliffhanger when Erica and Blake both realize Richard may be connected to the tangled web of events that's coming together. What part do you think he plays in all of it? What do you think his motives are for getting involved?

13. The Hacker Series is full of supporting characters that round out the series and make it whole. How do you think these characters and their different dynamics affect the outcomes and events of the book? How do the relationships and friendships developed in this book add to the events that are happening?

14. Both Erica and Blake need control in different aspects of their lives. When Blake asks Erica to give up control to him, what is he really asking of her? Why do you think Erica is hesitant to give up this level of both emotional and physical control? What does giving up control to Blake in that way signify for Erica, and in turn, what does Erica giving it all to Blake signify for him?

15. There are many instances in *Hardline* in which Erica and Blake are at their most vulnerable. What moments specifically evoke these feelings and reactions for both Erica and Blake? At what point do you think they are their most vulnerable emotionally?

ACKNOWLEDGEMENTS

This book would not have been possible without the daily encouragement of my fans. Each and every message and comment fills up my cup more than you could possibly know. To be able to write and know that so many of you are eagerly anticipating the next installment of my imagination is a blessing beyond words.

Special thanks to my betas and the members of my *amazing* street team for your unwavering support and patience! Team Wild is a force to be reckoned with. Love you ladies something fierce!

Many thanks to every single person who promised me that writing this book could be done despite a crippling deadline, a ton of pressure, and everything else life decided to throw my way in the meantime, which was a whole lot more than I ever expected. Thanks also to my Mom who reminded me to sleep, take breaks, and remember the big picture. Even though I mostly ignored all that advice and forged ahead anyway, thank you for reminding me that I'm human and not super woman.

I would like to thank my author friends too, for their support and kind words. I'm not sure how I would have survived without the regular check-ins and virtual whiskey dates with my sexy soul sister, Mia Michelle. On that note, thanks, Jack. You got me through a few tough spots too.

As always, I am forever grateful for my editor, Helen

ACKNOWLEDGEMENTS

Hardt, for making last minute miracles happen. My books aren't officially born into the world until she sprinkles her magic editing dust over them. Thanks to Amy and Jon for dedicating time to proofing!

Thanks also to Remi for introducing me to the stars and shining a light on elements of this chapter of Blake and Erica's story that I may have never otherwise discovered.

Last but not least, thank you to my staff for keeping my business alive while I disappeared into Blake and Erica's world for days at a time. Special thanks to Kurt, whose help in redesigning the series covers saved me mountains of time and stress. You have the patience of a saint!

ABOUT THE AUTHOR

Meredith Wild is a *New York Times*, *USA Today* and international bestselling author of erotic romance. She lives in Boston with her husband and three children. When she's not writing or interacting with fans, she's working with high-tech start-ups. Her dream of writing took a back seat to college, parenthood and eventually entrepreneurship, which led her into the fast-paced high tech industry. With enough life experience to fill a few lifetimes, she now devotes her hours to writing contemporary adult romance, with a hint of kink. When she isn't writing or mothering, Meredith can be found sunbathing with an adult beverage.

You can find her at www.facebook.com/meredithwild
and hear more about her writing projects at
www.meredith-wild.com